THE BADGER'S REVENGE

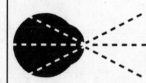

This Large Print Book carries the
Seal of Approval of N.A.V.H.

A JOSIAH WOLFE, TEXAS RANGER NOVEL

THE BADGER'S REVENGE

LARRY D. SWEAZY

THORNDIKE PRESS
A part of Gale, Cengage Learning

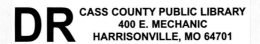

GALE
CENGAGE Learning™

Detroit • New York • San Francisco • New Haven, Conn • Waterville, Maine • London

GALE
CENGAGE Learning™

LIBRARY OF CONGRESS CATALOGING-IN-PUBLICATION DATA

Sweazy, Larry D.
   The badger's revenge : a Josiah Wolfe, Texas ranger novel / by Larry D. Sweazy. — Large print ed.
     p. cm. — (Thorndike Press large print western)
     ISBN-13: 978-1-4104-3996-3 (hardcover)
     ISBN-10: 1-4104-3996-8 (hardcover)
     1. Indian captivities—Fiction. 2. Texas Rangers—Fiction. 3. Revenge—Fiction. 4. Large type books. I. Title.
PS3619.W438.B33 2011
813'.6—dc23
                             2011021409

Published in 2011 by arrangement with The Berkley Publishing Group, a member of Penguin Group (USA) Inc.

Printed in the United States of America
1 2 3 4 5 6 7 15 14 13 12 11

This book is dedicated to the memory
of my uncle,
Robert "Bob" Byrne,
the first writer to ever inspire me.

ACKNOWLEDGMENTS

No book ever gets written alone, and no book ever finds its way to a reader alone. As I wrote this book, several of the bookstores that had previously supported my work closed their doors, and it didn't seem right not to acknowledge their passing.

I walked in the doors of The Mystery Company in Carmel, Indiana, for the first time in the spring of 2004 after making my first professional short story sale to a western anthology (*Texas Rangers,* edited by Ed Gorman and Martin H. Greenberg, Berkley Books, 2004). Jim Huang, the owner, happily agreed to stock the book and host a signing for me — my first. The Mystery Company has been my "home" bookstore ever since. The staff has always promoted my work, and I count many of them as my friends. Thank you, Jim, Austin, Edna, Moni, Jennie, Jaci, and everyone else at TMC for all that you've done for me over the years. You all will be sorely missed.

The Wild in Noblesville, Indiana, was primarily a children's bookstore, but the owner, Jane Shasserre Mills, welcomed my books and hand-sold a great many of them. Noblesville will not be the same without you or the store, Jane.

I briefly met the staff at the Waldenbooks store in my hometown of Anderson, Indiana, but Eric and Stephanie went above the call of duty to host a great book signing for me. Thank you. I hope you both have found careers that allow your love of books to carry on.

Finally, to all of the booksellers who have been gracious and kind to me, especially Margi Kingsley and the staff at the Noblesville Barnes & Noble, who are still fighting the good fight, making sure books find their way to readers' hands every day, thank you for all that you continue to do.

Also . . . this book wouldn't have been possible without the continuing support from my writing friends (you know who you are) and those who have helped guide my books to their final form: John Duncklee; the Berkley production team; Faith, Cherry, Liz, and Chris; and most importantly, Rose, whose confidence in me never wavers.

AUTHOR'S NOTE

The challenge of mixing fiction with history is never ending, especially when the mix includes a venerable organization such as the Texas Rangers. In each of my books, I have tried to capture the high-quality character and spirit of the Rangers, most eloquently described by Walter Prescott Webb in his highly respected book *Texas Rangers: A Century of Frontier Defense* (University of Texas Press, 2008): "No Texas Ranger ever fanned a hammer when he was serious, or made a hip shot if he had time to catch a sight. The real Ranger has been a very quiet, deliberate, gentle person who could gaze calmly into the eye of a murderer, divine his thoughts, and anticipate his action, a man who could ride straight up to death."

Mr. Webb's ideal of a Ranger is a high standard. One that continues to be apparent in the modern Texas Ranger organization. It is my hope that every time I tell a

Ranger story, I uphold the character and honor of all Texas Rangers, past and present.

For other historical works concerning the Texas Rangers and the Frontier Battalion, the following books have served me well: *Lone Star Justice: The First Century of the Texas Rangers* by Robert M. Utley (Berkley, 2002); *The Texas Rangers: Wearing the Cinco Peso, 1821–1900* by Mike Cox (Forge, 2008); *Six Years with the Texas Rangers, 1875–1881* by James B. Gillet (Bison Books, 1976).

Online resources such as *The Handbook of Texas* and *Texas Ranger Dispatch* magazine, have also been helpful in portraying the Texas Rangers as accurately, and honorably, as possible.

PROLOGUE

October 1861

The forceful north wind pushed through the walls of the cabin, searching out every nook, cranny, and snake-sized hole it could find. It was a harsh cold that was nearly bone chilling, a surprise to a young man's skin that was more accustomed to long, hot, Texas summers than the mystery of the Dakotas or the promise of constant blizzards in the faraway land of Montana. It was the first hint of the coming winter, and the certainty of the change of seasons was not lost on Josiah Wolfe, who slowly stirred awake under a thin blanket, wholly unprepared to step foot on the floor and get a start on the day.

Winter in East Texas was mild, and the deep drop in the temperature was an anomaly, a drop more akin to late January mornings, though rare even then, than October ones. Beyond the suddenness of

11

the cold, roiling clouds were visible through the window, lighting the room in gloomy shadows instead of the happy sunshine Josiah had hoped for the night before. He'd finally drifted off to sleep, fear mixing with excitement over the new adventure that lay in wait for him the next day.

Josiah pulled the blanket over his head and tried to snuggle deeper into the feather mattress and fall back asleep.

He had dreaded the coming of this day, even though he had been more than excited by some of the prospects of it.

He was sure he was ready for whatever was coming his way. He had to be, but . . . the pine cabin had always been just over the next horizon, even when he had ventured into Tyler or Waco as a boy, then as a young man, with his father or a friend nearly always at his side. Texas was all he knew, the only part of the world that made sense to him. Leaving it made him nervous, but not in a can't-breathe kind of way, just nervous in a not-knowing-what's-next kind of way.

If only the cause of his leaving Texas were to see the world for fun and profit and not to take up arms in a war he had yet to understand, then he would have been truly excited. But that was not to be. He *was* off to war, as an infantryman in the newly formed Texas Brigade. A young soldier, green to the sight of death outside of the barn, or the sight of blood rushing out of the body of a wounded Union soldier, perhaps at his hand, instead of a pig or a cow. Battle, and its consequences, was just too uncomfortable to imagine.

The day of his departure had arrived with the push of a cold, hard wind — whether he was ready or not.

Below, under the loft where he'd slept since he could remember, his mother moved about as quietly as she could, preparing the morning meal. The deep aroma of coffee reached his nose, further provoking him to climb out from underneath the comfortable blanket.

He glanced out the window as he stood, searching for the silhouette of his father walking the land, or coming out of the barn, easing through his morning chores. But Josiah saw nothing moving. It was almost like the world was frozen in the thick gloom of the perpetually gray morning — the same color of the uniform he would soon be wearing — and neither his father, nor any other living creature it seemed, dared set foot on the ground before Josiah did.

The fields beyond the cabin were freshly

harvested; the smell of decay yet to set on the wind, but there was still work to be done on the small stretch of land that Josiah Wolfe had called home his entire life.

Firewood still needed to be chopped, feed gathered for the horses and sole surviving cow, which had been mated with the Halversons' bull for next year's meat, and whatever other provisions needed to be put up in the larder to get his mother and father through the winter. None of those chores were his concern now. The burden of providing for the farm would fall squarely on the shoulders of his father — who was more than able, still a strapping man as the age of fifty rapidly approached. Josiah knew his parents' life would have been made more comfortable if they would have been blessed with another son, or even a daughter. But that was not to be. Josiah was their only son, their only child — and now he was duty-bound to leave home for points unknown, where a battle waited to be fought and blood waited to be spilled.

Thunder boomed in the distance, so far away the claps were more like drumming echoes — or cannons firing in a war that had yet to reach the confines of Texas, but surely would soon enough.

The thunder drew Josiah's attention away

from the window, and then, without one quick look of regret around the loft, he shimmied down the ladder.

"Where's Pa?" Josiah asked, rubbing his forearms, shivering, as he planted his bare feet on the cold plank floor.

His mother had her back to him, standing over the stove. He was at least a head and a half taller than she was, had been since he was nigh on fifteen, a summer when he'd shot up as quick and tall as a hearty corn stalk. Her hair was pulled back and wound up off of her shoulders for the day's work ahead. There were faint brittle streaks of gray mixed in with her soft dark brown hair. Age was marking his mother with thin wrinkles and those hints of gray, almost too invisible to see, but she still looked young to Josiah.

The smell of hot bacon grease met with the aroma of coffee, and Josiah's stomach complained loudly. A piece of bread sizzled and fried in the skillet, and a pot of beans began to bubble.

"It isn't much." His mother turned and faced him. Her eyes betrayed any strength she may have found in her morning routine; they brimmed with tears, a dam ready to burst. She spun quickly back around to the stove, flipping the bread, so, perhaps, he

15

would not see her cry. There was no need. He had heard her soft cries throughout the night. There was no comforting her. He had tried for days after his enlistment, to no avail. She opposed the war inside the walls of her own home, and she was opposed to Josiah fighting in it no matter the reason or cause.

Josiah took a deep breath and bear-hugged his mother from behind. "I'll be fine."

"I know. That doesn't make it any easier."

"Where's Pa?"

His mother wiggled a bit uncomfortably, and Josiah eased back, freeing her from his gentle embrace.

"He went into town," she said.

"Seerville?"

She shook her head no. "Tyler."

"But the boys are mustering in Seerville, then we're off north to meet up with the rest of the Brigade."

"I know. I tried to talk him out of it. But you know how your father is." She served up his breakfast on an enamel plate and handed it to him, forcing a smile. "Eat up. We haven't much time."

Josiah did as he was told, hurried to the small table and sat in his regular chair, glaring at the empty one that was his father's.

The year before Josiah was born, his father

had fought in the Cherokee War of 1839. The Battle of Neches occurred just a few miles outside of Tyler. Three Texans were killed and five wounded. One of the wounded was Josiah's father, and he had walked with a limp in his right leg ever since. Josiah had never known his father when there wasn't some pain to bear because of the injury, but it was never discussed, never talked about, never given credence or used as an excuse. More than a hundred Indians were killed in that battle, the rest driven into the Arkansas Territory, and after healing, Josiah's father lost his taste for war and killing, but he had not tried to stop Josiah from joining the Texas Brigade.

Leonard Wolfe knew better than anyone that Josiah would be subjected to unbearable scrutiny and prejudice if he did not go off to war like the rest of the boys in the area. Josiah was healthy, of age, and it was his duty to prove his love of Texas, and now the Confederacy. But Leonard Wolfe did not encourage the enlistment, either, or show any more joy than his wife did, when Josiah made his decision to follow his friends into battle. Instead, he acted as though nothing had happened at all.

The storm that had been on the horizon

settled squarely above the cabin. Josiah finished his breakfast and hurried to get ready, ignoring the push of rain and cold wind under the door.

It only took minutes for him to prepare to leave; everything had been packed and readied the night before. A satchel and a long gun stood waiting at the door. He would travel light until he was given a uniform and the rest of what he needed for battle. Skills, he hoped, waited, too. His mother stood, her head down, waiting next to the door, along with his gear, a tin of warm biscuits in her hand.

Josiah stood before her, trying to be the man he knew he had to be, walking away from his boyhood home.

"Don't be angry with your father, Josiah. You are his only son, and he knows the cost of war more than we."

"He should be here."

"He has done his best."

"I'm not sure I believe that."

His mother's chest heaved heavily, the air deflating out of her body in a certain and sudden sigh of resignation. "You are too like him to leave your anger behind. Write to me." She hugged him quickly, kissed him on the cheek, then threw open the door, and said, "Be careful now, you hear?" She thrust the tin into his hands.

Josiah took it, setting his jaw hard in place, grinding his teeth so he would not allow a tear to be shed. "I will do my best, Ma, I promise."

"I know. But stay clear of bad sorts. Pick your friends carefully."

"I have friends."

"Charlie Langdon is not your friend."

"Ma," Josiah protested.

"Don't argue. Be wary — the Langdons have always had a troublesome, untrustworthy streak. Now, go. Go, before I lock you inside the house and never let you leave."

Josiah hesitated, then returned his mother's kiss, grabbed his gear, and headed out into the raging, cold wind, ignoring the thunder, lightning, and the sound of his mother sobbing behind the door like someone had died in her arms.

He ran toward town, toward the regiment that was waiting for him, hoping that his father would be waiting for him along the road. But he wasn't. His father was gone, and Josiah was left to face the most important day of his life without a word of advice, a comforting nod, or a wink of the eye that acknowledged an inkling of pride. He could barely contain his rage.

CHAPTER 1

November, 1874

The first shot didn't come as a surprise.

Josiah Wolfe and two other Texas Rangers from the Frontier Battalion, Scrap Elliot and Red Overmeyer, had tracked a lone Comanche scout easing into a dry creek bed, taking cover in a thin stand of brittle switchgrass.

The Comanche had seemed certain he hadn't been seen — but now he knew he was wrong. The trio had been aware of the scout's presence for more than a couple of miles, following after him, as stealthily as possible, to a spot where they were certain they had enough cover to engage the Indian and return him to camp for questioning, as they had been ordered to do by the captain of their company, Pete Feders.

Indians had been rustling cattle, and the Rangers had been charged with bringing a stop to the practice. Good, bad, or otherwise, there didn't seem much end to the rustling. Josiah hadn't objected to the assignment, but he did find it curious that Feders wanted a Comanche captured, not killed. The only thing Josiah could figure was the Rangers were getting a reputation for shooting first and asking questions later and Feders had been instructed by the higher-ups, more specifically either Major John B. Jones or Governor Richard Coke himself, to polish their reputation a bit. Didn't make much sense though, since killing Indians did more for their reputation than anything else.

Whatever the case, Josiah was in no position to question the motives behind the orders. He was in charge, a sergeant to the two men, one a fine weathered Ranger, the other a boy still trying to prove his manhood, as far as Josiah was concerned, as he eyed the Comanche cautiously.

A soft glow of fresh morning light covered the rolling ground leading to the creek, the land dropping slowly in the distance toward the struggling San Saba River. The cool November air was salty, and the creek the Indian lay prone in was a brine spring all used up, still crusty and white with alkali. Nothing could live off that soil, or at least it didn't make sense for any kind of critter to be able to, other than the mass of flittering insects that hovered inches off the ground.

Even on a cloudless day, there was a depressed, hopeless feel to the place. A few gnarly live oaks and mesquites dotted the hill country landscape, and the Rangers had taken refuge behind a small crop of boulders once Red Overmeyer was certain the Comanche scout had detected them.

The first shot pinged off the straight-edged rock just above Red Overmeyer's head, echoing in the crisp air, announcing to any creature or man within a few miles that something was amiss.

"Dang, that foul Indian damn near took my ear off." Red raised his carbine in retaliation but did not immediately pull the trigger, looking to Josiah for permission to start returning fire.

"He's lookin' to do more than that," Scrap Elliot said.

"Careful with your aim, men. Captain Feders was strict with his orders about bringing the raiders to justice. The scout needs to be interrogated." Josiah focused on the spot where the shot had come from, then glanced over at Scrap Elliot. Scrap had an itchy trigger finger.

"You talk Comanche, Wolfe?" Scrap asked.

"Not my job, that's Feders's worry."

23

"Justice ought not to be none of the captain's concern, either," Scrap said. "He obviously ain't seen what a Comanche'll do to an innocent family."

Scrap's family had been killed by Comanche, or so he claimed, and his anger still clouded his judgment, at least as far as Josiah was concerned — so he ignored the comment as best he could. There was no use arguing with the boy at the moment — though that's usually what happened when they were in each other's company.

"You can take that up with the captain," Josiah said, raising his own Winchester rifle to aim.

The rifle was a model '73, not as difficult to handle as the Sharps 50 he used to carry, the rifle Overmeyer still called his own, but still, the rise of his arm brought a quick pain that ran across his chest like a hot piece of iron burning him from the inside out.

The shot of pain was a reminder to him that it hadn't been so long ago that he'd been stabbed in the left shoulder by a knife in an attack by a Kiowa in Lost Valley. It was July when that skirmish had happened, and the wound was scarred over now, healed thinly, he thought, but a quick reaction still brought pain, telling him the wound wasn't as healed it appeared to be. It was still tender. Sometimes, he wondered if it would ever be healed at all.

"You all right, there, Wolfe?" Red asked.

Josiah nodded. "Take a shot. Let him know we mean business. Elliot, scoot around to the other side of this rock, and see if there's a way in behind him. We'll get him pinned in, then we'll take him alive like the captain wants." He hoped that neither Red nor Elliot sensed his own discomfort or his nervousness. This was his first real engagement under fire since he'd been wounded.

"Careful now," Red warned. "There'll be more than one. Always is. I ain't never seen none of them scouts stray too far apart."

"You said there was only one," Scrap said.

"Is. For the moment. Like those flies, there, though. Do more damage in a swarm than alone. No such thing as just one Comanche scout. No such thing as just one Comanche, period."

"Ought to just kill the savage, and be done with it," Scrap replied.

Josiah nodded forcefully beyond the rock, silently ordering Elliot to get a move on.

"He'll learn to trust what I say one of these days," Red Overmeyer said.

Red was an old hand when it came to dealing with Indians. Probably fifty years old, or older, he wore a long beard — faded red, closer to orange with age — that made him look more like a mountain man on a beaver hunt than a Ranger out scouting for a Comanche raiding party. Red's stained buckskin shirt looked nearly as old as he was, and it barely covered his rounded belly that hung over a leather belt. The shirt looked like it was about to pop apart at any second. A full complement of bullets sat waiting underneath his belly, and a Bowie knife sat firmly on his hip in a hand-tooled leather scabbard that looked old and worn, too, from plenty of use.

It was not uncommon among Rangers to dress in the fashion to which they were comfortable, since there were no required uniforms.

One of the appeals for Josiah of signing up back in May, when the Frontier Battalion came into proper being, was the lack of regimentation. He'd had enough of tight military control in his younger life when he'd served in the First Infantry, the Texas Brigade, in the War Between the States, and he didn't care for that kind of strictness in his life these days.

Red rarely talked about his encounters with Indians, and Josiah suspected he had lived among the plains Indians at one time or another, married to a Sioux or Shoshone, judging from the minimal tales he told. Red loved Indian women, which was obvious from the way he spoke of them.

Regardless, it was good to have Overmeyer along, his knowledge paramount in assisting the cause of taming the Comanche, even though it was not a battle Josiah had ever chewed at the bit to engage in in the first place — fighting Indians. Staying close to Austin, a day-and-a-half ride away to the north of the capital, was as important to him as remaining a Texas Ranger. At least, until now.

Elliot had not moved from his spot, almost daring Josiah to formally command him to do as he was told.

Josiah nodded again, more firmly, his eyes hard as the metal that had been forged to make the rifle barrel he was holding.

With a loud "Humpf!" Elliot spit on the ground, glared back at Josiah, and did as he was told, carefully edging along the rock, his own Winchester cocked and at the ready.

Josiah thought Scrap Elliot an impetuous sort, never really trustworthy with his intentions or mood, but *always* trustworthy when it came to shooting and horse riding.

The kid, that's how Josiah thought of the boy, since he was hardly twenty years old, had certain talents that had proven effective in the recent past, and even though Josiah rarely said anything aloud, he admired Scrap's talents to a high degree. They'd saved his life more than once. His history with Elliot allowed for a certain discounting of youthful enthusiasm. He worried now, though, if he could hold Elliot down, get him to toe the line, and let the plan at hand fall into place. So far, events were occurring without any hint of trouble.

"That boy's gonna either get us all kilt one of these days," Red said, "or be a hero in the annals of time. Got the spirit of a warrior, and the brains of a thick piece of granite."

Josiah chuckled — and at the same time the Comanche fired another shot into the clump of rocks. The chuckle faded quickly, as he and Red both returned fire.

White dust popped up into the air along the dry creek bed. The scout's rifle went silent almost immediately.

Josiah pulled back and faced Red. "You think he's hit?"

"Won't know till I see a dead body. Sneaky bastards, these Comanche are. You know that, though, don't you, Wolfe?"

Josiah nodded, listened for Scrap, and heard nothing.

There was little wind, no birdsong, not even a hawk lifting higher on the warm currents in the clear blue sky. The day had yet to fully grab hold, but it was going to be a warm one, especially for this time of year. It was like they had stumbled into a desert, devoid of any life at all.

He peered over the rock again, and saw no movement along the creek.

"Anything?" Red asked.

"Nothing."

"I'm worried about that Elliot now."

"Me, too."

"Should I go after him? Take a look and see if I got lucky and kilt that there scout?"

"Yes. Go."

Red pulled himself out of the cranny he'd positioned himself in and disappeared behind the same rock Scrap had.

It only took a second for the silence to return. Now it belonged entirely to Josiah. All he could hear was the beating of his own heart.

He looked over the rock again, angling the barrel of the Winchester toward the creek.

Unconsciously, he balanced the barrel with his left hand, eased his finger onto the trigger, and let his right hand fall so it was touching the butt of his pistol, a single-action Colt .45-caliber, most often called by him, and other Rangers, the Peacemaker. Settling his arm as he had had allowed the burning sensation around his wound to fade away, but not fully disappear.

This time, he saw movement, but it was only a snake, a small rattler slithering along the white, sandy bank of the dry creek. It was hunting quietly, searching for anything that moved. It was a futile quest as far as Josiah could tell.

He was starting to believe Red had gotten lucky with the shot . . . until he sensed a bit of movement behind him.

"Don't move," a strong male voice said forcefully, but almost in a hush. "Or I'll shoot you dead right here. Let the guns go — but don't turn around until I tell you. Understand?"

Josiah nodded. He could not help but catch sight of his oppressor out of the corner of his right eye as he did as he was told. It was a Comanche. The same scout he'd thought — had hoped — Red had killed. There was a rifle in the Indian's steady hand, pointed directly at Josiah's head.

There was no way he could spin and shoot, just kill the Indian outright. There was no room, and he knew better than anyone that he was not fast enough to pull off such a feat.

First, Josiah pulled the Winchester down over the rock and let it fall out of his grasp. The rifle kicked up a cloud of dust at Josiah's feet, but not enough to distract the Indian, nor enough to create an opportunity. Josiah's options were fading fast.

He was curious, though, why the Comanche didn't just shoot him. Most would have. Normally in this circumstance he'd already be a dead man, if everything were as it seemed.

"Now the pistol," the Indian said.

The scout's English was halting and had the regular start-stop that accompanied many of the Indian speech patterns Josiah had heard in the area. Probably taught by Christian missionaries in an attempt to civilize them. No chance of that, Josiah thought, not at the moment, not with a war taking place north, up Red River way.

He pulled the Peacemaker slowly out of the holster and eased it to the ground next to the rifle.

"The knife in the belt, too."

Again, Josiah did as he was told. He had no more weapons, other than his fists and. hopefully, time — time enough for Red and Scrap to return and discover the lone scout and rescue him. For that reason, each of his

31

movements was slow and methodical, not out of fear, but out of hope for an opportunity to strike back at the Comanche.

"Now," the scout said, "take off your boots and turn around slowly."

Josiah did as he was told, emptying his boots of dirt, but no weapons as the Comanche had suspected, then faced the Indian for the first time.

There was no recognition. He had never seen the scout, or the other Comanche who stepped out of a shadow behind the rock where Scrap and Red had disappeared, a rifle in his hand, aimed directly at Josiah's head.

Both men had long black hair, a feather braided into the right side of the taller one. They both wore shirts that looked to be made for an Anglo instead of an Indian; gingham, light blue, with a mosaic of circles and squares. The second Indian's shirt was faded red, striped instead of dotted with shapes.

Each wore necklaces that draped low from his neck and looked more like breastplates than jewelry, except the necklaces stopped at the top of the gut and were made of wood or a smooth bone, it was hard to tell which, instead of metal. Both men wore long pants and riding boots. These two looked more like outlaws than Comanche rustlers, and for a moment Josiah was confused.

"Hold out your hands," the original scout, and taller of the two, ordered Josiah.

The second one, who Josiah decided was taking orders and was subservient to the tall scout, rushed forward and quickly bound Josiah's hands with a heavy rope.

"Don't think your friends are going to rescue you. It is too late for that, Josiah Wolfe," the scout said, a slow smile coming to his face. "Put your boots back on."

The mention of his own name surprised Josiah, but he tried not to show it. "You killed them?"

"Not yet."

"I didn't hear a thing. Why should I believe you?"

"Why do you think I care if you believe me or not? I am the one holding the gun at your head," the scout said.

The short Comanche yanked the rope tight around Josiah's wrists, finishing off the binding so tightly it nearly cut off the circulation.

It was all he could do to not cry out in pain. "How do you know my name?" Josiah asked through clenched teeth.

"We have a mutual friend."

"And who would that be?"

"You call him Liam O'Reilly. My people call him the Badger."

CHAPTER 2

The Comanche pulled Josiah out into the open. Josiah gave up any thought of struggle when he saw that Scrap and Red were tied to opposite sides of a towering elm tree. They were bound tightly with a heavy rope that looked more suited to being used as a hangman's noose than holding two Texas Rangers captive.

The trunk of the ancient tree was so broad that Josiah doubted that a big man like Red Overmeyer could get his thick arms all the way around it, but it didn't matter — Red and Scrap were tied to the tree with their backs to it, their stiff and unmoving arms pinned tightly at their sides. They were facing opposite directions, their mouths gagged securely with their own kerchiefs. Rescue or death would be their only escape.

Death was not an option as far as Josiah was concerned. Even less so now that the name Liam O'Reilly had been mentioned.

If it were possible for Josiah to feel hate against a man, then there was no question that he felt that emotion for O'Reilly. The redheaded Irishman was as mean as a motherless snake and just as unpredictable, too. Even though Charlie Langdon, the leader of the gang that O'Reilly originally belonged to, was long dead and buried, his power and anger still seemed to haunt Josiah, this time in the form of O'Reilly. It was not that long ago that Langdon and O'Reilly had gone after Josiah's son, Lyle, and held him as bait to lure Josiah home. Langdon was captured and eventually hanged. O'Reilly escaped, stepping head-first into the leadership role that Langdon had left vacant.

Now there was cause to be concerned about the past meeting the present.

But the men that were captured and bound were Josiah's charges, entrusted to him by Pete Feders. Duty would not be clouded by emotion, and Josiah swore silently that he would not let anything happen to his men.

Josiah had hand-picked Red and Scrap for the mission to capture Indian rustlers, to gain more information from them, find out their sources.

The situation Josiah now found himself

in, being a captive instead of a captor, was not one he had even considered a possibility before leaving Austin on the short trip.

Scrap pushed against the rope and struggled to escape when he saw Josiah being pulled out from the rock maze where they had taken refuge, but he could barely even breathe, much less struggle. The two Comanche didn't even glance at their captives. Acknowledgment would have surely brought a certain and swift end to both men's lives.

Josiah felt a push of the rifle against the back of his head, warning him off any sudden, or stupid, movement.

He acted like he didn't notice the push, and glared at Scrap silently, ordering him to quiet down without saying a word. But Scrap didn't respond — he needed forceful vocal orders to behave — he just struggled more valiantly, showing as much nerve as he could, bound like a wet pig about to be butchered, knowing full well his life was at stake, certain to cease in seconds, rather than years.

Josiah was almost positive the Indians would slit the two fellow Rangers' throats and leave them there for the coyotes, vultures, and flies.

He was shocked it hadn't happened at the

outset of their attack, when the Rangers had first been captured. It was a well-thought-out plan that had been perfectly executed by the Comanche.

Any man who thought the Comanche lacked intelligence had never been the mouse in one of their catlike games.

The Comanche weren't always so generous in sparing a life, which made something about the entire situation seem odd. There was a strange air about the Indians that didn't feel quite right to Josiah. It was like something was turned on its side, and he was looking at everything before him all wrong, unclearly.

Josiah just kept telling himself to stay vigilant, to watch and wait for that blink of an eye at the wrong turn by one of the Indians, so he could make a move to save himself and, more importantly, to save Scrap and Red.

He knew, though, that if both men did die on that tree, he would spend the rest of his life knowing he had let them down. He would have lost all of the stakes that mattered in the cat-and-mouse game, and surely, his days as a Texas Ranger would come to a quick and unceremonious end. The deaths would be too much for him too bear. Josiah was certain he couldn't live with himself, constantly blaming himself for two more senseless deaths.

"Liam O'Reilly is not a friend of mine," Josiah said to neither Comanche in particular, hoping to distract the two from Scrap's efforts to free himself.

The mention of Liam O'Reilly sent a chill rumbling up and down his spine.

Josiah had always suspected that O'Reilly had headed up Charlie Langdon's gang once Charlie had dangled lifelessly from the hangman's noose, and he'd suspected, too, since crossing paths with O'Reilly in Waco during the previous summer, that there was a score to settle, a grudge to be revealed at the point of a knife or in a shower of bullets. Now he knew it to be true. O'Reilly was close, and the promise of the grudge and its consequence was coming to fruition at the hands of two Comanche scouts. "Langdon *was* your friend," the tall one said.

"How do you know so much about me? I don't even know your name."

"My name is not important to you at the moment. Your life is in my hands. That's all you need to know."

"If you say so. You're right, though. Charlie Langdon was my friend a long time ago, before the war."

"Your war? The Faraway War between the whites? What a shame you didn't kill more of your own kind. Our war has been here since the White Disease appeared unbidden one day, and has refused to leave ever since. Your likes have driven us to the four corners of our lands, and yet here we are — holding a gun to the back of your head. Some wars never end. Your personal war with Charlie Langdon still rages, as does my war with the foulness of your white breath on the land my grandfathers walked on."

"Yes," Josiah said, "me with a gun to the back of my head. Charlie Langdon betrayed me more than once, and he continues to reach from beyond the grave to pursue his quest to see me done in. He was my deputy when I was marshal of Seerville and he abused the power of the badge. He still thought he was at war, that there were no rules that applied to him. Once he stepped foot into the clothes of a murderer and thief, they fit him like a glove. I'm glad he's dead, but obviously I'm not free of him yet."

"You could all be dead, but yet we stand here talking," the Comanche said.

"No need to do these fellas any harm," Josiah answered, dodging the reality of the truth of the Indian's statement. "I'm the sergeant. They have no quarrel with you."

"They are Rangers, and they are white. That is enough of a reason to kill them. The young one would shoot me in a second, given the chance."

Josiah silently acknowledged this was true. The Indian wasn't stupid.

They stopped then, about ten yards past the tree.

Both Comanche exchanged a set of glances that were surely prearranged and meant something to each but nothing to Josiah.

There was no evidence of a greater plan that he could see, but Josiah's mouth went completely dry. It felt like the saltiness that hovered over the brine creek was caked on his tongue.

"I will order them not to shoot," Josiah said.

The Comanche laughed, then drew his eyes and mouth tight. "There's enough innocent Comanche blood in this ground for us to hate them until the moon falls from the sky for the last time."

"You have no say in that matter, Ranger Wolfe." The short one finally spoke. The one Josiah had decided to call Little Shirt since they were not going to tell him their names.

Little Shirt's voice was gravelly and held a strong, no-nonsense tone — a direct contradiction to his size. Maybe Josiah had been wrong, he thought. Maybe Little Shirt was in charge. Not that it mattered. He, too, would kill both Indians at the first chance to be free of the situation he found himself in.

Killing didn't come easy to him like it did some men, but he would fight to the death, there was no question about that.

"O'Reilly has nothing against them," Josiah said. He wanted to keep the Comanche talking as long as possible. It seemed to be working so far.

"You think you know what the Badger holds as currency to kill a man, Ranger? If a man has no red hair or lacks that melancholy Irish lilt in his voice, then Liam O'Reilly would just as soon see him dead. Flayed open is more like it, his guts burned to a crisp so nothing can gain satisfaction or sustenance from his flesh. Feels that way about Comanche, too. His hate knows no boundaries. His spite is a source of pride. But you should know all of this — you gave him more power once you marched Charlie Langdon to his hangman's noose. How does it feel to know you gave power to an evil man?"

Josiah could not challenge the statement, though he didn't know much about Liam

O'Reilly, just recent actions, since the spring, since running down Charlie Langdon — before then, he'd never heard of this Liam O'Reilly, this man the Comanche referred to as the Badger. "Is O'Reilly your friend or not?"

"You should hold your lips together, Ranger Wolfe, or you will lose your tongue," the tall one said. He would be called Big Shirt if the short one was Little Shirt. "And the ability to assume, as well, that we are only doing O'Reilly's bidding."

They pushed on, walking beyond Scrap and Red, without further incident. Josiah was relieved, but far from certain of Scrap and Red's fate. Or his own, for that matter.

Their horses, including Josiah's Appaloosa, Clipper, were tied to trees near the barren creek fifty yards off to their left.

Josiah had to restrain himself from violently protesting at the thought of leaving Clipper behind, but decided to heed Big Shirt's warning. He had no guns, no knives, no power . . . and nobody covering his back. As hard as it was, though, as long as they were walking away from Scrap and Red, then he was just going to go along and not make waves until the right opportunity presented itself.

The Indians' plans seemed even more

43

certain, and since they had the upper hand and had not killed all three of them in one fell swoop, their action propelled Josiah to believe even more that something was afoot that he did not understand.

What lay ahead of him was well within the grasp of his imagination, though.

He had seen firsthand what a swarm of Comanche or Kiowa warriors could — and would — do to a defenseless man. Their savagery was firmly planted within the locality of his nightmares, even worse than any of the hauntings he had brought back to Texas from the War Between the States.

And leaving Clipper behind was like leaving family. Other than his two-year-old son, Lyle, who was his only living flesh and blood, back in Austin, the horse was almost all he had to care about in this world.

Big Shirt said something to Little Shirt in Comanche, in a knowing, and hard, whisper.

There was no way to translate the language; the words were a jumble of nasally grunts and sounds that didn't make any sense to Josiah. Still, it was obvious that the Indians had come to the next part of their plan, and Little Shirt was giving orders of some kind, since Big Shirt nodded, his eyes unblinking until the last syllable was spoken.

Little Shirt whistled, and within a second or two, a trio of horses appeared from behind the closest outcropping of rocks.

There was not a man, or Ranger, in Texas who wasn't aware of and did not silently respect the prowess most Comanche demonstrated when it came to horsemanship.

They were legendary trainers and riders, the success of many of their battles based solely on the abilities they put to use atop their mounts. All three horses were mustangs, one tall, fully chestnut mare, that had a hard look in her eyes, like she was full of rage, and two paints, one mostly white with small blotches of chestnut.

Little Shirt pulled back, leaving only Big Shirt with his rifle barrel pushed against Josiah's skull. There was no chance, yet, to break away. The short Indian grabbed the three horses' leads and walked them over to Josiah and Big Shirt.

"Get on. But don't try to be brave, Ranger. Your life means nothing to me," Big Shirt ordered.

"Where to?"

"Do you believe in Hell?"

Josiah hesitated. "I've been there before."

"Get on," Big Shirt repeated. "The missionaries would be disappointed in you, Josiah Wolfe."

"They need to get a look at Hell for themselves," Josiah said.

"Something we agree on," Big Shirt said.

Josiah felt the pressure of the rifle barrel leave the back of his neck. But Little Shirt had him square in his sights, Red's long gun, a .50-caliber carbine, aimed straight at Josiah's head.

It was no use trying to escape.

He could not abide being a prisoner, but leaving this world because of that, leaving all that he held dear and had managed to love again, was not worth it.

He heaved himself up on the horse, the tall chestnut mare. She was not amused, and snorted and rustled backwards as he got settled on the horse's strong back. There was no saddle, just a well-worn blanket.

Big Shirt mounted his horse, a smaller paint, and took over holding Josiah at bay as Little Shirt followed suit and mounted his own horse.

Now that all three of them were atop their respective horses, Little Shirt eased into the lead and let out a shrieking hoot and holler, a scream that was more suited to a night-time attack from a cougar or coyote than a man.

The Comanche legged his horse deeply

with his knees, urging it to break away and run.

Before Josiah knew what had happened, Big Shirt slapped the rump of the chestnut mare, and she tore out after Little Shirt. Big Shirt was close on Josiah's tail, and both Comanche had their rifles in hand, a bullet just a pull of the trigger away from cracking his skull wide open, putting a permanent end to his conscious knowledge of daylight and his pursuit of a full, satisfied life.

Dust obscured Josiah's vision, but he could see enough to know that they were going to circle the tree that Scrap and Red Overmeyer were bound to.

He had no control of the horse. The mare acted like he did not exist on her back.

Both Comanche continued their screams and yells. *"Yip, yip, yaw!"*

Josiah could see Scrap struggling against the bindings of the rope, though it did him no good. At that moment, Scrap's fate was far from certain, and it looked like the boy could barely breathe.

Fear was not a characteristic Josiah was accustomed to seeing in Scrap's eyes. He had only known the young Ranger since May, since joining up with the Frontier Battalion in San Antonio. Since then, the two had been thrown together in a few skir-

47

mishes that could have gone badly for Josiah if it hadn't been for Scrap's shooting and riding skills. There were times when Josiah liked Scrap well enough, like when he kept his mouth shut, and there were other times when the kid just plain got on his last nerve. Scrap was moody and unpredictable, traits he needed to shed if he was going to be a good Ranger — if he got the chance, if he survived.

As they rounded the tree, Red Overmeyer made eye contact with Josiah.

Unlike Scrap, Overmeyer did not struggle, did not try to scream through his gag. Instead he looked away from Josiah, then lowered his head to the ground, like he had already surrendered to a predestined fate.

In a swift and sudden pull of the trigger, Little Shirt fired the carbine, his aim perfect.

Red Overmeyer's head slammed back against the tree in an explosion of blood and bone. The only scream to rise into the air came from both Indians in a victorious cheer. Scrap's scream was frozen in his throat, muffled by the kerchief stuffed in his mouth and his own fear.

Josiah jumped at the explosion, expecting it but shocked and scared by it nonetheless. He feared Scrap was next, then his turn, too — but it did not escape Josiah's attention that Red had just been shot by a bullet from his own rifle.

The three circled the tree again. Big Shirt fired his rifle this time, hitting Red directly in the heart. If there was any chance that Overmeyer was suffering, that thought came to a quick end. He was dead, though his eyes were wide open, fixated on the ground, unfazed by the cascading blood from the first shot.

With that, the two Comanche brought all three horses nose to nose, putting Josiah and the angry chestnut mare even more tightly in between them, the reins of Josiah's horse secure in Big Shirt's hand.

They pushed around the tree again in a fast circle, without firing another shot, then headed south, leaving Scrap Elliot in a cloud of dust, blood, and flies that already smelled opportunity, the hoots and hollers of the Indians rising to the clouds, along with Red Overmeyer's soul. If a man believed in such a thing.

CHAPTER 3

A solid blanket of gray clouds had pushed its way east to reveal the promise of a beaming, late autumn sun and a pure cloudless sky. There was no weather, or any other apparent obstacle, that would slow the unlikely trio down.

Big Shirt said they were going to Hell for a visit.

As far as Josiah was concerned, there was no turning back now. Elliot would have to fend for himself, find his way out of the bindings and off the tree — or die there from starvation, if Josiah couldn't escape and turn back to free his fellow Ranger.

At the moment, there were some questions to be answered, and the only Hell that Josiah could conceive of was the Hell that Big Shirt and Little Shirt were going to pay at the first opportunity he could deliver it.

The method of delivery was immaterial. A rock, a fist, a kick with a hard boot heel to the throat, crushing the Adam's apple of either of his captors. He liked the thought of them suffering, dying a slow death, like what was promised him and delivered to Red Overmeyer. It would be interesting to see who the promise came to first.

Josiah was not encouraged by the clear sky.

The coming of a near perfect day offered little hope that everything was going to be all right, that it would work out — his life didn't work like that. A storm would provide more opportunity for escape. As it was, Josiah's blood ran hot, and his hands, though still bound tightly, ached to get a hold of a gun. But all he could do was ride the angry chestnut mare and spit at Little Shirt.

Little Shirt pulled a pistol from a holster belted on his side, Josiah's .45-caliber Colt, his Peacemaker, and pointed it at him in one swift, angry pull. "Do that again, Ranger, and I'll kill you."

"What's stopping you?" Josiah spit again, this time hitting his target right between the eyes.

Josiah had decided he wasn't going to wait to get to Hell. He was already there.

Little Shirt was either going to kill him right then and there, or he was going to give

Josiah an opportunity to break the horse he was riding out of the Indian's grip and flee toward the perfect blue sky.

Josiah was willing to die trying to save himself — therein saving Scrap, too, if he could make it back to the kid. He wasn't willing to be a passive captive. He wasn't willing to live with Red Overmeyer's untimely death on his shoulders and just surrender to the two Comanche, and let them lead him to Hell or beyond.

Little Shirt screamed something in his own language from deep within his heaving chest, then wiped away the wad of spit as quickly as he could.

Comanche was just as baffling a language to Josiah as Spanish was, but there was no mistaking that the Indian was angry. Josiah chuckled. "Kill me now."

Without warning, Little Shirt brought his horse and Josiah's adopted ride to a sudden stop, the Peacemaker still aimed at Josiah's head. Little Shirt raised the barrel and pulled the trigger.

The blast nearly shattered Josiah's eardrums as the bullet whizzed by his temple, barely missing him.

The bullet was so close he felt the breeze and energy of it, felt the reverberation of the report, could taste and smell the gunpowder. Breathing was like eating fire; his throat was immediately raw.

For a second, Josiah Wolfe thought he was a dead man.

Only then did he realize how foolish he'd been, allowing his anger to get the best of him.

His life did not flash before him. He had been in too many tough spots for that to happen. Sometimes, he was certain that death was riding sidesaddle along with him. The ghosts of his past, his wife Lily and their three daughters, trailing after him in an ethereal form, biting at the bit, waiting on the chance for a long overdue reunion. It was nonsense, the thought of eternity with those that he had loved and lost, but at the moment, the fleeting thought of it gave him an odd bit of comfort.

Big Shirt screamed back at Little Shirt in Comanche.

Whatever was said forced the Indian to drop his aim. It sounded like gibberish. A coyote calling in the evening for its mate. A snarling cougar, set on its prey, cornering it, offering the weaker opponent one last moment to consider escape. There was nothing about the Comanche language that Josiah found beautiful or lyrical. It was all hate and anger. Especially now.

53

"I am stopping him, Josiah Wolfe. You are not to be killed, or we will be killed," Big Shirt said.

Josiah cocked his head. How odd was it that the Indians had received nearly the same order he had — bring them back alive. But for what? And why?

"Why did O'Reilly put you up to this?" Josiah forced the words out of his dry mouth, unable to restrain his curiosity any longer.

The cloud of gun smoke wafted away behind them, slowly dissipating into nothingness. The ringing in his ears continued, though, providing enough evidence of the shot for him to continue on.

"I have no reason to answer your questions," Big Shirt said. "But know if you try to escape, or attempt to provoke my brother again, I will shoot you myself and suffer the consequences. We are not far from our destination. If you run, you will be caught, and you will die a slow, painful death. The vultures will tear at your skin as you take your last breath. That is my promise. Do you understand?"

Josiah thought about spitting at Big Shirt, but quickly thought better of it. Big Shirt and Little Shirt were brothers. That was news. They didn't look anything alike.

54

"What are your names?" Josiah demanded, not taking his eyes off his Peacemaker that now rested tightly on Little Shirt's hip.

"There is no need for names. We will not be friends, Josiah Wolfe," Big Shirt said. "You can count on that."

The killing of Red Overmeyer was not the first time Josiah had witnessed the death of a fellow Texas Ranger at the hands of an Indian, nor did he expect it to be the last.

Even though he had known Red a short time, since July, when Josiah had first joined the company of Rangers at the Red River camp, he'd considered Red a friend as much as a partner on the trail, and had been more than glad to have him at his side on the mission assigned to him by Pete Feders.

Overmeyer was trustworthy, or seemed to be in the short time they had known each other. Josiah had never detected a lie, or even a hint of dishonesty, in their many conversations. The man was a handy scout, as well, but this time out, the tracking skills that had led to a long and productive life, if it were to be judged by the oversized belly Red sported and the tales he told, had failed to detect Big Shirt's brother.

At the moment, Red Overmeyer seemed to have suffered the harshest punishment possible for his failure, and there was no way to know what had happened to Scrap, or what lay ahead for Josiah.

He had no idea where they were heading — they had gone north, then northwest. The old Corn Trail was not that far away, a military supply road that would lead right up to the town of Comanche — settled and occupied by Anglos, not Indians, so Josiah thought that Big Shirt and Little Shirt would probably avoid that town at all costs.

Unless, of course, they had left their band and joined up with Liam O'Reilly and his gang — which was the implication, since they knew who Josiah was and had specific knowledge of O'Reilly and his wicked demeanor.

Still, the two Comanche had not declared allegiance with the man they called the Badger. O'Reilly's name could have been a ruse to instill fear in him — which, if that were the case, was a mistake. All the Irishman's name did was provoke anger, and the only fear Josiah had was of losing control of his actions again.

The two Comanche brothers had drawn Josiah in even tighter with a rope around his waist tied to Big Shirt's horse.

Little Shirt had control of the rope that held Josiah's hands, as well as the reins to the chestnut mare.

Josiah missed being on Clipper's back. He had ridden the tall Appaloosa for several years now, and the horse knew his touch as well as any horse could. It was like they were one full being when they rode together, especially under duress. Josiah was certain that Clipper could read his mind, know when to turn before Josiah knew he was even going to turn, or cut when the call for a quick escape demanded it. But now Josiah was on his own. The mare he was riding did not respond to the pressure of his knees or the sharp jabs of his boot heels. He could have been a dead man for all the horse seemed to care. It understood Comanche, not English.

In the past, there had been a few times Josiah had been left to his own devices. Even as a member of the Texas Brigade, he had rarely found himself so ill-equipped to save himself. He had fought hand to hand next to Charlie Langdon, the former, and now dead, leader of the gang Liam O'Reilly was a member of, and had possibly re-formed and now headed up.

The men of the Brigade were the first men into battle and the last out. Josiah had seen so much blood and death that his own perception of mortality had been tried and tested on multiple occasions — preparing him for this very moment, for what lay ahead.

Getting out of his current situation alive, intact, and healthy seemed unlikely unless he stumbled across a windfall. And luck was not something Josiah Wolfe was accustomed to having on his side. He wished he had acquired the vice of gambling. At least then he could figure his odds.

He was stuck with his own survival skills, which were far from weak, though they went unused in many cases. Even recently, a man named Juan Carlos had saved Josiah in San Antonio, and was still on the run for killing the man that would have killed Josiah — one of Charlie Langdon's men sent to settle their ongoing feud and stop Charlie from being escorted to the hangman's noose. The noose finally came, though, and much to Josiah's regret, he had not been there to see Charlie Langdon dangle at the end of the rope.

It was hard to say where Juan Carlos was now.

The fact was that Juan Carlos was a Mexican, a Mexican to the Anglo world, but half-Anglo if the truth was known. As relevant as Juan Carlos's heroic actions seemed in San Antonio, in the last few months, since joining the Frontier Battalion, Josiah had been saved by more men than he could count. These included Scrap Elliot and his expert aim and sharp-shooting, not once but twice saving not only Josiah's life, but that of Josiah's two-year-old son, Lyle, too.

The suddenness of Josiah's disregard for his own life when he'd spit at Little Shirt was a surprise to him.

Lyle would be left an orphan, left to face an uncertain world without anyone to show him how to be a man, a Wolfe. There was no way Josiah was going to let that happen. So he castigated himself silently, remembering the hard lessons his own father had taught him, lessons that Josiah couldn't have learned otherwise, like picking good, solid friends and standing up for them, and for yourself, when times got tough — like now.

The last several months had been difficult, moving to Austin, not knowing anyone, and sleeping in a lonely bed by himself. Mostly it had been difficult being away from Lyle. It seemed like he was always working his way back to his son, at least since rejoining the Rangers. Somehow, that needed to change — if Josiah survived, was able to make it back home, one more time. Or it would be a sad certainty that Lyle would grow up alone, never knowing what had become of his father.

There had been outlaw trouble in the town of Comanche earlier in the spring. John Wesley Hardin had been in town celebrating his twenty-first birthday, and a deputy sheriff recognized the noted gunfighter. When Hardin asked the deputy if he knew who he was, the deputy, a man named Charlie Webb, lied and said he didn't. Instead, Webb followed Hardin into a saloon for a drink, pretending to be part of the celebration, and pulled his gun on the outlaw, intent on taking Hardin down. But one of Hardin's friends saw the ploy play out and yelled out to warn the criminal. John Wesley Hardin killed Charlie Webb at close range, then ran out of town like a cockroach encountering sudden daylight.

A lynch mob was quickly formed, and most of Hardin's family was taken into protective custody — to save them from the angry townspeople. But a group of men, supposed loyal, law-abiding citizens hiding under the cover of darkness, broke into the jail where the family was being held and pulled out Hardin's brother, Joe, and two cousins. All three men were hanged without the luxury of a trial, and it is said they were all hanged with a rope too long, the promise of a slow, strangulating death more than certain, since all three men had grass between their toes when they were discovered the next day.

So Josiah was more than surprised when their trio topped a slight, treeless, rise, and the town of Comanche sat in the middle of the road, about a mile away.

Embers from the troubles in the spring still burned among the townsfolk, even though Hardin had fled, reportedly out of Texas, to Florida. But there were rumors of revenge from the remaining Hardin family, against the ruthless tyrants of so-called justice, for the senseless killing of Joe and the cousins.

The town was small, a supply base for the surrounding ranches. There was a courthouse built of hand-hewn log; a small post office since the town was the county seat; a dry goods, and a general store; along with the expected livery, blacksmith, and jail. Several wood frame houses sat along a couple of dry, dirt streets. Rain was obviously an event of long memories — perhaps winter would be a relief and bring a spattering of much needed precipitation to the parched town. Snow was shared only in imaginations and once every hundred years or so, this far west.

A dog barked in the distance. The sun fell below the horizon, and a wind picked up, swirling dust into tiny, harmless, cyclones. A chill touched Josiah's face, and he shivered from the sudden burst of cool air — a reminder that it was November, that a change in seasons was under way, no matter how brief or unnoticeable that change would be.

Little Shirt pressed his mustang paint closer to Josiah's mare. "Listen, Ranger, one wrong move and I'll kill you. Right in front of the sheriff. He's not going to do nothing. You understand?"

"He's warning you not to shout out, Wolfe. He won't kill you." Big Shirt cast an angry glance at Little Shirt. "But we know your name — you remember?"

Josiah nodded.

"We also," Big Shirt continued, "know of your little house in Austin, and the wet nurse, Ofelia, who tends to your only son."

"I will kill *you both* the first chance I get if anything happens to my family," Josiah said through clenched teeth. Instinct demanded that he reach for his gun and end this game now, but the ropes were so tight on his wrists that he could barely wiggle his fingers. He felt a throbbing pulse from his fingernails to his toes.

Little Shirt laughed. "Mexicans are not family, Wolfe. You are Anglo through and through. What are you thinking?"

Josiah ignored the taunt. His mouth was foaming like that of a rabid dog.

"You will be free of us soon enough, Josiah Wolfe," Big Shirt said. "We will collect our reward and be on our way."

"Your reward?" Josiah demanded. "Why is there a reward?"

This time Big Shirt laughed — only it was a slight, knowing laugh with the turn of a lip instead of the deep antagonizing laugh of his brother. "You did not know that you are a wanted man, Josiah Wolfe? What a shame. You do now."

CHAPTER 4

Evening was settling in as the trio eased into the town of Comanche at a slow gait, taking full advantage of the falling shadows and thick gray light.

It would have made sense for them to ride right down the main street to the sheriff's office if what Big Shirt had said was true, that Josiah was a wanted man, but that was not the track that the Indian brothers took leading their prisoner into the quiet, almost dead, town. They avoided the main street and cut down the first alley they came to, coming to a stop directly behind the Tall Gate Saloon.

The thought of being a wanted man played heavily on Josiah's mind — but not as heavily as remaining a captive of the two Comanche, who he figured were loyalists to the Badger. Whether they wanted to admit it or not.

He'd encountered Liam O'Reilly, briefly,

64

at a distance, in Waco in July, riding with a posse of deputies. Word was the sheriff had been bought out, was operating at the will of an outlaw gang, most likely O'Reilly's. Hiding behind the badge was not an unusual ploy for the despicable and unworthy — so it came as no surprise to Josiah that O'Reilly had worked his way into Waco after Charlie Langdon's demise.

When Josiah was a marshal himself, Langdon had taken up a lawman's position as a deputy, taking advantage of their friendship and the bonds that had been created fighting together in the Texas Brigade — all for the power, or the perception of power, that being a lawman offered.

Charlie had quickly twisted that power into an ugliness that led to the deaths of four innocent people — and from there he had gone on an all-out rampage, with disregard for the law and justice itself. Charlie had been a great soldier, excelling at killing the enemy. So it was entirely possible that Langdon had clued in his protégé, O'Reilly, to use the badge and hide behind it, as well.

But what if there was an unknown warrant, a wanted poster with Josiah's face on it? he wondered silently to himself. Would being a member of the Texas Rangers save him from prosecution?

He knew the answer to that question before it had completely vanished from his mind. The answer was a resounding no.

There would be no protection against the law, not if a crime was provable — even though Josiah could think of nothing that he had done in the recent past for which he would be considered culpable. He had plenty of enemies, though, enemies who would see him harmed any way they could — and, of course, O'Reilly fell right into that bunch.

"You get down easy, now, Josiah Wolfe," Little Shirt said.

Josiah sneered at the Indian. He could smell the sour yeast permeating from the kegs sitting along the back wall of the Tall Gate Saloon. "How much am I worth to you, little man?"

Big Shirt swiftly intervened, saying something to Little Shirt in a calm but forceful voice, in their native Indian tongue, then: "As for you, Wolfe, we are finished."

"You didn't have to kill Overmeyer," Josiah said, again, trying to get Big Shirt to tell him why the tracker had been killed.

"You do not know what I had to do, or why. Perhaps you never will. It does not matter to you. My duty is done, and I can get back to my own life now."

"Back to stealing cattle and killing white men?"

"You think too little of the Comanche."

"A war is coming."

"It is already here," Big Shirt said, pulling his rifle, a war-era model 1865 Spencer .56-50 carbine, out of the scabbard and pointing it at Josiah's head. "Get him down off the horse, brother, before I decide to end his war myself, with a pull of the trigger."

Josiah took a deep breath but tried not to show any movement.

He was sitting stiffly on the back of the angry chestnut mare, watching everything around him, scanning for an opportunity and a way out of the mess he'd found himself in — other than a swift death.

A ramp led up to the entrance of the back of the saloon. Lamps already burned brightly in the cathouse windows upstairs — business was slow. There were three floors, and all of the windows on the top floor were encased in heavy iron bars.

The building wasn't a jail. The windows were barred so the whores wouldn't flee after they had completed their nightly routines. A lot of the women did not choose to stay in the occupation they found themselves in. They were forced into a kind of slavery that Josiah thought was far worse than just about anything he could imagine. Some women were even chained to their beds after their work was done, so they could not escape.

For a brief second, Josiah let his mind wander, forgetting for a moment any opportunity for his own escape, as he thought of two whores he'd known in the last few months.

One he'd slept with, Suzanne del Toro, dead now, killed at the hand of her own brother — she was a victim of greed and jealousy. Suzanne had shown Josiah a moment of comfort and offered herself to him as a woman, not a professional, when he needed it the most. He was still troubled by her death, but only because he knew he could have loved her in a way he had never thought possible. But that was never to be, now that her charred bones lay buried in a cemetery outside of Austin.

The other whore, Maudie Mae Johnson, was a woman Josiah and Scrap had rescued on their way to the Red River camp to join up with the Frontier Battalion, in July, when Josiah had encountered Liam O'Reilly the last time.

Mae, as she liked to be called, was a mad

cat full of sharp claws, but she also had a tender side that showed when you least expected it. She was one of the most confounding women Josiah had ever met. He suspected the girl was sick — sick with the disease of whores — but he wasn't sure.

As far as Josiah knew, and hoped for her sake, Mae was still in Fort Worth where they'd left her, at the boardinghouse Scrap's aunt Callie managed. Mae had told Josiah she could have loved him, but he doubted that was true. At least not the kind of love that he understood and knew.

An out-of-tune piano started to play, banging loudly from inside the Tall Gate Saloon, and it recaptured Josiah's attention from the third floor.

There wasn't any singing, and the roar of the usual crowd did not exist. There were no horses or wagons to be seen in the alley behind the saloon — maybe they were all out front.

The town was a quiet one, not like the cow towns that grew up next to the cattle trails, the populations exploding with the drives north and cowboys seeking ways to quickly rid themselves of hard-earned wages on women and whiskey. But it was entirely possible that the earlier incident with John Wesley Hardin had cast a dark and fearful pall over the place. Josiah had seen the effects of violence strangle the life out of a town, drain every man, woman, and child who had seen it of hope or promise.

A cantilevered roof covered the back entrance to the saloon. The shadows were even denser here since there were several buildings built within a few feet of one another. All of the buildings were three to four stories tall. Night had not completely fallen, but it might as well have been midnight in the alley.

Josiah slid off the back of the horse and planted his feet firmly on the dry ground.

The rope loosened a bit at his ankles, and Little Shirt let the rope that bound Josiah's wrists briefly go slack — but just briefly enough to give Josiah a bit of room to put all the force he could into a double pump of the elbow to Little Shirt's face.

If ever there was a time to make a move and try to escape, now was that time.

Josiah's elbow caught Little Shirt directly under the chin the first time, then square in the nose, sending the Indian tumbling backward.

The blow allowed Josiah to yank free from the Indian's grip on the rope that held his hands.

The Comanche screamed, and a mass of

blood spurted from his mouth and nose — the sudden blows having broken his nose and causing him to bite his tongue.

Josiah jumped back with all of his might, pulling the rope that was holding his feet from Little Shirt's hand, then dove under the chestnut mare, hoping to avoid a shot from Big Shirt's trusty Spencer rifle.

"You are a fool, Josiah Wolfe!" Big Shirt yelled.

But he did not shoot. Josiah was too close to the horse, lost on the other side of a deep shadow that he had seen from atop the mare.

He scrambled to his feet, all the while pulling at the rope, trying to free himself of his confinement so he could run full out into the dark alley next to the saloon.

It only took Josiah a few seconds to free his feet from the rope — but he knew that he couldn't completely unbind his hands. The rope was loose enough for him to work his fingers and wrists, but that was it.

He hated to do what he was about to do, but he had no choice — and there was no time for hesitation.

He cold-cocked the chestnut mare, punched her square in the mouth twice for good measure, making sure his goal was accomplished.

The horse screamed, then reared up on her two hind legs. Big Shirt had to whirl his horse around, sending him halfway out of the alley, to avoid the screaming, bucking horse.

Josiah dove away from the mad horse, then rolled across hard ground and came up to squat with his back against the saloon.

Big Shirt fired the rifle, and the bullet pinged off the side of the building, a foot over Josiah's head.

Even though the air was cool, sweat poured down Josiah's face.

He could hear Little Shirt moaning. His hand hurt like hell, and his knuckle was bleeding from catching a few of the horse's teeth with the hard punch.

He felt around the edge of the building and hoped he could slide between the saloon and the neighboring building without getting stuck — or shot at and killed — and make a run for it.

One more deep breath and Josiah was up on his feet, pushing sideways between the two buildings and down the wall as quick as he could, fleeing the Comanche brothers.

Little Shirt was still on the ground, rolling around in agony, and Big Shirt was still on his horse, shooting into the darkness, shouting, swearing he would not sleep until he saw Josiah Wolfe dead and buried.

CHAPTER 5

The entire town of Comanche came alive at the shots from Big Shirt's rifle. Bright light erupted from the Tall Gate Saloon like it was morning and a gold rush had been feverishly announced. The buildings across the street blazed alive with light and activity. There was a rise of noise, chairs scooting furiously on wood floors, spurs jangling, horses reacting to the shots, prancing at their posts, snorting, tugging, nervous to flee.

Josiah moved slowly, hugging the side of the building, glad that he was wearing dark clothes, making him less of a target — for the moment. His mind was running like an unattended train as he pushed toward the light and commotion, toward the main street that cut through the middle of Comanche.

To say he was in between a rock and a hard place was an understatement. His choices were extremely limited. His hands were still bound with rope, and he had no weapon, no horse, and no idea where the hell he was.

Turning back to face Big Shirt was certain death. He had no choice but to make a run for it — somehow, to somewhere.

He came to the end of the building, his back flush against the outside saloon wall, and stopped to consider what his next move would be.

An empty keg nearly blocked his exit from the compact alleyway, if it could be called that, but Josiah was certain he could jump it.

Another shot rang out behind him, and a bullet dug into the dirt a couple inches from the heel of his boot.

Josiah jumped but did not run out into the light. Not yet.

Another shot came. This time, an inch closer. The next one would be right on target if Josiah didn't move quickly.

Big Shirt was yelling at the top of his lungs in his native tongue, as he and his horse danced at the other end of the building — a raging silhouette born of wartime nightmares that ended in nothing but blood and death.

Without warning, Big Shirt jumped off

the horse and disappeared briefly into the darkness. The shooting stopped, and Josiah saw Big Shirt return and lift Little Shirt to his feet, forgoing a shot at Josiah, instead offering aid to his brother.

There was only a matter of seconds to decide what to do next. Hurrying footsteps through the saloon grabbed his attention as precious seconds ticked away.

Three men pushed through the batwings of the Tall Gate Saloon, turning their heads up and down the street, searching for the cause of the ruckus, each with a gun in his hand, his fingers ready on the trigger.

It only took one short second for Josiah to determine that one of the men was Liam O'Reilly.

Just as Josiah had thought, the outlaw was riding with the law, even though he wasn't wearing a badge. Not like in Waco. The other two men were unfamiliar to Josiah, but both of them were wearing silver stars on their chests.

If Josiah had been a praying man, he would have started a conversation with God right then and there — or earlier, when he'd been taken captive by the Comanche. But the fact was that Josiah Wolfe wasn't much of a churchgoer or a praying man. As far as he was concerned his own fate rested squarely on his own shoulders.

He'd never had the curiosity or the push toward church from his parents to decide one way or another whether the promise of eternal life was real or a tall tale. His folks had left that choice up to him. The war had almost made him a believer, his survival a testament to something other than luck . . . but even then, he couldn't bring himself to ask an invisible force for help as so many of his brethren soldiers had done. But it was his wife Lily's death that had put the final hard glaze on his heart and shut out any possibility of belief in an all-knowing, all-loving and -forgiving God who had time to come to his side when Josiah needed help.

As his wife and three daughters lay dying from the fevers, the preacher man from Tyler wouldn't come out to the cabin, though Lily had requested his presence — since she *was* a believer — to pray them into Heaven, for fear of contracting the sickness himself. Lily was heartbroken and lapsed into a forever sleep, then died, with the certain fear she was on her way to Hell because she had not been blessed by a man of God.

There was no forgiving that man as far as Josiah was concerned.

Big Shirt fired another shot blindly into

the alley. This time the bullet grazed Josiah's calf.

His first instinct was to scream out, but Josiah put his wrist up to his mouth to shield any sound of breathing that might clue O'Reilly and his men in to the fact that he was only a few feet away from them.

He restrained himself as much as he could, bit into the cloth of his shirt, trying his best not to scream out, not to make any noise at all.

Big Shirt called out again, this time for help, clearly in English.

"Damn it, they've let loose of Wolfe." There was no mistaking the Irish brogue, no mistaking Liam O'Reilly's angry voice. "Stay here, Clarmont, just in case he comes up this way."

The man nodded in agreement, then O'Reilly and the other man turned and disappeared back into the saloon.

Josiah assumed the two were hustling to the back of the saloon to help Big Shirt. It looked like it would be a one-on-one fight, if it came to that, with the remaining man, Clarmont.

Josiah wanted to avoid fighting the man at all costs. The pain in his leg was worsening, and his pant leg was wet with blood. The air smelled of gunpowder and death, an all too familiar odor that Josiah hoped never to become immune to. But it was *his* blood he smelled, and the pain was excruciating.

Without any further hesitation, Josiah picked up a rock and chucked it as hard as he could down the boardwalk, opposite the entrance into the Tall Gate.

He quickly scurried to the ground and found another rock that fit neatly into the palm of his hand, a crude weapon, but a weapon nonetheless, which might help even the stakes if he did have to take on Clarmont in a hand-to-hand fight.

The rock clunked on the hard, dry wood, capturing the man's attention.

"Hey," Clarmont yelled out. "Who is that?" He walked right by Josiah, who had ducked back behind the keg.

Behind him, Josiah could hear yelling — Irish and Comanche, a mix of anger on two foreign tongues that needed no translator to understand.

Clarmont had his back to Josiah, went about ten feet past him, then he stopped.

It was now or never, so Josiah mustered all the energy he had, kept his mouth clamped so he wouldn't cry out in pain, jumped over the boardwalk, and took off straight across the street — hoping like hell he could disappear into the shadows before

O'Reilly's man was able to get a shot off at him.

The door to the Darcy Hotel was ajar, and Josiah pushed it open without slowing his run from across the street.

Somewhere behind him, a shot was fired, and Clarmont yelled for him to stop, but Josiah didn't stop running, he just kept on pushing, the burning pain in his leg not slowing him down, hanging on to the rock like it was a brand-new Peacemaker made out of solid gold.

A tall woman dressed in the latest fashions gasped and pulled her daughter close to her, most assuredly assuming that Josiah was an outlaw on the run, as he ran into the hotel lobby.

The woman had perfect blond hair, suddenly reminding Josiah of Pearl Fikes. Pearl was the daughter of the late Captain Fikes, and the first woman since Lily had died that had caught Josiah's eye. This woman wore an elegant, tall, dark blue velvet hat with several white and gray bird feathers sprouting from the center. Her jacket covered a blouse of scalloped lace, with a standing pleated collar, and she was wearing a long skirt the color of which perfectly matched her blue hat. She was a fine-looking lady, well put together, probably waiting for a Butterfield to points unknown.

The Darcy Hotel was a three-storey affair, an example of perfection and high manners rarely seen in such a small town as Comanche. Josiah wouldn't have noticed the stateliness of the lobby and the hotel itself if it wasn't for the woman and child, who was probably about twelve, near the age of his oldest daughter — if she had lived.

"Sorry, ma'am," Josiah said, slowing to doff his sweat-soaked brown felt Stetson.

The woman stepped back, fear frozen hard on her face as she gripped the little girl tighter.

Josiah stopped for just a second to get his bearings, looking for a way out of the hotel. "I'm not here to cause anyone harm," he said, making eye contact with the girl. The thought of causing a child any undo stress was unthinkable to Josiah.

"You will have to leave this instant, sir!" A mousy clerk yelled from behind the marble counter just inside the door.

The clerk's collar was pressed into high wings, a black ribbon tie pulled tight at the neck, making his Adam's apple bulge unnaturally. He looked proper, well scrubbed, like he'd been a fixture at the hotel for a long time. For all Josiah knew, the man was the owner.

But it didn't really matter.

Josiah took a deep breath and ran directly toward the clerk, propelling himself over the counter with one hand, trying his best not to land on his injured leg, making sure at the same time he didn't lose the rock.

The clerk screamed and went tumbling backward, trying to avoid Josiah's perceived attack.

The noise from the clerk's mouth sounded more like something that would have come from the woman's daughter than a man. His rimless glasses went flying into the air, the shattering of the lenses mixing with the commotion as the glasses smashed to the floor in a thousand tiny pieces.

Josiah stumbled over the man and yelled in pain as he landed on his ankle. He quickly righted himself and kept on going, rushing through a curtain that led to an office and, hopefully, to the outside of the hotel.

Just as the curtain was about to fall and close off any sight of what was behind him, Josiah looked over his shoulder and caught a glimpse of Clarmont, followed by two more men, pushing into the lobby, causing even more fright to the woman and child. They had rifles in their hands now, as well as their six-shooters, drawn and ready to fire.

Sweat dripped from Josiah's forehead. His heart was pounding a mile a minute, and worst of all, he was leaving a bright red trail of blood with every step he took.

Once he ran out of the office, Josiah suddenly found himself in a long hallway. He ran toward the back of the hotel, disregarding the shouts and screams behind him to stop. He expected a bullet to pierce his back at any second.

CHAPTER 6

The Chinaman held no emotion on his face at all. He stood at the door of the kitchen, a collection of pots boiling on an iron wood stove filling the air with the aroma of simmering chicken broth, mingling with the pungent odor of bread set out to rise. The yeast was not so stinging to the nose, since it was offset by the sweetness of the broth, but the smell of food of any kind was an unwelcome encounter for Josiah. His last bit of food had been early in the morning when the world had been right, when Red Overmeyer still had the ability to smile and laugh aloud, and did so frequently.

It looked like the Chinaman, who was dressed in traditional black garb, with shaved head, pigtail and all, was standing there just waiting for Josiah to arrive. He was less than well scrubbed though, and there was a hole in his boot, large enough for his big toe to be sticking out.

Truth be told, the cook was probably alarmed by the commotion in the lobby, fidgety as a rabbit to loud noises, uncertain about what violent act was coming his way next, and wondering if the violence, as it probably had in the past, was going to be directed toward him.

Just as Josiah ran by the Chinaman, not slowing down since he didn't sense the man as an immediate threat, the short little man shook his head no, put his hand out, and said, "Not that way."

Josiah stopped dead in his tracks, trying to catch his breath. "It's the only way out."

"They probably have a man there waiting."

"Where then?"

"Upstairs. Go to the end of the hall, jump across the roof."

Footsteps rushed closer, pushing through the office just as Josiah's had. The rumble on the wood floor was like thunder, a coming storm, the ground shaking, but instead of lightning, there were rifles and anger, a score to settle from days long past that could not be solved in a gentlemanly way.

"Then what?" Josiah asked.

The Chinaman shrugged his shoulders, then walked back into the kitchen. One of the pots was boiling over.

Josiah decided to take a chance with what was behind the door. Jumping from rooftop to rooftop sounded like certain death to him.

The air was cold. Night had not hesitated but had fallen in a thick black curtain, covering everything in its path as if a load of coal dust had fallen unexpectedly from the sky. It was not cold enough to snow — that would have been all too rare, but the glow of light would have been welcome.

Josiah did not rush headlong out the door.

He pushed it open slowly, as slowly as he could, looking over his shoulder with sweat pouring from his forehead, the burning in his eyes matching the burning in his calf. He was certain his boot was full of blood.

He did not have time for his eyes to adjust to the darkness, but he slipped out of the door, sliding along the outside hotel wall, gripping his weapon, the simple rock, as hard as he could, hoping upon hope that the Chinaman was wrong.

Maybe there had not been time for the man, or men, to reach the back of the hotel.

At the moment, Josiah's gamble seemed to be paying off. But he had to decide quickly what to do next.

He could make a blind run for it.

There seemed to be houses in the distance, oil lamps just starting to burn in the windows. There were no other tall buildings behind the hotel. Nor was there an alley as there was behind the saloon. Since he had no idea where he was and had no knowledge of the lay of the land in and around Comanche, running into the darkness seemed to be a huge gamble.

Or he could find a place to hide and hope he would be safe.

It only took Josiah a second to decide to run.

But the decision came a second too late.

The back door of the hotel pushed open and slammed against the wall with a loud bang. The darkness was immediately cut with bright, intense light, shadows, movement, and the smell of anger and sweat, as well as that of fresh coal oil. A torch had been lit.

Clarmont pushed out the door, leading with his rifle.

Without a moment's hesitation, Josiah swung the rock as hard as he could, smashing it into the man's skull with as much force as he could muster.

He didn't want to maim the man; he wanted to stop him dead in his tracks. It was a life for a life — war had been proclaimed, in Josiah's mind, the moment his hands had been bound and he'd been taken captive by Big Shirt and Little Shirt.

Clarmont yelled out in astonishment and pain. His surprise was mixed with the sound of shattering bone, blood escaping his brain through any avenue possible; ears, mouth, and nose.

The damage done, Josiah let go of the rock, and tackling him with all of his remaining strength, he jumped at Clarmont, who was already halfway to his knees.

Josiah only wanted one thing now: Clarmont's rifle.

The rifle looked to be a Spencer repeating carbine, in which case, if Josiah was right and the man had a fully loaded the rifle, he would have seven shots to protect himself and flee.

There was no mistaking that Liam O'Reilly and the Comanche brothers were not far behind.

Tackling the man was another risk, another gamble, but it was the only option Josiah had. A rock against a gang of men was less than practical. He needed a gun to protect himself.

Clarmont fell to the ground with a heavy thud, now silent. More footsteps followed down the hall past the hotel kitchen, and two more men pushed out the door. One of them was holding a blazing torch, trying to see what was going on. The other one had a new model '73 Winchester in each hand, cocked and ready.

Josiah had judged the motion and gravity of the tackle correctly when he dove at Clarmont, and he was able to grab the Spencer before it hit the ground.

And as he rolled, all of the action had loosened the rope on his wrists, and it fell away completely with one final hearty shake, freeing his hands once and for all.

In a quick series of maneuvers, Josiah was up in a squat position and firing the first round, catching the man with the two Winchesters square in the right shoulder.

The man fell back into the hotel, knocked back partially by the force of the shot, but also by his own will, realizing that the upper hand was no longer theirs, since Clarmont was lying on the ground, nothing more than a mound of lifeless flesh, his lifeblood quickly draining out of the gaping hole in his head — and Josiah now possessed a rifle of equal power.

For good measure, Josiah fired off another shot. His aim was certain, catching the man just above the ankle, fully eliminating his ability to give chase.

The man with the torch also jumped back into the hall, tossing the flaming club toward Josiah.

Josiah dodged the flame and realized that in freeing his own hands, the man was set on taking up one of the fallen Winchesters.

There was a gang rushing the hall behind the injured man, and a rousing crowd had fallen out into the street in front of the hotel in search of the latest round of trouble to befall Comanche.

A fire bell clanged, and in the distance, a trio of dogs started barking. And to add to the chaos, there were more rising voices, screams and shouts and orders, and the sound of gathering horses.

Josiah took a deep breath, then turned and ran toward the edge of the darkness as fast as he could, trying with all of his might to ignore the growing pain from the gunshot wound in his calf and the weariness that was rapidly draining his energy.

His failing physical capacity was being overridden by the heavy rush of fear that had settled in him, along with the strong need to survive, with the warning of certain death or something worse: recapture by the Comanche and Liam O'Reilly's gang of men.

A solid wall of black clouds hid the moon. Pain ran up Josiah's leg like it was venom from a rattlesnake bite. Sweat from exertion, fear, and pain mixed and dripped onto his lips, reminding him of his thirst, of his need to find someplace to hide.

Buildings were nothing more than shadows, and there was no way he was going to rush into a house with a burning lamp set in the window, causing more fear and unwelcome attention. He wanted to avoid human contact at all costs.

There was still a rise of orders and furious movement behind him, in the center of town and surrounding the Darcy Hotel.

Josiah worried about the little girl, certain he would be responsible for her nightmares once her head hit the pillow and sleep swept her away from the violent world she walked in during the day.

Running full out at night came with its own causes for serious concern.

A hole could take him down, making him an easy capture for Liam O'Reilly. Or he could stumble over a watering trough, smack his head on an unseen post, and die trying to escape. But thankfully, Josiah had a little experience running at night.

It was one of the skills that had saved him during the war.

Once he reached a certain level of fear or anger or need to flee, it was like his body no longer belonged to him but moved on its own accord, his feet dancing on pure instinct, his eyes cutting a path that a cat would have been lucky to see.

He could only hope that his skills would rise from wherever they slept and save his life one more time, like they had in Chickamauga and Knoxville.

His heart was beating so hard Josiah was certain his chest was rolling like a wheat field facing the wind, the rhythm of blood wild and fast, the organ preparing to jump out of his skin if he ran any faster. But he did. He had to. A quick look over his shoulder gave him even more reason to fear. There were several riders on horses, all carrying torches, heading right for him.

He zigged, then zagged, pumping his legs furiously, the concern about his beating heart gone — he was only worried about saving his hide. Plain and simple, that seemed like a slim possibility.

Ahead, he saw two barns, both small — three or four stalls at the most. The closest barn sat a fair distance from a well-lit house.

The other one, a run of about five hundred yards, sat in near darkness. If there was anyone at the house it seemed to belong to, then the barn looked empty, dark, and unattended. He hoped his instinct was right.

Josiah gripped the Spencer, knowing for certain he had five shots left, and made his way to the farthest barn, sure that he was about to make his last stand.

CHAPTER 7

The posse thundered by the barn, but it was easy to tell that a few of the riders had dropped off to conduct a close search.

Josiah could only hope that there wasn't a discernible trail of blood for them to follow. He'd scooted his feet upon entering the barn, wiping away as best he could any sign of entrance in the ankle-deep straw. But he knew that any man who could track a rabbit on hard dirt could see right through his feeble ploy to hide any evidence of his existence.

A dark corner of the barn beckoned as Josiah was able to adjust his eyesight. He had to trust his feet to find a high pile of straw and hay.

He burrowed inside, destroying well-established mice and rat tunnels. The smell of rot and rodent piss was strong, but it didn't matter, he could go no farther. He would die where he lay, or live to fight another day. It was that simple.

Regulating his breathing took a second, then he pushed the barrel of the Spencer to the edge of the pile of straw and cleared enough of it away to have a line of sight to the huge double doors that he'd just entered through.

There was nothing to do now but wait for his pursuers.

He was too close to town for them not to check the barn. It was just a matter of time before they came looking for him. Through the thinly planked walls he could hear the slow and steady trot of horse hooves, circling the barn, looking for any sign of him.

A small glint of light passed by the other side of the barn; a torch and murmured voices.

The loss of blood had weakened Josiah to the point of fearing for his next breath.

Not only did his leg hurt, but the pain had traveled all the way to his chest, even reigniting the tender pain of the old knife wound.

Chills began to travel across every inch of his skin. He was sweating profusely. The inside of his mouth tasted like old dirt, metallic and unhealthy. It was the taste of death, and Josiah knew it.

But he held his breath and tried his best

95

not to move, as the barn door creaked open. Odd thing was, this all seemed very familiar to Josiah, reminded him of fighting the Northern Aggressors in Antietam a lifetime ago. As it was, this was not the first time he had thought his shallow breath might be the last one he'd ever take.

The war never left him — or any man who saw battle, for that matter. Most days he could push away the ghostly battle screams, disassociate himself with suitable tasks of some kind to make the memory vanish.

But today was not most days.

The only comfort that came to his mind now was the pure and true fact that he had lived to see another day — then, and hopefully now.

Survival of the battle in Georgia came mostly at luck's hand. Most men didn't have such good fortune — his mother prayed for him, he knew that, but he couldn't credit her holy actions as the cause of his survival.

Antietam was a bloody day, the casualties so deep it was said that nearly eighty percent of the Texas Brigade had been killed on that single day. It was a larger loss than any other brigade suffered in the whole war, on either side, from beginning to end. And Josiah had been there in the thick of it. He still bore his own scars from the battle, though he tried to ignore them. Now it was impossible not to consider his own mortality, just like he had in the last moment of retreat to the West Woods at the end of the battle, broken, bleeding, running for his life, stumbling over more dead men than he had ever seen in his life, or hoped to ever see again.

There were streams of blood running in every direction, moans and groans filling the air.

If the Grim Reaper was actually working the field, then he must have been sweating at the brow — working hard carting off the dead to whatever realm the wraith came from in the first place.

The surgery tents were in full bloom, the surrounding ground red and muddy with blood, crates overflowing with amputated legs and arms. Screams mixed in the air, too, and as night fell, the cries of pain did not stop. The owls remained silent. Gone. Or watching, from atop the trees, the madness of men.

Josiah had been certain it would be impossible to survive another day after that. But he had.

The win at Antietam was a fragile but certain victory for the Union. In the days that followed, the blood that was left behind on the fields of Sharpsburg and Antietam gave Lincoln a window to fight back with his words and ideas. He released an early version of the *Emancipation Proclamation,* further isolating the rest of the world, particularly England and France, against the Confederacy — at least to the point of ceasing to offer any financial aid to the cause.

It was a blow from which the South would never fully recover.

There had been no way for Josiah to know, of course, that he was fighting a losing battle on that bloody day — just as there was no way now to know the outcome of his current, dire circumstance in an unknown barn in Comanche, Texas, nearly twenty years later.

This day, and Antietam, all felt familiar. Too familiar, and that was the troubling part. Coupled with his own physical weakness, he felt like he had given every ounce of his being to win a futile war, and it still was not enough.

Josiah held his breath, tried not to move, steadied the barrel of the Spencer the best he could.

A mouse ran over his right hand, flittering across his skin in fear, fleeing as quickly as it could.

The rodent didn't startle him. He was aware of its presence, as well as the village of them that lived in the hay mound, so he was not surprised when they decided to run. He just hoped they would go one at a time, scurry from the light deeper into the hay instead of outward, drawing attention to his position.

He remained still, unfazed, as the light inside the barn grew brighter.

The smell of coal oil filled the interior, the threat of fire a concern to animal and man alike, but more so to Josiah. He had seen the aftermath of a fire in a barn, seen the charred human bones of someone left behind, and now that fate could very well be his.

Odd thing was, he was certain he heard the horses outside fade into the distance. They had not stopped scouting, searching for him, so he was a little confused — but nonetheless aware of the threat coming his way.

Silence filled the barn.

Sweat dripped from the tip of Josiah's nose to the top of his lip. He tasted his own salt, feared for his own life, and pressed his finger tighter on the trigger — just as the light pulled back and disappeared.

The barn went black.

Sometime in the middle of the night, Josiah slowly stirred then started awake, suddenly aware of the passage of time.

The riders had gone on, and the torch had vanished. Though Josiah was not sure if he had lost consciousness before or after the torch had come and gone.

It didn't matter; at the moment, he seemed to be safe. Not to mention alive and armed, still equipped with the Spencer and five cartridges to protect himself with. That was more currency than he had had since first catching the trail of Big Shirt — which now seemed as much a trick as the attack on Lost Valley by Lone Wolf in July. Still, he didn't know for sure that he, Scrap, and Red had been lured to the cropping of rocks by Big Shirt and Little Shirt. Or if the Indians' true cause all along had been to take Josiah hostage.

It was the first time that he'd had the strength and clarity of thought to question the events of the day.

Not that he was healed. But the bleeding in his leg had stopped, congealed as he slept. It was apparently just a flesh wound, though at the time the bullet hit him, it had felt like a full-on shot. He couldn't be sure that he was right now, and he would have to wait until daylight to make sure, but he thought he knew the difference between a graze and a direct hit, and he was almost certain that he didn't have lead lodged in the muscle or next to the bone.

He was hungry, thirsty, and weak, but the fear of death — at least impending death and doom — seemed to have passed.

Josiah was reasonably certain at that moment that he was going to live to see another day. Then the questions crept back into his mind as he lay there, still afraid to move in the solid darkness, unsure of where he was or what was next.

If it had been Big and Little Shirt's intention, or mission, to capture him because he had a reward on his head — most likely posted and sworn out by Liam O'Reilly — then why did the Comanche shoot Red Overmeyer? Kill him like a trapped animal, tied to the tree . . . and leave Scrap there alive?

At least that was the way it had appeared.

The last time Josiah had seen Scrap, the boy's eyes were filled with fright, and he was tied to the tree, struggling to escape with Red behind him, his head half blown off.

Not much of it made any sense at the moment to Josiah.

Suddenly he was an outlaw being pursued by an outlaw — for what cause? A price on his head for what crime? He was a Texas Ranger, damn it, not some low-life gunslinger who killed for the pleasure or power of it.

How did a simple expedition to scout out Indian cattle rustlers turn into a trail of confusion, leading to the death of a good, solid Ranger like Red Overmeyer?

Josiah exhaled. Just thinking about all of it made him weak, and he decided that there was no place to go at the moment. What he needed most was more rest. Hopefully, there would be plenty of time to get his answers once the sun broke over the horizon.

The first question: Was Scrap Elliot still alive?

If he could get free of the town of Comanche, then Josiah knew he had no choice but to head straight back to that tree and see what had become of Scrap — and Red.

CHAPTER 8

Nobody likes to wake up with a gun barrel firmly lodged against their lips.

"You move one muscle, mister, and I'll blow your fool head off."

Josiah flickered his eyes open.

His vision was blurry, and he was weak — but not stupid. He restrained himself. He was not going to move an inch, but instead, he would do as he was told, and not search out the Spencer that had fallen from his grip sometime during the night. Josiah still wasn't sure if he was awake or in the midst of one of his common nightmares.

"What the hell are you doin' in my barn?"

Josiah started to answer the question, but stopped when the barrel of the rifle at his lips was pushed just a little harder. This person meant business. Josiah was fully awake now.

"Don't answer that. I know why you're here. You're that Ranger that the sheriff's lookin' for, ain't you?"

Josiah didn't move, just blinked his eyes, clearing his vision. He saw his accuser clearly now, at the other end of the rifle, a .50 carbine, and was a little surprised.

The gun was held by a girl, well not quite a girl, a young woman, maybe twenty years old.

Tangled brown hair fell over her shoulders, and she was dressed in a blue cotton dress that matched the color of her eyes, topped with an oversized woolen, four-button man's sack coat. The color of the coat had nearly bled out of it, and it was as gray as the coming winter sky. The girl's eyes were cold, hard as the metal of the rifle in her hands, not showing fear but outright anger and indignation.

The dress would have been loose-fitting at any time, but now she looked to be in the late stages of pregnancy. Her belly was full and rounded, dropped low at the waist, protruding like she'd stuffed two full-grown pumpkins up under the dress. Her breasts protruded, full and ripe obviously, the cleavage deep, but thankfully hidden mostly by the pull of the simple sack coat. Her feet were bare and dirty.

"Well? You are, ain't you? You're that Ranger everybody's lookin' for?" the girl demanded, pulling the rifle away from Josiah's dry mouth about an inch. "You best answer me, mister. I'm in a foul mood the way it is, lackin' sleep like I am."

Josiah nodded yes. "I am."

"Now what in hell's tarnation does the sheriff want with a man like you?"

"I don't know."

"What you mean you don't know?"

"It's a long story."

"I ain't got the time nor the patience for long stories or tall tales at the moment. Stand up."

"I didn't do anything wrong."

"Do I look like I care? You're in my barn, causing me grief and they're certain to come back once they figure where you done hid the night out. Ain't that enough?"

"I didn't mean to bother you."

"I said stand up." The girl bounced the barrel of the carbine, motioning for him to move sooner rather than later.

"I don't know if I can."

"Why's that?"

"Got a wound. A flesh wound I think."

The girl stared at Josiah for a long, hard second, running her eyes up and down the mound of hay he'd buried himself in. There was a dried puddle of blood at his feet.

"Now all of this is about to cause me to

scream. This is the last damn thing I need right now. Can't you see I'm about to birth a baby?"

"I can see that," Josiah said, looking away.

There was no way the girl could understand his sadness at the sight. The emotion trumped his fear, but only for a moment. He knew he had to push away any thought of his lost family and his living son if he wanted to get out of the barn, and Comanche, alive.

Dull morning light filtered into the barn. The double doors were open, and it looked to be a rainy day outside. The coolness of the night had yet to fade, overtaken by the wind of the day, running due west from one side of the barn to the other, droplets of rain pushing in through the cracks. It was easy to tell it was going to be an uncertain November day, the chill hanging on every breath of air like a bad memory.

The rain was steady — and from what Josiah had seen on the ride the day before, the town looked like it needed a big drink of water. But as far as he was concerned, the change in weather couldn't have come at a worse moment.

If it were possible for him to flee, to escape unseen, then his footprints would be even easier to track in the fresh mud.

Somewhere in the distance, thunder clapped.

The girl looked over her shoulder and shook her head. "Ain't liking that. Doc Foley don't like coming out in a storm. His horse spooks easy the way it is."

The barn smelled heavily of manure. Mixed with the natural rot of the hay, it added to Josiah's sense that the barn hadn't seen the work of human hands anytime in recent memory. There were no horses or other animals living in the barn. Maybe they were outside.

"My rifle is to my right. I'm going to move away from it," Josiah said.

"Good idea."

"Where's your husband?"

"You need to mind your own damn business, you understand, Mr. Ranger?"

Josiah nodded again. "Sorry, ma'am, I didn't mean to offend you. Just looks like you're in a delicate condition. You got pains?"

She stared at him, bit her lip, then nodded yes.

"Pretty close together?"

"Close enough. Baby'll be early by a month if it comes anytime soon."

"I don't know that I can help you."

A cloud crossed the girl's face. Something

107

caused her concern, and her mood went right back to where it had started; foul and mad.

"You just need to shut the hell up right now and stand up and do what I tell you." The girl looked over her shoulder quickly, like she'd heard a sound that Josiah didn't. "Or you're gonna be a dead man if you don't do as I say and hide."

It was then that Josiah heard the thunder of horse hooves, rounding the rear of the barn, heading right toward the open doors.

The girl stood squarely in the center of the open double doors, the rifle resting across her left forearm, her finger hovering over the trigger. Beyond her, three men sat on horses. Two of them Josiah didn't recognize, the other one he did.

The man was Liam O'Reilly, there was no mistaking that. His hat had fallen back off his head, held by the string around his neck. His thick red hair glistened, soaked with rain but still bright as a redbird strutting around in full breeding feathers, trying to entice a female. O'Reilly's hair was as tousled as the girl's, and he looked like he'd been riding all night. His clothes were muddy, and the other feature that stuck out to Josiah from his position, hiding in the hay mound — where the girl had instructed him to go just moments before the riders arrived — was that O'Reilly didn't wear a badge now, while the other two men did.

"Morning, Billie," the man in the lead said.

He sat comfortably on a black stallion. The man was wearing a tall black Stetson, a black vest with a five-point star pinned to it, muddy riding boots, and a slicker opened up over his shoulders.

"What can I do for you, Sheriff?"

"We're looking for a man."

"Figured as much. That Ranger?"

Josiah stiffened. He still wasn't sure if he could trust the girl — Billie, he figured, since that was what the sheriff had called her. But she'd told him to hide, and hide he had. He had no choice. Running was out of the question.

The sheriff eased the horse up a step, and he looked past Billie, peering curiously into the barn. "You seen him?"

"I heard your men out searchin' last night. They stirred me out of my bed. Thought we was bein' attacked by Comanche."

"Nothing to worry about."

"That's what you say. I just came out to check the barn. Ain't nothin' missin' or anybody around that I can see."

O'Reilly pushed his horse up next to the sheriff's. "Come on, Roy, let's get on with it."

"Billie deserves a moment." The sheriff glared at O'Reilly. "Don't you know who she is?"

"I know who she is. Everybody in Comanche knows who she is. No offense there, little lady," O'Reilly said, the Irish in his voice not a lyrical lilt, but hard, like a cold-edged Bowie knife, "but we don't have time for such niceties."

"That Ranger killed Bill Clarmont last night. I lost another deputy," the sheriff said.

"Something you're gettin' good at, Roy," Billie snapped.

"Doc Foley's busy tending to some of the other men who were hurt. You need me to send him out?"

Liam O'Reilly slid off his horse, a tall chestnut mare, and walked up to Billie like he'd known her all his life. He stopped inches from her face.

"He's supposed to be out this way soon." Billie didn't flinch, didn't seem to be intimidated by O'Reilly's glare.

"Easy there, man," the sheriff said to O'Reilly.

Josiah's vantage point was partially obscured now, but he could still see the third

110

man sitting on a horse next to the sheriff. The deputy was a brute of a fella, round like a big boulder, with a long, black beard, almost all covered up with a pommel slicker to protect himself from the rain. The man had access to his six-shooter on his hip, the rain shield open enough to expose the badge on his chest and any other weapons he'd equipped himself with. He held a Winchester, ready for anything out of the ordinary, or anything foolish enough to move. Whoever he was, the deputy didn't look familiar, nor did he appear to be a man who would hesitate if it came down to killing a Ranger.

Josiah was surprised that the Comanche brothers weren't riding alongside O'Reilly. It was a relief as well as a revelation. The Indians could have roused Josiah out of his hiding place, tracking him by sight and smell, far easier than the sheriff and his deputy.

O'Reilly glanced over his shoulder, scowled at the sheriff, then turned his attention back to Billie. "You got reason to hide a man in the barn, Billie Webb?"

"Not sure that it's any business of yours."

"Against the law to harbor a fugitive of justice."

"You ain't the law."

O'Reilly laughed, then as if a curtain had

fallen across his face, the muscles in his cheeks froze in anger.

He flipped up his gun from his swivel-rigged holster, a Peacemaker like Josiah's, only with fancy pearl white grips, and in rapid succession fired all six rounds blindly into the barn, taking aim at nothing in particular, but scanning the barn from one side to the other, each bullet piercing the hay mounds or a dark corner — where a man running from the law just might hide.

CHAPTER 9

Billie stood in the doorway of the barn and watched the three men ride away. When she turned to face the inside of the barn, it looked like all of the blood had drained from her face. She was white as a Christmas goose whose neck was being firmly held on the cutting block.

"You still alive in there, Ranger?" Her voice was a whisper, and she kept looking over her shoulder, still untrusting of the sheriff and his men, maybe uncertain about whether or not they'd left a spy behind, just waiting to call them back.

Josiah stirred in the hay, then sat up slowly, his rifle appearing before he did, clearing his face of the debris. O'Reilly's shots had missed him. He sighed deeply.

"I'm fine."

Billie exhaled. "Good. I was afeared he got lucky and kilt you."

"I got lucky."

"Best not use all your luck up at once."

"I'll keep that in mind. Are they gone?"

Billie eased back to the door, her right hand unconsciously massaging the crest of her massive stomach. "Looks like."

Josiah stood up, teetered on his leg, grimaced as a shot of pain nearly toppled him over. He was weak from the loss of blood, but more than that, the long ride and chase the day before had left him weary, hungry, and feeling less capable than he'd felt in a long time.

"We need to get you inside the house," Billie said, rushing over to Josiah.

Josiah shook his head. "I can't risk getting you in any kind of trouble. I've got to get on out of here."

Billie slid underneath Josiah's arm, shoulder first, steadying him with all of her weight. She was nearly a head shorter than he was, but strong and hearty, given her current condition.

"It ain't but twenty feet to the house. Those fellas who are after you need to be locked up inside a jail cell them damn selves. Ain't a one of them worth an ounce of dirt. Especially that red-haired one."

"O'Reilly," Josiah said.

"You know him?"

"We have a history."

"That figures. He's lower than a rat, and meaner than one, too." Billie exhaled, then clenched her teeth, fighting off a pain.

"You all right?"

"Baby's lit my heart on fire, that's all."

Josiah nodded, then pulled away from Billie, his feet a little more sure now that he'd had the chance to stand. The wound bled a little, but it wasn't going to stop him like he'd first thought it would. He walked to the barn door, limping noticeably, and peered out.

"All this excitement has got you riled. You need to forget about me and go on back in the house, take it easy till the doctor comes along," Josiah said.

Billie Webb's head drew back like she'd been punched. Her face hardened as fast as hot gunmetal set in a cooling pot. It would have only taken a smidgen of imagination to see the steam blasting out of her ears.

"Just who in the hell do you think you are, Ranger, comin' in here and tellin' me what to do? You just go on, then. Go out there in broad daylight and get yourself kilt. See if I give a damn."

With that, Billie stalked straight out of the barn, her eyes focused solely on the tiny clapboard house — but she stopped midway, turned, and surveyed the landscape, then walked back to the barn door. "You won't last for ten minutes outside of here. Now, come on, don't be a damn fool. I ain't gonna ask you again."

The rain had continued to fall steadily in thick sheets. The entire world was cast in a blanket of grief, all blacks and grays. Even though it was morning, it looked like night was about to fall. A breeze had turned into a healthy wind, pushing up from the south. Rivulets of water ran down Billie's face, but she stood unmoving, her jaw set hard, giving Josiah the solid impression she was not going to take no for an answer and leave him to fend for himself.

"It's now or never, Ranger. Once this weather passes, the sheriff'll be back. You can count on that. Him or that ugly Mick."

Josiah pushed off the door, sliding the Spencer up under his arm, his finger on the trigger. He knew Billie was right. O'Reilly would come back for certain, so there was nothing to do but take advantage of the rain or face the consequences.

Billie waited for him to catch up and then walked shoulder-to-shoulder with him to the door of the small house.

The grounds around the house were barren, save a towering live oak, reaching into the unruly sky like a giant pole as thick around as three whiskey barrels tied together. The gnarly branches looked like arms reaching up in need of something unseen. They, too, were thick and barely moving in the steady wind. The tree was not a threat, unless lightning took a liking to it, and would no doubt offer immense shade and comfort on a long, hot summer day. Pleasure of that type seemed a luxury at Billie Webb's house.

Mostly, though, Billie's place looked plain uncared for, neglected for some time. Goat-bush and hackberry had about taken over the switchgrass beyond the barn. A gate to the pasture had come off its hinges, blocking entrance or exit for any creature, man or beast, and making it difficult to come and go. Even the barn itself was in need of serious repair. Most notably, the roof had holes, as big as a dog's head, peppered on both sides of the steep incline.

Josiah could not restrain himself from noticing the condition of the homestead. He had spent nearly all of his life on a similar piece of land in East Texas, just outside of Tyler, and he knew, firsthand, the trials of keeping up with one thing after another on a farm — especially when you were alone. And making that assumption about Billie didn't set well with him, considering her current physical condition and quick temper. There was more going on in her life than he knew . . . and he wasn't sure he was in much of a hurry to find out all of the details of her reality.

He had other things on his mind at the moment — but had no choice but to take refuge inside the small house.

Josiah stopped at the stoop and let Billie lead the way into the house. He scanned the gloomy horizon for any sign of the sheriff, O'Reilly, or any other riders, and saw nothing. Not even a cow or a horse. The weather wasn't welcoming for a duck, or bird of any kind, either.

Billie slid out of the oversized sack coat, hung it on a peg just inside the door, then made her way to the woodstove.

"I'll get that," Josiah said, shaking off the rain.

He was soaked to the bone. If his boot had been full of blood earlier, then it certainly had washed away by now. Still, he felt cold and shriveled. The heat from a hot stove would be a welcome development.

Billie ignored Josiah's offer and slid a healthy piece of wood into the stove. Orange embers filled the bottom of the stove, and the heat rushed out into the small interior, filling it comfortably. The wood caught fire immediately, the crackle of it the first happy sound Josiah had heard in nearly a day.

"There's a trunk in the next room. You'll find some britches and socks there. Help yourself," Billie said.

"I can just stand by the stove and dry out."

"This ain't no time to be nice, Ranger," Billie said, pausing, a curious look passing across her face. "What's your name, anyways?"

"Josiah. Josiah Wolfe."

"I'm Billie."

"Billie Webb," Josiah said, nodding his head.

"Guess you already figured that out."

"Yes, ma'am."

A slight smile replaced the curious look on Billie's face. "Been a while since anyone's called me ma'am. I haven't been out much since Charlie . . ." She stopped, cut the sentence off with a tongue sharp as a knife, then turned away from Josiah and threw another log into the stove. "Well, go on now, don't just stand there like there's nothin' to do. Get out of those clothes so I can take a look at your leg. I don't figure we have much time to get you cared for."

The inside of the two-room house was just as unkempt as the outside. Clothes were tossed about on the floor like rugs kicked in fury, and the bed in the other room looked like Billie had just rolled out of it. The floor had not seen the touch of a broom in a good while, and cobwebs in the corners certainly held insect nests, they were so thick. It was a welcome environment for scorpions and spiders, among other creatures that could cause the girl harm.

The trunk Josiah had been instructed to open was easily found sitting in a corner undisturbed, and the inside was as neat as any military locker Josiah had ever seen.

For a matter of privacy, Josiah slid against the wall, propping himself up as he peeled off his wet clothes.

The wind outside found its way through the walls and wrapped itself around Josiah's ankles. A chill ran up his leg and didn't stop until it reached his ears.

His leg was bloody, and the wound was still seeping, the wetness preventing complete clotting. Josiah touched the graze, pressed it, and slid his finger around the upper edge just to make sure there wasn't any lead to be found inside. He didn't think so, even though it hurt like hell, almost as much as the stab wound in his shoulder.

There was no question he needed to be bandaged. All things considered, his whole body hurt. He caught the first whiff of coffee boiling on the stove and realized how hungry he was, too. He quickly discarded the rest of his clothes and found a pair of trousers, socks, and a simple tan cotton twill shirt. He dried himself with a wool shirt that had been eaten up by a cadre of unseen moths, and changed into the clothes. They fit like they had been made for him.

When Josiah walked back into the room, Billie was standing over the stove with her back to him. She was frying up some bread and bacon. She must have heard him come in. She turned to say something, but the words caught in her throat. Nothing came out of her mouth but a surprised cry, followed by tears bursting out of her eyes, cascading down her full cheeks as if a dam had been breached after a devastating storm.

CHAPTER 10

"For a second, I saw Charlie standing there," Billie said, wiping her face dry. "I'm sorry."

"It's all right." Josiah stood a good ten feet from Billie, across the room, and had his own visions of ghosts. There was no way Josiah could not have thought of his wife, Lily, silhouetted against the window, her stomach swollen with child. They'd had four children together. He was no stranger to the beauty of pregnancy — and the tragedy of it, too. "I take it Charlie Webb was the one John Wesley Hardin killed in the spring," he said.

"Shot him in the back is what he did. The coward." Billie hesitated, scowled, and looked away, fighting back even more tears. "Don't ever mention that man's name in this here house again, you understand?"

"Yes, ma'am, I'm sorry."

"No need to be sorry. But I won't rest till

I hear tell that son of a bitch is dead and buried. I'd've gone after him myself if I'd been able, but I'd figured out that me and Charlie was gonna have a young'un to look after right before then." She exhaled heavily. "It's not your problem."

"You don't have a family to go to, I take it? No one to help you out?"

"None that's worth the powder and lead to blow to hell. Charlie was my family. All we ever wanted was a little piece of land and a family to look after. He took to bein' Roy's deputy to make a little extra money. I never figured he'd get kilt."

"I've questions about the sheriff."

Billie let out a quick laugh that originated deep in her chest. "That man's scared of his own shadow. My guess is he let the fools into the jail that pulled out Hardin's brother and started all this meanness. Look at what it's done. Nobody feels safe. You're a Ranger, can't you do something?"

Now it was Josiah's turn to exhale. "The county sheriff pretty much has authority over all of the Rangers. He's got to ask us for help, and we're not lawmen. Not in the sense that the sheriff is. Jurisdiction is a topic best left to Governor Coke and the men in Austin who make the laws. They don't want us to wear badges or interfere in

123

county business. There's not much any Ranger could do. Especially one who's just been shot and chased after like he's an outlaw himself."

"Well those stuffed shirts ought to get out of the city more often."

"You'll get no argument from me on that."

The room was warm and the smell of bacon strong, carried about on the drafts that were poking in all through the house as the storm carried on without any sign of letting up outside.

Billie had set two plates on a small wood table. A cup of steaming coffee sat waiting for Josiah — but he didn't move. His feet were suddenly frozen to the floor. He was afraid of what he was walking into, certain that if he sat down at the table, leaving would become difficult, if not nearly impossible. And he had to leave. He just had to — and soon.

"Let me take a look at that leg." Billie slid a piece of fried bread onto a plate and set it on the table along with a small bowl of beans.

Josiah still didn't move. He just stared at her, uncertain of what would be next. He understood Billie's bitterness and pain more than he could say. It had taken him nearly two years to pick himself back up after burying Lily and his three little girls. He couldn't imagine what it must be like for a woman left to fend for herself, at the worst possible time in her life, pregnant, her husband shot in the back by a heartless outlaw set on making a name for himself.

"Well?" Billie said, a questioning look falling across her face. "You surely ain't bashful, are you?"

"No, no." Josiah stepped forward, remembered the pain, and limped over to the chair, pushing any thought of his family — living and dead — as far away from his mind as possible.

Billie rolled up his pant leg. "It needs cleanin' out and bandaging up real tight-like. I got some salve that Charlie brought back from the war that ought to stop the infection from spreadin', if'n it shows up. Don't look to be too much trouble. You're a good healer, Josiah."

Only on the outside, Josiah thought, but he didn't say it. "I don't think there's any lead in there."

"Don't look that way. I couldn't help you if there was. We'd have to wait for Doc Foley."

"That might be too long."

"Ain't a concern. He won't do nothin' for you I can't." Billie stood up, walked over, pulled a pot off the wall that was hanging just above the stove, then headed for the door. The water pump sat like a lonely sentinel just outside.

"I'd like to be on my way before the doc shows up," Josiah said.

Billie ignored the comment. "Go on, get yourself somethin' to eat. You need to regain your strength." She seemed reenergized now that her attention was focused on someone else. Any pain she might have felt before was minimized as she prepared to take care of Josiah's wound.

Josiah thought she had the makings of a good mother.

Billie grabbed the sack coat off the peg and threw it over her shoulders. She pushed out the door, unconcerned about the weather or anything else — like somebody watching from a distance. But Josiah was concerned. He scooted back against the wall, out of the line of sight from the doorway, eyeing the Spencer that he'd stood in the corner, just next to the door.

He couldn't resist any longer and took a deep swig of coffee. It was hot and strong and had the flavor of Arbuckle's, for which he was glad. He breathed deeply after the first swig, then took another drink. The coffee was nearly gone by the time Billie came back inside with a pot full of water.

She had barely dried herself off from being outside in the first place, and now she was soaked from head to toe all over again. The rain didn't appear to bother her.

"Not lettin' up out there. I think it's gonna be a long storm," Billie said.

"Looks like you all needed some rain."

"The land's been pretty much on its own since Charlie died. Not gonna be long before one of the outlying ranchers moves in and takes it. Probably come spring. Baby'll be here anyway, and I can't keep up with it the way it is. Can't imagine runnin' after a young'un and tryin' to do all of Charlie's work, too."

"I'm sorry," Josiah said.

"Just the way it is. I couldn't just stop, not with my belly growin' every day. Maybe if'n I would've been without it, then I could have."

Josiah fidgeted in the chair. "I understand."

"I imagine you do." Billie put the pot on the stove to boil. "You look like a man who's seen more than his fair share of ugliness. You was in the war, wasn't you?"

"Yes, ma'am. The Texas Brigade."

"I figured. Looks like you came back all in one piece."

"Mostly."

"That's what Charlie would've said, too. I knowed him since I was knee-high to a grasshopper, but I sure didn't know him when he came back from that fight."

"War changes a man."

"Ugliness does. Sure does. Charlie softened some after we married. But some nights he'd scream out, tremble like a scared little feller. You know what I mean?"

"I do," Josiah said. "I do."

"I 'spect bein' a Ranger is a lot like still bein' at war."

"Not so much. It's a different war, at least."

"They're all the same."

Josiah nodded in agreement.

"You got family?" Billie asked.

"A son, in Austin. He's two."

"No momma?"

Josiah shook his head no. "Her and my three daughters died. Fevers took 'em." He wasn't about to tell Billie that Lily had died giving birth to Lyle.

Billie took in a deep breath. "I'm sorry to hear that."

"Thanks."

Neither of them said anything for a minute or so. A long minute. Time enough for the drafts to push much of the sadness and

128

death out of the house — at least as much as was possible.

"You drink all of your coffee?" Billie asked.

"Nearly."

"Not hungry?"

Josiah nodded his head yes. "I was waiting for you."

Billie smiled. "You go on while I get out of these wet clothes."

"You sure?"

"I appreciate you bein' a gentleman and all, Josiah Wolfe, but I'm not much for food at the moment. Now, go on, eat."

"Yes, ma'am." Josiah didn't need to be told twice. He dug into the plate as if he hadn't had a decent meal in a year, like he had upon returning home that first day from the War Between the States.

Billie disappeared into the same room Josiah had changed clothes in. The house creaked as a gust of wind pushed against it. Rain pelted the single window, and for a brief moment, Josiah felt safe.

He lost himself in the meal, in the warmth from the stove, in Billie's kindness. He nearly forgot about everything. The pain in his leg. O'Reilly's presence in Comanche. Scrap's fate . . . And most of all, Lyle and Ofelia, waiting for his return in Austin. He was only supposed to be gone two days.

It was a moment to savor, just like the bacon, the fried bread, and the beans . . . because just as soon as he finished eating the meal, Josiah heard a loud thump in the other room and felt the floor shake.

A scream that matched the wind and the storm outside echoed inside the house, and without thinking, Josiah was on his feet, knowing full well what the tone of the scream meant.

CHAPTER 11

Billie lay on the floor motionless. Her face was drained of color, and there was a huge puddle seeping out from underneath her. The room smelled wet and sour.

"Somethin' broke," she whispered, her eyes flickering in pain — or maybe fear.

Josiah nodded, and exhaled deeply. "I sure wish Ofelia was here," he said, looking to the ceiling. He was kneeling at her side.

They never had got around to bandaging his leg, but that seemed to be a distant concern at the moment. The wind outside whistled as loud as a locomotive, and rain hit the roof like stones dropping from the sky. Josiah sure hoped the house was built solid.

Billie put her hand on her belly and tears began to stream down her face. "Damn you, Charlie. Damn it all to hell. Why ain't you here? You promised you'd never leave me."

Josiah ignored the plea. There was nothing he could say to her to ease her pain and he knew it. Neither of them had the ones they loved in their lives to call on, to lean on, when they needed them the most.

"Come on, let's get you some dry clothes on and get you in bed. That baby's gonna come whether the doc's here or not," Josiah said, standing up.

It was a struggle, but with Josiah's help, Billie pulled herself up and sat on the edge of the bed, groaning softly, her hand never leaving her stomach.

"You've done this before, ain't you?" she asked, her mouth wide as she breathed in quick bursts.

"No, ma'am. I wish I could tell you I have."

"But you had four children. What did you do? Go huntin' while your wife laid in misery?"

"I stood outside the door, watched the little ones after there was more than one. Ofelia, the *comadrona,* um, the midwife, was there for every one of the births of my children."

The scowl returned to Billie's face as she regained normal breathing patterns. "You weren't there for any of them?"

"The last one. My son." Josiah hesitated, tried to force the memory out of his mind, but that was impossible.

Lyle was born nearly a year after they had buried the last of their children. Lily's pregnancy was a new hope, a rebirth of their family. But it wasn't long into it that she started to grow weak. By the time the baby was due, the fevers had come for her. She died in labor, and with little time to spare, Josiah's son, and only living child, was cut from Lily's belly by Ofelia — with Josiah's help.

It was the saddest moment of his life.

". . . But it was a difficult birth," Josiah added, looking away from her, away from her stomach. Tears settled in his eyes, but he refused to let them fall.

"This one ain't gonna be easy," Billie said.

"I suppose it's not. It's your first pregnancy?"

"Yes," Billie said. "And from the feel of it, I ain't gonna be in no hurry to ever do it again."

"Can you change yourself into a dry dress?" Josiah asked.

He wasn't a praying man, although there were circumstances when he sure hoped for a certain outcome — but asking an unseen force for a favor seemed silly at the moment . . . when it was just the two of them, stuck in the middle of a storm, with Billie about to give birth.

When Billie nodded yes, Josiah was greatly relieved. "I'll be right outside the door if you need me."

"You're good at that."

"It's the last place I'd prefer to be at the moment."

"Beats bein' out in the storm, a wanted man, a posse on your heels that won't offer you a moment of justice," Billie said.

"I don't mean to sound ungrateful. That's not what I meant. I'm sure I'd be hanging from that live oak just outside the door, my feet dragging the ground, if it weren't for your generosity."

"This has to be hard for you. I can't imagine losin' a baby, much less three. But I don't think I can do this myself."

"I'm not going anywhere," Josiah said, easing out the door, closing his eyes, taking a deep breath, wishing he was the kind of man who could run right out of the house and not look back.

Billie's bloodcurdling scream matched the roar of thunder over the house. Sweat and tears mingled as they streamed down her face. She looked like she was standing outside in the storm instead of lying on her bed, her legs pulled up in a V, about to give birth to a baby.

Josiah could see the baby's head starting to protrude out of her body. There was no time for embarrassment or hesitation. Billie needed his help, needed him to be strong, to be there for her in a way he couldn't be there for his own wife when she was alive. He had no choice but to put his hands down between her legs and guide the baby out into the world.

In his memory, Josiah heard Ofelia speaking in Spanish, *"Empujar al bebé hacia fuera."* And then in English: "Push, Miss Lily. Push hard."

Josiah repeated what he remembered. "Push, Billie, push."

"Oh damn it. Where's Charlie?"

"Push, Billie."

The baby's head was halfway out.

"Push harder, damn it," Josiah demanded.

Billie screamed again, and with a swift and surprising thrust, the baby was in Josiah's bloody hands.

For a second, he was in shock, holding the wet and warm little thing. It wasn't moving. It was all red and wrinkled like a prune. Honestly, the baby scared him, covered in mucus and blood like it was. He'd only seen one that wasn't cleaned up, and that was Lyle, cut out of his dead mother's stomach. Josiah had tried to forget that.

Billie was panting, catching her breath, staring at him. Her eyes were all glassy.

Josiah stood back, brought the baby up to his face, and tapped it between the shoulder blades gently. The baby didn't hesitate. It gasped, let out a whimper, opened its eyes, and began to cry, filling the room with life — and relief.

"What is it?" Billie whispered.

"A girl," Josiah said. "You have a daughter, Billie Webb. You have a healthy little girl."

The day had passed right on by with Josiah completely emerged in the drama of the baby's birth.

The strongest part of the storm had passed over them, too, but the rain per-sisted, steadily now, tapping on the roof comfortably instead of with the threat of menace or destruction.

There was some coffee left, and Josiah poured himself a full cup. He wasn't sure what time it was. Coming up on evening. It was hard to tell with the continuing cover of grayness that seemed like it was never going to go away.

Billie and her daughter lay sleeping in the bed. Josiah had done what he could to clean the two of them up, but eventually Billie ran him out of the room, certain she could do it herself. Another relief.

The coffee was strong and only lukewarm since the fire in the stove had nearly died out. After a couple of deep drinks, Josiah set the cup down and tossed a few pieces of wood inside the stove. The pile was getting low and probably wouldn't last another day. The thought caused Josiah some deep concern. He had no idea how Billie was going to take care of herself.

There was nothing he could do at the moment to help her out, other than warm up the beans and bacon and fry up some bread. He figured Billie would be pretty darn hungry when she woke up.

He wasn't totally inept when it came to women's work. He couldn't be. There were a lot of things he'd had to learn after Lily died. Ofelia was a great help, but in the beginning she wasn't around all the time. That didn't happen until Josiah moved to Austin, and Ofelia had decided to come along with him.

He eased over to the window, then eyed all of the ingredients he'd need to get supper going.

The land was flat beyond the barn, and the horizon was a good distance off. It was

137

hard to tell where the rainy sky left off and the earth began.

The ground was soaked. Newly created streams crisscrossed the yard, rain cutting through the dry, unsettled dirt around the house. Puddles looked like ponds, and the pasture appeared more like a lake than a field left unattended.

Wispy clouds rolled east, pushed by a strong unseen breeze. Rain fell from the sky in a slant, and there was no brightness in the distance. Not a single hint that the storm and the rain had run their course. The only certainty, the only promise, was that night was coming soon.

Josiah was, in a gentle way, glad of that. It would be nice to settle in for the evening. Build a fire. Tend to Billie's needs as best he could. And worry about what lay ahead of him tomorrow . . . with the hopes that the weather would pass, allowing him to figure out what to do.

Any thought of comfort left Josiah immediately as he took a swig of coffee, still standing at the window, surveying the landscape, peering over the top of the cup. He stopped drinking and blinked his eyes to make sure he was seeing what he thought he was seeing.

It only took a second to realize he was

right. A lone rider, sitting on a horse, about fifty yards north of the barn, sat staring at Billie's house.

The rider was well protected from the rain, a slicker in the shape of a poncho covering his guns — with the exception of the rifle that was settled firmly in his hand. It was hard to make out any definite features through the gloom and rain, the horse and man were black to the eye; an unknown silhouette on the horizon.

But there was no mistaking who the rider was. It was Liam O'Reilly.

Josiah turned away and fetched the Spencer from next to the door, moving quickly but trying to be quiet so he wouldn't alert Billie.

When he got back to the window, O'Reilly was gone.

Gone like a wraith disappearing into the depths of Hell.

CHAPTER 12

A warm ray of sunlight filtered into the cabin through the window. Sometime during the night, Josiah had awoken from his spot on the floor and realized the rain had stopped. The storm was over. The only sounds he could hear were Billie breathing gently and rain dripping off the roof. He'd stirred at daybreak, then pulled himself up off his makeshift bed of clothes and blankets. His leg hurt and he was stiff, but the bleeding had stopped. There didn't look to be any infection.

Now that it was full on into the morning, with the sun up, the ground was soaked and muddy but navigable.

Josiah had kept himself busy. He tried to be as quiet as he could, stacking a fresh pile of wood by the stove, gathering whatever he thought Billie would need, without his assistance, in the coming days.

A few times he was certain he'd heard

Billie and the baby stir in their bed, heard suckling sounds, figured if there was any need for him to invade the girl's privacy, she would call out for him. She hadn't.

"What are you doing, Josiah?"

Her voice caught him unaware. Josiah turned his head to see Billie standing in the sunlight, cradling her baby, a certain glow about her that Josiah recognized from his days as a new father. Lily was never more beautiful than right after she'd had a baby.

Billie had combed her long brown hair and let it fall over her shoulders. She had on a fresh yellow dress and was barefoot. Her feet even looked like they were sparkling. Her eyes, nearly the same color as her hair, twinkled, too, and her skin looked healthy and well scrubbed. Somehow, she had managed to clean herself up without Josiah knowing it.

The baby girl was wrapped in a blanket, but Josiah could see her head topped by a full head of hair that was black as coal. A hand reached up out of the blanket, fingers reaching and grabbing for the first time.

He'd been stooped over, straightening the last bit of wood into a proper stack. "Making sure you have everything you need," he said.

The color drained immediately from

141

Billie's face.

Josiah stood upright then, still dressed in Charlie's clothes, and exhaled deeply with resignation. "I think it's best if I go."

"You can't leave in broad daylight."

"They know I'm here, Billie, I'm sure of it. If they don't, they will soon. Daylight will be their chance, too. I saw O'Reilly watching the house. My presence is putting you and the baby in danger. It's hard telling what they'd do to you for helping me."

Billie walked over to him, her eyes hard and unyielding. The baby gurgled and cooed. "They won't hurt me."

"I can't take that risk."

"They'll hunt you down. You think I want to live knowin' that you died because of me?" Billie said.

"If they kill me, it won't be because of you. I told you, O'Reilly and I have a history."

"Looks more like unfinished business to me."

"I suppose you're right. Neither of us will rest until one of us is dead. If he found out for certain you gave me food and shelter, he'd take his anger out on you, I'm sure of it."

Billie turned away from Josiah, tears streaming out of the corners of both her eyes. She was biting the corner of her lip to restrain a full-out cry. The beauty that had previously held her in such grace was now completely gone. She stopped at the door, her back fully to Josiah, and rocked the baby.

"I was hopin' you'd stay," Billie said, softly, staring down at the baby. "I knew you'd have to leave sooner or later. But I was hopin' to have at least a day or two with you here. More really. At least till I got my strength up. I could keep you well hid, Josiah. There's a root cellar out yonder that ain't too infested with critters. If the need arises for you to disappear there."

"It'd be the first place they'd look. I'd have no way out."

"In the barn, then," Billie pleaded.

"I'm sorry," Josiah said. "I don't think we have a day to spare. The sooner I leave, the better off you and the baby will be."

Billie turned and faced Josiah. "There's nothing I can do or say to make you change your mind?"

"No, ma'am, there isn't."

He wasn't sure of her offer, but there was a different look in Billie's eyes. One he knew, too, and it was not just the glow after having a baby. She was lonely. She missed her husband. She needed a man. But Josiah was not that man . . . and they both knew it. Or, at least, he hoped she knew that was true. He had a life in Austin that was as fragile and new as Billie's baby. He needed to go home — or at least, try to go home.

Billie said nothing as she let a look devoid of emotion fall over her face. She disappeared back into the room where she'd given birth, back to her marriage bed, back to her loneliness and new responsibilities.

The baby began to cry. After a long minute or so, the baby's screams and whimpers were matched by Billie's sobbing, echoing a hunger and need that could not be filled.

Josiah grabbed up the Spencer, peered out the door cautiously, then walked outside into the bright sun, more determined than ever to face Liam O'Reilly one last time.

The horses had obviously weathered the storm, huddling in a lean-to about twenty yards beyond the barn. Josiah didn't even know the lean-to existed, or that there was any livestock at all on Billie and Charlie's farm, until he'd set about replenishing the wood for the stove.

At first glance, the little farm had looked to be in serious disrepair, suffering from neglect because of Charlie's death and the effects of the lingering summer drought that had just been sated by the torrential rains. Now that the sun was out, the air clean, and the wind gone, Josiah could see beyond the neglect.

The degradation and disrepair was a recent occurrence. There were signs that at one time, not so long ago, the farm had been well tended; the fences whitewashed, the barn stalls cleaned regularly, the house well cared for. All of the prideful chores had since gone by the wayside, lost in the depression and reality of death.

A few chickens appeared out of nowhere, happily pecking at the mud, searching out gravel and dirt anywhere they could find it, clucking as if they didn't have a care in the world. They didn't notice the red-tail hawk circling overhead, but Josiah did.

A small garden stood at the back of the house with herbs and a few stalks of corn still struggling to survive, even though it was November. Weeds were thick, gone to seed, and there would surely be no sign of the garden next year if Billie's luck continued on as it had.

The horses didn't look like they had been cared for properly in a good while, either. Josiah couldn't fault Billie for the neglect. He just felt sad for her. Surely there were town folk that could have come out to help her, but it didn't look like that had happened. He wondered why.

Of the two horses, only one looked to be of use. It was a tall palomino mare, her buckskin coat still shiny, but not nearly as much as it could be with some tending. Her mane was almost pure white. She looked to be about fifteen hands tall.

The other horse was a mare, too — a swaybacked black horse, graying at the snout and a good deal shorter than the palomino. The black mare eyed Josiah cautiously, backing up and snorting as he made his way toward the lean-to.

He found a catch box about a third full of moist oats, scooped out a handful, and offered it to whichever one of the horses would come to him.

"That there black one is Sulky. I've had her since I was a little girl. She's been skittish and leery of men ever since I knowed her."

Sulky looked up and seemed to calm down right away at the sound of Billie's voice. Billie had a habit of sneaking up behind people much like Josiah's old Mexican friend Juan Carlos.

Josiah spun around to see Billie standing a few feet behind him. He had not heard her approach. She'd startled him, and his hand immediately went for his six-shooter, which, of course, wasn't there. "Sorry, you caught me unaware."

The baby was nowhere to be seen.

There was still no emotion on Billie's face. None that Josiah could read, anyway. She seemed as cold as a block of ice in January.

"The other one is Charlie's horse. Lady Mead. He just called her Mead, but I liked it when he said her full name. He was awful damn proud of that horse."

The palomino accepted Josiah's offer and took the oats from his hand eagerly.

"She likes you," Billie said.

"Seems so."

"She tries to bite me when she thinks I'm not lookin'." Billie walked up to Josiah's side as Lady Mead finished the oats. "You're really leavin'?"

"Yes."

"What are your plans? Runnin' off in the daylight don't seem to be too wise, to me."

He turned and faced Billie. "I'm not running."

"What do you mean?"

"Rangers don't run."

"So you're just gonna waltz right into town and confront that ugly Mick?"

"Something like that."

"Something like that?" Billie echoed, putting each hand firmly on a hip, digging her feet into the ground. "They'll kill you. They'll just straight-out kill you. Do you want to die, Josiah Wolfe? Is that it?"

"No, Billie, I don't. You know that. I got reasons to live, but this fight needs to be over. If I run, I'll be looking over my shoulder the whole way. Even worse than that, I'd just be leading them back to my home. I've already seen my son in the hands of an evil man intent on doing me, and him, harm once. I'm not about to let that happen again."

"Your son ain't gonna have a ma or pa the way you're goin'. It ain't gonna matter whether you're brave or not. Dead is dead. I know that firsthand."

"I know you do, but I'm not changing my mind. I figure if I go into town I can appeal to the sheriff's sense of justice. If I'm guilty of a crime, I deserve a fair trial. I just need to get to him and tell him my side of the story. I was captured by two Comanche, because O'Reilly has a bounty on me. He doesn't have the right, or the power, but somehow, he's using it. Used it to bring me here."

"Are you just foolhardy? There's a mob in town that dragged two men out of the jail and strung them up without one mention of a trial. Now, I ain't defendin' that dead Hardin boy, he was rotten to the core and all, but he got nothin' but a long rope, and not a second of justice. If there was such a thing for him. You think you're any different?"

"I'm a Ranger, not a gunfighter's brother." Josiah stared at Billie. "And, it's the only way you'll be safe. Today, tomorrow, and thereafter. They won't ever know you helped me. It's the only way, Billie."

Billie drew in a deep breath. "They'd kill you if they thought I'd had anything to do with you. I don't want you to die because I gave you shelter, I couldn't live with myself, not after losin' Charlie like I did."

"I won't."

"All right then . . . there are a few things of Charlie's I want you to have so you can at least have a fightin' chance. The first being Lady Mead. She can run like the wind when she has to."

"I can't take the horse," Josiah said.

Billie exhaled. "It's one less thing I have to care for, all right?"

"I'll consider her a loan."

"Consider it what you want. It tears out my heart just to look at that horse. Now I got Charlie's eyes starin' right back at me from his little girl's eyes. Ain't that enough of a reminder of what I don't got?"

The palomino nudged Josiah with her long, elegant nose, begging for more oats. He couldn't tell her no any more than he could decline Billie's generous, but painful, offer.

CHAPTER 13

Once Josiah cinched the saddle tight on Lady Mead, there was nothing else left to do but leave.

Billie stood on the stoop holding the baby. "You sure I can't talk you out of this?"

"I'm sure, ma'am."

"All right, then. I guess I understand. No man wants to live his life lookin' over his shoulder. I could tell certain things about you the second I laid eyes on you, and that was one of 'em." Billie's eyes looked past Josiah to Lady Mead. "That rifle all you got?"

Josiah nodded. "It'll be enough." It was a lie, and he knew it. He had five shots left in the Spencer. He was a good shot — but he wasn't a great shot. Every one of them would have to count — and even then that probably wouldn't matter at all. He knew he was most likely walking into a firing squad.

"Hold on," Billie said.

She didn't give Josiah time to protest — she disappeared back inside the house in the blink of an eye.

For once, Josiah didn't voice an objection, though his instinct told him to get on the buckskin palomino right then and there and take off at a good run, test out the horse and see if she ran as fast as Billie said she did. But he couldn't leave without a proper good-bye. At least a proper thank-you. Josiah wasn't real good at saying good-bye.

Billie returned quickly. She'd left the baby behind, inside the house, but was carrying a hand-tooled leather gun belt with a full holster that was packed with a six-shooter and enough bullets to get him through a long gunfight. Billie held it out to Josiah. "Here, take this, too. I ain't got no use for it."

"I can't take Charlie's gun, Billie. You need something to protect yourself with."

"I got a shotgun. If that ain't enough, then I got more problems than I can handle anyways."

"You're sure?"

"Lord almighty, Josiah Wolfe, consider it a loan, too, if you have to. Either bring it back when you can, or I'll have Roy pick it off your dead body and return it to me. He'll

152

know where it came from once he sees it."

"Thanks for the vote of confidence."

"You're the fool that's walkin' into a hornet's nest in broad daylight. Ain't got nothin' to do with confidence."

"All right." Josiah walked over and took the gun belt. It only took a second to realize that the gun was a Colt Frontier.

Colt had introduced the Frontier not long after Winchester came out with the new Model 1873. It was chambered to handle the same .44-40 cartridge. That way a man only had to buy one kind of shell for the rifle and gun he carried. "Frontier" was acid-etched on the barrel or Josiah wouldn't have recognized it so readily. The interchangeable cartridges wouldn't do him any good since he was carrying a Spencer — but the thought made him wonder if Charlie had a Winchester, too. Billie had just said she only had a shotgun to protect herself.

Josiah pushed the thought out of his mind; questioning Billie was of no use to him. In reality, Charlie Webb had himself set up with a good horse, a good gun, and most of all, a good woman.

Life had obviously been pretty good for Charlie — at least until he had the misfortune of recognizing John Wesley Hardin. There was no need to question anything beyond that tragedy now — Billie had shown him a kindness that was too deep to ever be repaid in full. Taking out Liam O'Reilly was the only thing he knew to do that would help Billie see a future void of any kind of trouble.

"Charlie liked that gun a lot," Billie said.

Josiah strapped on the gun belt but resisted the temptation to pull the gun out of the holster and feel its weight, see how it handled. He'd wait until he was out of sight before he did that.

"Thank you," he said.

"This is it, then?" Billie said.

They were about a foot apart. Josiah could smell fresh soap on her skin. He looked down to the ground, away from her deep blue eyes. "I have to go, Billie."

"I know you do." There were tears welling up in her eyes.

Behind her, from inside the house, the baby whimpered in two short bursts, growing louder, until the whimpers erupted into a full cry.

Billie turned to go inside, and Josiah walked away, his back to her, without saying another word.

By the time she came back to the door, Josiah was nearly past the barn. He looked over his shoulder, waved, then urged Lady

Mead on to a full-out run.

If Billie said, or shouted, anything after him, he didn't hear it.

Josiah stopped just over a slight ridge. Billie Webb's house had disappeared from sight behind him, and the town of Comanche lay fully in front of him on the horizon. Coming in from the north, the town looked bigger, more sprawled out than it had coming in from the south. Still it was a decent size for a supply town.

Lady Mead had proven to be a comfortable ride right out of the gate. The mare was no replacement for Clipper, but she would do — at least for getting him down the muddy road to meet his fate, and hopefully beyond.

The Spencer was tucked lightly into the scabbard, and Josiah took this as the first opportunity to handle Charlie Webb's Colt Frontier.

The six-shooter handled fine and felt comfortable in his hand. Still, there was a hesitation in Josiah's grip. The fact that he was wearing a set of dead man's clothes, riding his horse, and holding his gun did not fail to escape his attention. He figured that, from a distance, he just might look like Charlie Webb's ghost, come back from the

155

great beyond to claim his revenge.

It was not a thought he relished, being mistaken for a ghost. But it just might help throw O'Reilly, or his thugs, off Josiah's trail long enough for him to get to the sheriff's office — which was his plan. The other side of things was a bit uglier. It wouldn't take much for anybody to figure out where Josiah had re-outfitted himself. Somehow, he had to manage to keep Billie Webb safe.

The only way he knew to do that was to stay alive. Which was the other part of his plan. He wasn't sure how that was going to happen. Just that it had to.

A mangy black-and-white dog ran from behind the first house Josiah passed and started barking its fool head off. The door to the house was open, and so were the windows. Pale blue curtains flipped in the breeze, and other than the dog, the house was silent.

The sun beamed down from overhead, the cold thrust of yesterday's rain a thing of the past. The day was warm, especially by November standards. Sweat beaded under the brim of Josiah's felt Stetson — his own — and the clothes he was wearing felt itchy against his skin. They still held a hint of lye in them, and mixed with the heat and the task he was riding into, the smell made him more nervous and uncomfortable than he already was.

The Colt Frontier was loaded and ready. Josiah usually wore a swivel rig, but Charlie preferred a Mexican loop holster. Another odd choice, akin to the lack of a Winchester, but the Mexican holster was functional, though it told nothing of Charlie's past or the reasoning for his choices. Not that it mattered.

What was really important was that Josiah remember the limitations of the simple holster when the time came to use the gun. It really wasn't much more than a piece of tanned cowhide with a couple of nails holding it together.

Josiah shooed away the dog, annoyed at the alarm it was raising on the outskirts of town, but oddly, as he looked ahead, down the wide and muddy main street, the town seemed nearly vacant.

There were a couple of horses tied up in front of the saloon, and one in front of the Darcy Hotel, but no traffic coming and going. The Butterfield had probably come and gone, since it was past mid-morning, but it was unsettling not to see one soul, man or woman, making their way to and fro on the boardwalk.

Josiah kneed Lady Mead a bit, bringing her up to a trot to get past the dog. He scanned the tops of the buildings for lookouts and saw nothing, all the while easing the Spencer out of the scabbard and chambering a round.

He passed by a few more empty houses, and a chill ran down his spine. It felt like he had just ridden into a town besieged by some quick-acting sickness. Like it was a ghost town, even though Josiah knew better.

The heart of Comanche came up pretty quickly, and Josiah slowed the palomino to an easy gait. He headed straight for the sheriff's office, which was easy enough to find, since it was two doors down from the saloon.

He eased off the horse, all of his senses fully engaged. It felt like he was walking right into the heart of the land of Yankees without one soldier backing him up. The grip he held on the rifle was tight, but not so tight that it would hinder his aim or reaction if need be. The Spencer was an unknown and untrusted friend going into certain battle.

Just then, a man with a shaggy beard stumbled out of the bar. He stopped and stared at Josiah. "Hey stranger, you're late."

"Late for what, friend?" Josiah said.

"Bill Clarmont's funeral," the man said with a slur.

Josiah felt his heart skip a beat — or, at least, it felt like it. He'd killed Bill Clarmont. He was holding the dead man's rifle. The whole town was probably at the man's funeral, which explained the silence and the absence of commerce.

The shaggy man stroked his beard and steadied himself on one of the batwing doors to the saloon. "You look familiar."

Josiah stiffened. "I'm just passing through. Thought I'd stop in and speak with the sheriff."

"Well, he ought to be out at the cemetery, but that there's his horse."

"I'll just wait in the office for him to return then," Josiah said.

In the distance, a church bell tolled. Doom and finality carried on an unseen wind and the rays of sunshine. They'd obviously had to wait out the downpour to bury Bill Clarmont.

"Suit yourself. I'm not one for funerals myself."

Josiah nodded and pushed into the sheriff's office, the Spencer still in his grip. He took a deep breath and blinked his eyes, shocked at what he was seeing.

The sheriff, Roy something or other, Josiah hadn't picked up on the man's last name, was sitting in the chair at his desk, his head thrown completely back, a fresh bullet hole centered square in the man's forehead. Blood was still dripping on the floor.

The jail cells were empty, and all of the doors were standing wide open.

CHAPTER 14

A loud rush of noise out in the street — horses running at full speed — drew Josiah's attention away from the dead man. The thundering hooves were quickly followed by gunshots. There was nothing Josiah could do for the sheriff, so he dashed to the window.

Three men on horses sped past the sheriff's office, heading north, the opposite direction from which Josiah had come into town.

He recognized the three men immediately.

Liam O'Reilly and the Comanche brothers, Big Shirt and Little Shirt. They had bags thrown over their laps. Money bags, full and bulging.

Instead of rushing to the door, Josiah pulled the Spencer up and shot straight through the window.

Shattering glass exploded across the sill, but Josiah was ready for the fallout of his action; he dodged back quickly, dancing away from the shards as best he could, then returned to the window for another shot once the glass fell to the ground.

The three horses ran at a quick gallop, the muddy street holding them back slightly, but not slowing them enough for Josiah to get a great shot. There was a waterfall of mud flying behind the horses, globs hitting the ground in thumps, like someone was throwing muddy bombs from the roof of every building they passed. Two more breaths, and they'd be out of town, out of range — gone.

Josiah's second shot closed the deal.

Little Shirt tumbled off his horse, screaming, yelling words into the wind that only the breezes and his brother understood, his hand going for his blood-splattered shoulder rather than his gun.

The other two riders didn't even slow down, didn't offer to turn back and help if they could. Josiah didn't expect them to. He just hoped to get another shot off to stop them. He pulled the trigger on the second breath — the range too far, the shot too rushed to hit its target: the back of Liam O'Reilly's gnarly red head.

Little Shirt's horse reared back at the sound of the third shot, screaming and neighing wildly, frightened and confused by all the blasts, pulls, and tussles. Little Shirt had crashed into the mud, toppling without control, coming to a stop just shy of the boardwalk, stunned and injured — though how badly was hard to tell.

Josiah rushed out the door, putting himself behind Lady Mead. He had two shots left with the rifle, then the Spencer would become useless to him. At least, for the moment. So he had to make the shots count.

O'Reilly was certainly out of range, but still in sight.

The enraged Irishman was now fully aware of what had happened, though Josiah wasn't sure if the outlaw knew that he had been the one to take down Little Shirt. It didn't matter, other than making sure Billie Webb was free of retribution, so Josiah kept himself covered behind the horse.

They had been going in the opposite direction from Billie's house, so that was an immediate relief. O'Reilly was no fool. He would want to get as far away from Comanche as possible while the whole town was at the funeral. At least, Josiah hoped that was the case.

Josiah decided to try one last shot, so he laid the rifle across the horse's back, propped it up over his wrist, and sighted on

O'Reilly, rays glaring off his red hair, making his head glow like a setting sun on the horizon.

Just as he was about to pull the trigger, out of the corner of his eye Josiah saw Little Shirt begin to move. The Comanche was struggling for the gun in his holster, staring at Josiah angrily, muttering words that no one could understand.

Josiah had no choice but to pull his aim off O'Reilly. He turned the barrel toward the Indian and pulled the trigger, certain and intent on killing yet another man.

There was not an ounce of regret careening through Josiah's body as he took the shot.

His heart was racing with anger and rage — the score almost settled now for the deaths of Red Overmeyer and the sheriff.

The only recent death that caused Josiah any moral concern at all was that of the deputy, Bill Clarmont, but he could trace that occurrence back to Little Shirt's action as well. If Josiah hadn't been apprehended for a bogus reward on his head that O'Reilly had brokered with the sheriff, then he would never have stepped a foot into Comanche in the first place, and Bill Clarmont would still be alive. Who knew what side of the law Clarmont really worked? It was hard to say, and perhaps impossible to ever know.

All Josiah knew was that he was in the town of Comanche unbidden, forced there against his will, by the two brothers and their obvious allegiance to Liam O'Reilly.

This next bullet caught Little Shirt at the very base of his throat. His head jerked back, nearly ripped off with the sudden tear of flesh.

Blood sprayed every which way it could, a spiderweb of red fluid contrasting on the dark brown mud of the road. The sickening sound of certain death had probably been heard from a half a block away.

This time Little Shirt fell straight back into the mud, unmoving after the fall.

When Josiah looked back up, Liam O'Reilly and Big Shirt were about to vanish over the horizon. The shot was lost. It would be a waste of a bullet, and he didn't have the luxury to waste any.

Chasing after the two men now seemed like a ride into more uncertainty, and he'd had enough uncertainty in the last few days to last him a good long time.

The two outlaws had the advantage of knowing the land and of having a full cadre of weapons, fully loaded, unlike Josiah, who only had one cartridge left in the Spencer and a belt full of bullets for the Colt Frontier.

He eased out from behind Lady Mead, who had handled the rifle fire with grace and courage, hardly wincing at all when Josiah fired the final shot that had ended Little Shirt's life. Or at least he assumed that the Indian was dead. He still wasn't going to take any chances.

The round in the Spencer was chambered, and each step Josiah took toward Little Shirt was heavy with caution.

Somewhere in the distance a woman screamed.

The scream came from the direction of the bank, and that did not surprise Josiah in the least.

Once he made sure that the Indian was truly dead, he'd go investigate. But not until he was certain he'd been as successful as he thought.

The only Comanche he trusted was a dead Comanche.

The door to the bank was standing wide open, and a woman dressed all in black was bent over the floor, her back to Josiah. She was crying over a man in a brown tweed suit. A pair of eyeglasses lay shattered on the floor not too far from the man. A pool of blood surrounded the man's body.

There was no one else in the bank, at least as far as Josiah could tell. He'd left the Spencer behind, secured in the scabbard on Lady Mead's saddle, but for safety's sake, he had the Colt Frontier in his hand, loaded and ready.

Josiah was reasonably certain there was only a trio of outlaws, one dead, two on the run, but he couldn't be completely sure O'Reilly didn't have more men in Comanche, staying behind to do whatever meanness they could muster.

The vault door just past the tellers' cages was standing wide open. O'Reilly had robbed the bank while everyone was at Bill Clarmont's funeral.

"Excuse me, ma'am," Josiah said, stepping slowly into the bank.

The woman jerked her head back, startled. She immediately put her hands into the air, in fear.

"You have nothing to be afraid of, ma'am. I'm a Ranger. I'm here to help."

"How do I know that's true?"

Josiah nodded, emptied the bullets of the six-shooter into his hand, holstered the Colt, then raised his hands to the side away from his belt. "I mean you no harm."

The woman stood up, blood on the front

of her thick black skirt, making it look all shiny and wet. She was portly, a big woman, wearing a tall hat, the veil pulled upward. Most of her skin was covered by black cloth, her garb resembling widow's weeds. Bill Clarmont's funeral was probably not the first time the outfit had been worn in recent weeks or months, nor would it be the last.

"They've gone and killed Henry Peterson," the woman said. "Henry never hurt a fly. Not once. And he didn't have the cold heart of a banker, either. He was a fine man. Deserved better, he did."

"Did you see who did this?"

The woman shook her head no. "I was coming back from the doings, a funeral, you know."

"Bill Clarmont."

"Yes, a deputy in this town." She eyed Josiah from head to toe. "That why you're here, Ranger? To put a stop to this senseless violence?"

"I wish I could answer yes to that question." He refrained from offering his name, unsure if it was common knowledge that he had been the one to kill Bill Clarmont. There was no need to alarm the woman any further on a day like today. "So, you don't know who did this?"

"No, not for certain. But this town has

been overrun with thugs of late. I sure hope someone has the fortitude to go after these cold-blooded killers and give them the same treatment that Hardin boy got."

Josiah sighed heavily. He stopped at the woman's side and looked down at Henry Peterson. He'd been shot three times in the chest.

"Looks like the mortician is a busy man in this town," Josiah said.

"Lately," the woman said. "Him and the sheriff."

"The sheriff's dead, ma'am. There won't be any justice served to those killers right away. At least by him."

"Roy is dead?"

"Yes."

"You're certain?"

"Yes, ma'am."

"Then there is a Lord in Heaven. Our prayers have been answered," the woman said.

Josiah looked at the woman curiously and was about to ask her what she meant when he heard another ruckus outside: the arrival of several horses and riders coming to stop in front of the bank. He motioned for the woman to be quiet, then pulled the Colt from the holster and made his way to the door.

CHAPTER 15

The last thing Josiah Wolfe was expecting to see outside of the bank was a company of Texas Rangers. There were fifteen of them, two abreast, standing in wait in the middle of the street.

Captain Pete Feders headed up the troop, and Josiah was greatly relieved to see Scrap Elliot sitting on Missy, his trusted roan mare, three horses back in the mix of the boys.

Josiah stepped out of the bank, failing to tell the woman that all was well. "It sure is good to see you, Pete, um, Captain Feders." He walked out into the street and stopped a few feet from the captain's horse.

"Wolfe, you're alive," Feders said. His facial expression didn't change. He was stoic, his eyes hard, looking at Josiah head-on, then beyond, searching past him.

"Last time I checked."

"Elliot reported that you were captured,

carried off by two Comanche. Our hopes were not great in finding you among the living. But we set out for your rescue. It seems that our journey was unnecessary."

Pete Feders was a lanky man, a true son of Texas, born and bred in the state just like Josiah. They had ridden briefly together as Rangers, with Captain Hiram Fikes, before the Frontier Battalion had been formed and then again after. Both had been there when Fikes was killed, which was what ultimately led to Feders taking charge of the new company of Rangers, in the capacity of captain. Leadership didn't seem to fit Feders well at all — at least not comfortably, in a way that motivates other men to risk their lives for you. Riding second seemed to suit him more, taking orders rather giving them. Feders hadn't mastered that skill yet, even though he'd been in the lead spot for nearly six months now.

Feders was nearly as tall as Josiah, the two about the same age, and Feders was a veteran of the War Between the States himself, though not as a member of the Texas Brigade like Josiah had been. Feders had fought with an outfit from Alabama, which never made sense to Josiah.

Feders hailed from one of the counties in West Texas, where he fought the Comanche and the Kiowa plenty of times as a young man, braving the frontier before signing up in the army.

A thin but well-pronounced scar ran from the corner of Pete's right eye to his ear. Josiah tried not to stare at the scar, but he couldn't help himself. He had no clue of the scar's origin, whether it was produced at the hand of an Indian or a Northern Aggressor, or neither. Pete Feders was a private man — even more so since taking the reins as captain of the company of Rangers. He ate by himself and spent a good deal of time away from the shenanigans of the men when they weren't out on a mission: horse races, shooting matches, card games, and such.

Josiah thought that Feders's aloofness was to his detriment, a sign of the struggle he was having leading the company. Captain Hiram Fikes, Hank to his friends, had always been right in the thick of every aspect of Ranger life, whether it was eating, gambling, wrestling, or drinking long into the night. As far as Josiah was concerned, Pete would do himself a favor to remember Fikes's skills, but it wasn't his place to provide the reminder — or the lesson in leadership. Still it was good to see Pete Feders.

The captain dismounted his horse, a black

stallion that had come from the stables of Hiram Fikes.

The captain's widow favored Pete as a suitor for her daughter, Pearl, and had made it clearly known to everyone that he was her only choice — even over Major John B. Jones, who had taken a turn at courting Pearl.

The black stallion had been a gift made with the public intention of making sure the widow's wishes were met without question. It did not matter what Pearl herself wanted, since she had declined Feders's proposal of marriage more than once in recent memory.

Josiah wasn't sure of the entire reasoning behind her rejection of Pete's affections, but he had a pretty good idea — and that had more to do with her relationship with him, or a desire for one, than it did with the fact that Pete was a captain in the Rangers, where her father had lived a double life and, ultimately, lost his life.

"It is good to see you standing on two feet, Wolfe. I figured you for a dead man this time out. The fate of Ranger Overmeyer did not bode well for a positive outcome when we began our search," Feders said.

"I count myself a lucky man at the moment." Josiah looked past Feders and nodded at Scrap. The boy flashed a brief smile, then looked away.

Josiah had some questions for Scrap, like how he got loose and found his way back to the Ranger camp, what had happened to Red, and how they found him in Comanche. But those questions, and more, would have to wait until they were free of their current troubles. The hows and whys really didn't matter at the moment. Josiah was just happy to see Scrap Elliot alive and well, on his horse, continuing his life as a Ranger.

"It seems that way," Feders said. "I think the circumstances we all find ourselves in appear odd. Where are the people of Comanche on this fine day? The storm has passed. I assumed the streets would be jammed with citizens restocking their needs — grain, feed, libations, whatever the desire."

"There is a storm still raging on here."

"Explain, Ranger," Feders said.

"There is little time for that. The troubles are recent. Just happened minutes before your arrival."

"Our jurisdiction doesn't allow us to interfere, you know that, Wolfe."

"I'm aware of that, but I am not free of trouble, and neither is this town," Josiah said. "We have no choice but to interfere."

"What say you?"

174

"Liam O'Reilly robbed the bank within the last hour. He is on the run, heading north, out of town. They killed the banker, Henry Peterson, and the sheriff is dead, too. I believe at the hands of O'Reilly, though I don't know that for certain. He was riding with the sheriff, tracking me down after I freed myself from the Comanche brothers who took me hostage. Something must have gone wrong, or the sheriff stood up to O'Reilly, one or the other. Either suggestion is just speculation on my part. What matters is the sheriff is dead."

Feders waved his hand, motioning for a man, a Ranger Josiah did not know too well at all, B. D. Donley, to dismount and join in the conversation. "There is no county sheriff to take up the reins on this one?" He turned his attention back to Josiah. "What about a deputy?"

"That's part of the trouble that still remains with me, Pete," Josiah said.

"What do you mean?" Feders asked, an annoyed look flashing across his face. He had made it known that he didn't like to be called by his first name and found it a betrayal of rank and friendship. Josiah had known Pete Feders for so long it was difficult to call him anything else . . . especially Captain.

"I killed the deputy," Josiah said.

A final bell tolled in the distance, from an unseen church standing sentinel over an unseen cemetery. Bill Clarmont's funeral was now most certainly concluded, and the townsfolk were free to return to their daily lives — if they dared.

A few wagons appeared on the main street of town, the passengers and drivers dressed in full black attire, even though the day was more suited for something lighter, something that would denote more of a celebration. The riders in the wagon looked leery of the assemblage of Rangers.

Just as Josiah had heard the toll of the funeral bells, the mourners had surely heard the gunshots and the ruckus caused by O'Reilly. And seeing a troop of men, all dressed differently, not in military garb, with no markings to distinguish them as Rangers, probably brought more fear than curiosity.

Comanche had seen its fair share of vigilantes; lawless mobs that had wreaked havoc on those that followed the straight and narrow, living quiet, law-abiding lives.

The sun had risen high into a cloudless sky. The color of it was a solid blue, strong, not fragile like some November skies tended to be. It could have been a perfect summer day instead of a day drawing nearer and nearer to a brief winter. The wind was warm, pushing up from the south, and even in the center of town there was a flavor of salt and humidity to the air.

But Josiah's throat was dry. He stood over the dead Comanche, Little Shirt, uncertain of what to do next. The rest of the boys — Josiah's term, and most every other Ranger's term for the company — had followed him to the scene in the street, all mounted on their horses, ready for the next order from Captain Feders. B. D. Donley had followed behind Josiah, along with Feders.

"How come you were a-limpin'?" B. D. Donley asked.

"Caught a graze. I'm all right," Josiah said. In all of the commotion, the pain was a distant irritation, but there was no question that it still hurt and was open to the possibility of infection.

"You takin' the honors of the scalp?" Donley said, stepping past Josiah. Donley was a short fellow with a scratchy voice, a ruddy face, and a set of eyes that could have belonged to a crow; all black and beady.

Josiah shook his head no. He'd never scalped a dead Indian, and he wasn't about to start now.

"What's the matter," Donley continued, chiding Josiah and completely ignoring Pete Feders, "ain't you got the stomach for it?"

"I didn't kill this man for a trophy," Josiah said. "I killed him because I had to."

"Don't look like you're in a position to be all righteous, Wolfe," Donley said, his skinny chest puffing out, looking past Little Shirt at the gathering crowd.

"That's enough, Donley," Feders said. "You'll not make an exhibition of this."

"Ain't right, Captain," Donley said. He pulled his lips tight, till they almost disappeared. "This Comanch would scalp a live child. I know, I've seen it done. Ain't a purty sight, I tell you. Rots in your dreams so you can't make the bad pictures go away."

"This is not the place," Feders said, lowering his voice. "This town isn't anything but a powder keg waiting to blow. I want you to take two other men and go north after Liam O'Reilly. Track him as far as you can. Kill him if you get the chance, but don't stay out past three days."

"That it, Captain?" Donley said, a wide smile growing across his face.

"From you it is. Wolfe, I want you and Elliot to get out of here as quickly as you can. Head on to Austin and wait for word from me. Rangers or not, I don't think we'll be able to save Wolfe here from the rope once the crowd sees that the sheriff is dead and there's no law presiding over the town."

"I'm not running," Josiah said, stepping up past Donley, nearly knocking him off balance. "Don't even think about sending me out of here, Pete. I aim to finish what I started."

"It looks like you did. Now go. That's an order." Feders held Josiah's gaze. There was no question he meant business. The stare was cold and hard, and the scar on Feders's face pulsed bright red. "I don't mean to repeat myself, Wolfe. You need me and the boys right now, so I would take the opportunity to depart as quickly as you can before someone gets the idea that you don't need *your* scalp, either."

Josiah sighed heavily and started to turn away, but Feders stopped him with a quick grab of the shoulder.

"You call me Pete one more time, Wolfe, and you won't have to worry about me being your captain. Is that understood, Sergeant?"

Josiah nodded. "Yes, sir." He ignored the growing crowd around Little Shirt, kicked his boot into the muddy road, and headed for Lady Mead. "This isn't over," he said quietly, under his breath. "It's far from over, Pete."

CHAPTER 16

Josiah and Scrap rode south, out of town, both of them pushing their horses to a full run as soon as they had settled into their saddles.

Scrap took the lead, pushing his trusted blue roan mare, Missy, as hard as he could. Josiah let him have a couple of full horse lengths before urging Lady Mead to keep up.

He was glad to be heading south, toward home, toward Austin — but he slowed as they broke free of Comanche, hoping to catch sight of Billie Webb's house.

He silently hoped to see Billie outside, maybe hanging diapers to dry in the bright sun, or tending to what chickens of her flock remained. But he didn't see her. Only smoke rising lazily out of the chimney, casting a thin veil of black against an otherwise perfect blue afternoon sky.

For a moment, Josiah thought about pulling away from Scrap and taking Charlie Webb's palomino back to his widow, leaving her with something of value, at least to sell or trade when the need arose. But that would have to wait for another day. Pete Feders was unyielding with his orders: Go straight to Austin and wait there. No stops that weren't necessary. Get far away from Comanche as quickly as possible.

Josiah understood the reasoning and knew that if he didn't leave then, there might be more force in the town than the boys could handle or overcome. If all of Comanche had gone vigilante on John Wesley Hardin's kin, then challenging a troop of Rangers wasn't out of the question.

Seeing Billie and returning Lady Mead was not meant to be, and Josiah felt odd, full of regret at the thought. There was no way he was going to forget what she had done for him. Somehow, he was going to make things right, even though she didn't expect him to.

If it wasn't for Josiah, she would have had to birth her child alone, and that prospect was not lost on either one of them. Still, Josiah Wolfe was not the kind of man who rode away on another man's horse, or wore his clothes for that matter, without offering something of like value. But he was doing so now — for the first time in his life, at least that he could remember.

It seemed the only way to change any of that was to do as he was told and return to Austin.

He did feel like less of a Ranger, though — less of a man really — not staying to face the consequences of his actions head-on, but he silently agreed that Feders would have a better chance at quelling any disputes if Josiah wasn't there. Having Pete Feders act as his mouthpiece sure didn't feel right . . . but orders were orders.

There would be consequences to face, regardless of what happened in Comanche. Josiah was certain of that — knew that once they reached Austin, he would have to clear himself, and the reputation of the Rangers, directly to Major Jones, if not to Governor Coke himself.

He wasn't sure which group would be the toughest to face — the officers in the Frontier Battalion or the raging mad citizens of Comanche, Texas. Either way, he knew he'd face whatever came. Right now he just had a bullet graze in the leg. He hoped that would be the only scar from this incident.

Lady Mead seemed glad to be running, angling to keep up with Missy and Scrap.

Josiah let the mare have her head, let her go, and was surprised that she was as comfortable a steed as his own horse, Clipper. Scrap remained silent, distant, and that was just fine with Josiah. The last thing he wanted to deal with at the moment was the high spirits of Scrap Elliot. There were stories to swap between the two of them, there was no doubt about that — but neither man seemed in a hurry to chew the fat and recount recent events.

They skirted a town, Priddy, causing them to head due west for a few miles.

Well away from the town, or any other ranches or human habitation, a creek rose up out of the soft ground and snaked southeast, cutting through hundred-foot-high limestone bluffs. The creek was called Cowhouse Creek since there was enough room to shelter a good-sized herd of longhorns from weather or just to rest. Signs of recent passing herds were everywhere. There were hardly any grasses that didn't show sign of grazing, and the mud was dotted with hoofprints, hard and set, like artwork made of fired clay. But there weren't any cows moving through at the moment.

There was plenty of vegetation, drawing bird life and smaller critters, like squirrels and rabbits. The ground was a stony clay loam beyond the creek and sandy near the edge, and there were large groves of healthy oaks, walnuts, and other hardwoods to offer a fair amount of shade. The outlying vistas were dotted with mesquite, chaparral, buffalo grasses, hackberry, and thickets of heavy brush. A few mountains — two thousand-foot-tall hills — rose up in the distance as well. The remainder of their travels weren't going to be flatfooted, so they needed to be prepared.

Both he and Scrap had left Comanche without enough provisions, none as far as Josiah knew, to last the ride back to Austin, so the sight of the creek was a welcome relief since it looked to support a wide variety of wildlife to hunt — unlike the alkaline stretch of the San Saba lowland they had been captured in.

The day had stretched on, and now it was nearly evening. Daylight was fading gray. The perfect clear blue sky was being replaced by a melancholy one, dotted with thin vapors that looked more like veils than clouds. It would be a cooler night, but not cold, and for that, Josiah was glad. The bluffs would protect them from any high winds, but it would also make it difficult to escape any Indian attack if they chose the night for an assault. He still wasn't convinced that Big Shirt was aligned with any band of Comanche, but it was hard to say. Still, Josiah knew he had to be wary of both Big Shirt and Liam O'Reilly. It was hard to say how far their shadows fell and who they were truly aligned with out in the world, away from town.

Regardless, Josiah was ready to stop and make camp, at least water the horses and find something to eat before nightfall set in.

He urged Lady Mead to catch up with Scrap and Missy, and the mare obliged heartily, showing a burst of speed and dedication that surprised Josiah. He thought the mare must have been ready for a rest. But her spunk almost convinced him to continue on and ride through the night. He was ready to be in familiar territory, if the city of Austin could be called familiar. And Josiah was more than ready to see Lyle and feel the floors of home under his feet, instead of the uncertain ground he'd been walking on in the last few days.

"Let's make camp," Josiah yelled out to Scrap as he met him neck to neck.

Scrap glared at Josiah and yelled back, "You left me."

Josiah shook his head, not sure he'd heard Scrap clearly, but he had known the boy long enough to read the look on his face,

186

the hard set of his jaw, to know that he was angry and petulant — which was the last thing Josiah wanted to deal with at the moment.

He would rather have been riding with a stranger, one of the boys he didn't know very well, instead of Scrap Elliot. For some reason, Pete Feders seemed to think of the two of them as partners. Josiah certainly didn't feel that way. At least not at the moment.

"Have it your way." He yanked the reins and cut Lady Mead to the right, slowing her to an easy stop as gently as he could. He wasn't about to take his frustration out on a horse like he'd seen some men do.

The creek was about twenty-five yards off to his left, running swiftly. Shadows danced on the water, and there was a slight smell of dead fish in the air. It was like being let loose in the wild after being held captive longer than he ever wanted to be, and he took a deep breath of the acrid air and enjoyed every second of it. Oddly enough, his stomach grumbled with hunger.

Scrap had kept riding, disappearing quickly into the roll of the land and the chaparral in the distance. The ground was too hard for him to kick up a trail of dust, but Josiah was pretty certain that Scrap had slapped Missy on the rump, pushing her to run even faster.

Suit yourself, Josiah thought to himself. *Suit yourself.*

The fire reflected off the creek and played off the bluffs comfortably, like it belonged there . . . bringing light to a completely dark night. There was no sign of the moon, though the stars were pinpricks of sparkling silver for as far as the eye could see. Most of the insects that usually buzzed about at night had done whatever they do for the onset of winter — at least that was what Josiah thought, since it was nearly silent beyond the fire. The silence was a little unsettling. He felt like he was being watched — by more than just critters.

The Spencer was within reach, even though he only had two shots left. He still wore Charlie Webb's Colt Frontier on his side, so he was more than ready if he should come under attack. Paranoia was not a trait Josiah usually carried with him, but his capture by the Comanche brothers had unsettled him . . . and left him full of questions.

Being taken captive almost felt like it had been part of an elaborate plan — but for that to happen, then Liam O'Reilly and the two brothers would have had to have known he was leaving Austin with only two men, that he was vulnerable for capture. Could someone have told them about the orders he'd been given to go after Comanche cow rustlers and bring them back for questioning? If so, who? And why?

Perhaps the why wasn't such a difficult question to answer. Liam O'Reilly wanted him dead. And he would obviously go to any length to see that happen. The larger question, the one that was eating at Josiah the most, was who. Who could Liam O'Reilly recruit to get the information he needed from within the battalion of Rangers? Was there a spy within the ranks?

Josiah could hardly believe what he was thinking. He took a deep breath and looked out into the darkness. Something moved. Or at least he thought it had. It could have been a shadow swimming on the limestone, reflecting back off the running creek. Or smoke fading upward, caught by a breeze, then blown back to the edge of darkness. Or it could have been a cougar or a bear, attracted by the smell of what remained of the rabbit roasting next to the fire.

He grabbed up the rifle, eased it into his left hand, and unholstered the six-shooter.

"Don't go gettin' all trigger-happy, Wolfe,

189

it's just me," Scrap said, appearing out of the black of night, leading Missy closely by the halter. It was clear that she'd thrown a shoe.

Josiah relaxed. "You about got your head shot off."

Scrap nodded, tying Missy to a nearby oak. "Wouldn't be the first time."

The anger had gone from Scrap's face. Interpreting Scrap's feelings didn't take a medicine man; they were etched clearly on his features. Now he was just tired and about to give out after the long ride.

"Won't be the last time, either," Josiah said. He tried not to smile. He wasn't really that surprised to see Elliot walk into camp, his head down in defeat and resignation.

"Suppose not. Is that rabbit I smell?"

Josiah nodded. "My specialty."

"Mind if I join you?"

"Sometimes, but not now. Come on in."

"Thanks, Wolfe. I couldn't go on. Didn't want to hurt Missy running at night."

"I understand. We need to talk about some things, anyway," Josiah said.

"Yeah, I think we do," Scrap answered as he pulled a tin plate and fork from his saddlebag.

Josiah let his hand slide off the Colt Frontier, but he held on to the rifle. "You wouldn't have any reason to see me dead, would you, Elliot?"

CHAPTER 17

Scrap didn't answer until he'd filled his plate with meat and sat down next to the fire, opposite Josiah. "Why in tarnation would I want to see you dead, Wolfe? That's the silliest thing I've heard all day."

"Just sitting here thinking about everything, and a lot of things don't add up, that's all." Josiah toyed with a piece of the rabbit. It tasted good to him, but he'd had about enough.

Scrap grabbed up a leg and tore a chunk of meat off, barely chewing it. "Tastes like summer grass."

"If you say so."

"I do."

Josiah let the silence of the night push into the camp. He stared at Scrap Elliot, glad to see him but still uncertain if he would ever call him his friend. There was no doubt that the kid had true intentions — that he wanted to be a good Ranger and an honest man. But there was also the fact that he was young and wily, unpredictable as an unbroken mustang. Tragedy of one kind or another had shaped them both. Josiah was well aware of that. War had left its mark on him, and death and disease had afflicted him in a hidden manner. Some men lost an arm or a leg in the war. Josiah had lost the ability to trust — among other things.

For Scrap, the utter violence and rage employed by the Comanche had taken away the comfort that had previously existed in his young life. Murder had poured hate into his heart, and it coursed through his veins every day. The Indians had killed his parents outright, and that left Scrap and his younger sister, Myra Lynn, orphans. Myra Lynn lived with the Ursuline nuns in Dallas, while Scrap was left to fend for himself. His body might have kept on growing, but it sure seemed to Josiah that everything else, the things that mattered on the inside of Scrap, had stopped dead in their tracks when his folks were killed.

Josiah had seen the nuns once or twice on his travels. They wore long black dresses, black sleeveless cloaks, a headdress with a white veil and another veil that was black, too. It was hard to tell if the women were in mourning or practicing religion. He knew nothing about either, at least openly.

Still, Scrap rarely talked about his sister or family. Any bond that was shared by Josiah and Scrap would be the adventures they had experienced together since the forming of the Frontier Battalion back in the spring. And that had been a short time. Not time enough for a true friendship to grow as far as Josiah was concerned.

"What?" Scrap said, rabbit grease trailing out of the corner of his mouth. "Ain't you never seen a hungry man before?"

"Sure I have."

"Then why are you starin' at me?"

"Why'd you say I left you?"

"You did."

"I didn't have a choice."

"You let yourself get captured," Scrap said, setting his plate down next to the fire.

The air shifted, and the smoke enveloped Scrap like it had been called to him. The boy coughed, stood up, and moved away from the fire. The smoke followed him. "Damn it."

Josiah stood up, too, angered by Scrap's accusation. "You were the first one the Comanche took. You *were* captured."

"They tricked me. Overmeyer said there was only one."

Josiah sighed. Their voices were raised,

194

echoing off the limestone bluffs. Anger had invaded the silence of the peaceful November night.

"I would have never left you or Overmeyer by choice. You know that, right? Feders put me in charge, and I failed to keep you and Red safe. I brought trouble to the whole company, and I lost a man. He's dead because of what I failed to see, what I failed to do. I don't know if Rangering will ever be the same . . . if they'll even want to keep me on — if I even want to stay on with all that's happened."

"You or the rest of us," Scrap said.

"What do you mean?"

"The governor's put out an order to cut the Battalion down in size. Ain't enough money to pay everybody the wages they promised. I figure the pay I get in Austin will be my last."

"How many men are being cut?"

"They want twenty men to a company. You still got a chance to make the cut, Wolfe. You've known Feders a lot longer than I have. Rode with him and Captain Fikes. I figure you'll be fine in the end. I can do some cattle punchin', ain't like I'll be left out in the cold. I got skills. Horse skills. But I sure would like to stay a Ranger," Scrap said.

"You can't know anything for sure. They might keep you on." Josiah shifted his weight uncomfortably, standing back from the fire.

If the future had been uncertain before, it certainly was even more so now. He understood little about politics, or government for that matter. But he understood the lack of money in the state coffers. Since the Panic of '73 took hold a year prior, and nearly all the banking and railroad businessmen had lost their shirts, life had been hard going for most all of the United States and the territories beyond.

Governor Coke had gotten himself elected as the savior of democracy, promising a certain and final end to Reconstruction and all that had come along with it since the War Between the States had ended in 1865. Funding the Rangers had been a major initiative, promising to rid the state of the constant threat of Indian attacks and do away with the underfunded and corrupt State Police force. But Coke had obviously found out that funding a full battalion of Rangers was an expensive proposition. It was too expensive to sustain his original vision. No wonder Pete Feders seemed so strained when he arrived in Comanche. This was one more strike against his company, when his leadership was already fragile. Josiah's recent failures were surely just one more thing to make the company stand out as a bad example of Coke's original vision of the Rangers.

Josiah wondered if Pete knew more about the cuts and how they were going to occur. If so, then he probably wasn't able to say yet, adding to Feders's frustration.

"I don't think they'll keep me on," Scrap said. "There's men with more experience than me."

"You have a reputation as a great shot, and you're right, you've got horse skills. An exceptional sense that I've hardly ever been witness to. That'll go a long way. I wouldn't worry too much about staying on if I were you."

"You really think so?"

"I do. It'll be me that'll face the cut before you do. Feders isn't too fond of me."

"You know why?"

"I have an idea, even though I've tried real hard to stay out of his personal business, but I haven't been able to."

"Has to do with Captain Fikes's daughter, don't it?"

"It might. I don't know." Josiah sat back down in front of the fire and motioned for Scrap to follow suit. He did know, though

— at least his gut did. Pete Feders blamed him for Pearl Fikes's reluctance to be courted and ultimately to marry him, even though Josiah had stayed as far away from Pearl as was humanly possible. Early in the spring, Josiah had witnessed a full proposal, Pete on his knees in front of Pearl, and Pearl had turned him down flat. Josiah was hidden in the shadows, but he suspected Pete knew he'd been there. The man had treated him differently ever since.

"This whole trip turned ugly," Josiah continued. "I'd take back every decision I made since leaving Austin if I could. Change a lot of things. But life doesn't work that way. You know that as well as I do."

"You can't bring Overmeyer back." Scrap was still standing, pushing the toe of his boot into the sandy loam.

"Sit down. You're not going anywhere."

"I know that, but I'm still sore at you."

"Not anymore than I am at myself."

"I suppose not." Scrap sat down and picked his plate back up. The smoke snaked upward, leaving Scrap alone. The breeze died, as if it had never existed in the first place. "I suppose if there's any consolation, Overmeyer didn't suffer much."

"You're sure of that?"

"I couldn't see clearly, I was on the other

side of that big ole tree, but that damned Indian was a good shot."

"I saw it. Thought surely you were next."

Scrap looked down at the ground. "I nearly peed myself. I figured sure as there is a Hell and a Heaven that the Comanche was gonna jump off his horse and scalp Red Overmeyer, then come for me, too."

Josiah was quietly surprised by Scrap's declaration of faith. The boy had never mentioned much about his Christian beliefs, other than making note of his sister's life with nuns.

"That does seem odd, doesn't it?" Josiah asked.

"What?"

"That the Comanche didn't scalp Red, that they left you there . . . alive?"

"I wondered about it, but I sure didn't dwell on it. I was just glad to be free."

"How'd you get loose? Did you wiggle out of those ropes?" Josiah asked. "They looked awful tight." His tone was curious, and soft. He figured the memory was fresh, and being so close to Red in death, seeing and smelling his blood, had probably provoked a reaction from Scrap's emotional past. There was no need to get the boy all riled up again.

Scrap shook his head no. "No way I could

have got out of that binding."

"Then how?"

"Feders. He rode up with the company right near dark. I thought I was dreamin', havin' a hallucination. But sure enough, it was our company that rescued me . . . and you, too," Scrap said, a satisfied smile growing on his face.

Josiah caught his words before he said them out loud. He swallowed the question that nearly escaped his lips and let it settle deep inside him. But he couldn't let it go, couldn't keep from wondering why Pete Feders had been just a couple of hours behind them on the same day he had sent them out on a mission that Josiah thought was all his own.

CHAPTER 18

Austin came into view as Josiah and Scrap crested the rise of a hill. Josiah gently pulled in Lady Mead's reins and brought the palomino to an easy stop after a long, hard ride. Scrap followed suit, looking at Josiah curiously, but remained silent and didn't question the decision.

There was no joy in the homecoming for Josiah. Very simply, Austin still did not feel like home to him. The city was crowded, noisy, smelly, and the shadows were uncertain and mostly unknown. Josiah had yet to get his footing as a city dweller even though he had moved there on a permanent basis nearly six months earlier. The reasons, at least at the time, had seemed clear: He needed to move on with his life, and leaving his son on a small farm while he was away Rangering didn't feel right — especially after the outlaws — Charlie Langdon and Liam O'Reilly — had taken the boy hostage

201

and used him as bait. It had nearly ended in tragedy. Lyle was no longer safe in the piney woods of East Texas. But it was more than that. For a brief moment, Josiah had felt his heart stir alive, and he thought that being in the city and being close to those that stirred his heart — specifically Pearl Fikes — would help him step forward into a life worth living. Being a Ranger helped, but the recovery from the wound that had occurred in Lost Valley had set him back, and taken a lot longer than he'd thought it would. And Pearl Fikes was a grand catch, being pursued by Pete Feders . . . and Major John B. Jones. Josiah knew he could not compete with the stature of either man, so he had tried to avoid her as much as possible in the last few months. If there was one quality about the city that Josiah liked, it was the ability to get lost in it.

"What's the matter, Wolfe?" Scrap finally asked.

Josiah shook his head. "Nothing."

"It's a purty sight, ain't it?"

Josiah exhaled deeply. "I suppose so."

From their vantage point, they could see nearly straight down Congress Avenue. The Old Stone Capitol stood at the end of the road, a three-storey Greek Revival building, set in the middle of Capitol Square. The avenue was lined with buildings butted up next to each other, mostly two-storey, but some, including the hotels, were three stories.

The capitol building had a slight feel to it, and there were some who were demanding that a grander building be erected — but again the economic collapse had quelled any real momentum to rebuild. As it was, the election in 1850 had only named Austin the capital for twenty years, so there was a temporary feel to the building and what it stood for. Another election, in 1872, had settled the matter, making Austin the permanent capital of Texas.

It seemed there were buildings as far as the eye could see — churches and dry goods stores: Sampson & Hendrik's groceries and hardware, more than one mercantile, competing liveries, the Opera House, a few theaters, Republic Square and the county courthouse, nestled close to "Little Mexico," an enclave favored mostly by Mexicans and very few Anglos. Little Mexico was a rough section of town, but no more so than the section that served to provide entertainment for cowboys hot off the trail and looking for a good time in the bagnios, whorehouses, and saloons. That area, the first ward, was west of Congress

Avenue and ran to just north of the Colorado River. It didn't really have an Anglo name, like Little Mexico, other than Hell's Half Acre — but that was a Dallas name, and most Austinites refused to call it that — most cities had spots that were called that or something similar. It was one place Josiah rarely visited, but he could see it from where he sat on the ridge.

Very few trees were mixed in among the buildings, hardly any in fact, and what wildlife existed in town was mostly the two-footed, human kind. Even birds seemed wary of Austin.

Occasionally Josiah would look to the sky and see a soaring hawk or buzzard, and his mood would be lightened for a moment, memories of his childhood home rushing to the forefront of his mind. Then he would grow sad, longing for the birdsongs in the woods instead of the rumble of the train, the Houston and Texas Central Railroad, the hoots and hollers of teamsters, and the stagecoaches in a hurry to deliver their cargo, whatever it might be.

"If you don't like the city, then why in tarnation did you move here, Wolfe?" Scrap asked.

"It seemed like the right thing to do at the time. Still does for that matter. At least as long as I'm riding with the Rangers."

"Your boy ain't no more safe here than he was in Seerville."

"Ofelia has family here. They're not alone."

"I'd get rid of that Mexican woman if it was me. Your boy ain't gonna know if he's Anglo or a Mexican."

Josiah shot Scrap a cold, hard look, and Scrap immediately looked away. He'd voiced his opinion before about Josiah's choice to employ Ofelia as a wet nurse, a replacement mother, really, and Josiah had, in no uncertain terms, told Scrap to mind his own business. "If I was going to keep on Rangering, then I had to do something."

"Find a wife like every other widow man I know. Might be a place to start."

"It's not that easy."

"Would be for me."

"You need to . . ."

". . . I know, mind my own damn business."

"Something like that."

Scrap shrugged his shoulders. "What are you gonna do if you don't have to leave the city anymore?"

"I suppose if I'm cut from the company, then I'll look to move back home."

"Maybe that wouldn't be so bad."

"Hard to say," Josiah said. "Hard to say."

They took the ride into the city slow. The only hurry Josiah was in boiled down to two things. He couldn't wait to see Lyle, and more than anything, he wanted out of Charlie Webb's clothes. It was hard not to be grateful to Billie for her generosity, but how he had come to accept that generosity in the first place was hard to swallow. And he could not get Billie out of his mind. Her fate was worrisome, a waif lost in plain sight in the midst of an angry town — but there was nothing he could do to help her at the moment except what he had done: leave.

It would be good to step into a pair of boots that were his own instead of wearing Charlie Webb's and a shirt cut with his own scent and not a dead man's.

Josiah picked up the pace a bit when they crossed over the train tracks. His home was less than a block away now.

Scrap eased up alongside him, a comfortable smile on his face. "Your horse will be glad to see you."

"And I him. I thought Clipper was lost to me."

Scrap shook his head no. "He stayed close. Feders sent a runner back to Austin to make Major Jones aware of the attack from the

Comanche. They brung him back to the livery, like I told 'em."

"I appreciate it. Clipper and I have been through a lot together."

"That's a fine horse, too. What you gonna do with her?"

Josiah shrugged. "Haven't thought too much about it. I think the sight of her gave Billie Webb a heavy heart. Parting seemed to be a relief. I got other things to worry about at the moment. We'll keep her fed and tended to. That's the least I can do."

"Ought to bring a fair price if you decide to sell her."

"Now that doesn't seem like the right thing to do, does it?"

"I'm just sayin' . . ."

Josiah didn't answer Scrap. His attention was immediately drawn down the street as his house came into view.

There was a woman standing on the porch, looking up and down the street, nervously, like she was expecting someone, or had lost something, and the woman was not Ofelia.

There was no mistaking her identity. Her shoulder-length blond hair shone in the fading evening light like a golden beacon welcoming Josiah home. She had an hourglass figure and was dressed in clothes that suggested she was still in mourning for the loss of her father, though not the formal widow's weeds that her mother wore every minute of the day. She had on a comfortable black riding skirt, black boots, a black long-sleeved blouse, and no hat.

Still, even at this distance, Josiah thought that Pearl Fikes was one of the most beautiful women he had ever seen. Her face was sweet as a China doll's, and her eyes were cornflower blue, thoughtful and easy to read, but far from fragile. Pearl had received the lion's share of her good features from her father. There was very little of her mother in her that Josiah could see.

Regardless of that, of how he felt, her presence on his porch not only concerned him but frightened the hell out of him. She had never been at his house before, and he could not imagine what had provoked her to make a visit now.

He urged Lady Mead on, kicking a bit of dust up onto Scrap. The rains that had plagued Comanche had obviously not been as heavy in Austin. The street was dry, the ruts as hard as they normally were.

"What the heck is the matter with you?" Scrap yelled out.

Josiah didn't offer an explanation. He wasn't sure he had one. There was a deep rile in his gut, a familiar feeling, one that he usually trusted, one that almost always told him something was wrong.

Lady Mead played easily under his command, though not as easily as Clipper. The noise of the city didn't seem to bother her, though running full out in a street that had traffic — wagons, coaches, and lone cowboys — appeared to be something the horse wasn't too used to, or it had been a long time since she had experienced the exercise of ignoring city traffic. She lurched ahead of his directions, anticipating his moves wrongly, and then had to be pulled back.

Josiah brought the palomino to a quick stop in the middle of the street in front of his house.

Pearl had seen him by then, the expression on her soft face hard to read. But there was no mistaking the fact that she wasn't surprised to see him, nor did it appear that she was especially glad of his return.

No one else was in sight, not Ofelia or Lyle. Panic was setting in; memories of the past when both of them were in harm's way rushed to the forefront of his mind. His fear was real, and the only way he knew to counter it was to touch his gun — Charlie Webb's gun — and prepare to pull it if necessary.

Josiah nodded at Pearl as he ran past her to the front door. "Ofelia! Ofelia, come out here! Ofelia!" he screamed, coming to a stop. He could feel his heart racing, taste the fear in his mouth. He gripped the Colt Frontier so hard it shot a pain through his shoulder.

"She's not here," Pearl said. Her voice was soft, but the sad look on her face betrayed her intention, as her eyes grew glassy with tears. "She's gone. Ofelia is gone, Josiah. Ofelia is gone."

CHAPTER 19

All of the noise in the city vanished. It was like Josiah had stepped straight into a locked room made of six-inch steel. "Where's Lyle?" he demanded, more directly than he had ever spoken to Pearl.

"Sleeping. He was tired."

"He doesn't know you."

"We didn't have any trouble," Pearl said, never once breaking eye contact with Josiah. There was a strength about her that was just as present as her physical beauty, and Josiah found it easy to understand why so many men were in pursuit of her affections. "I've been around children before, Josiah Wolfe."

He took a deep breath. "Where is Ofelia?"

"She had to return home. There has been a tragedy in her family."

"What?"

"Her daughter is very sick. The details are thin. To me, at the very least."

Josiah knew almost every member of Ofelia's family. They were just like family to him, as well, even though there was a divide of culture and language. Ofelia's daughter, Lita, was older, had children of her own, and had taken over the midwife duties around Tyler when Ofelia had come to Austin with him. The sickness had to be serious for Ofelia to leave Lyle.

"I feared she was dead," Josiah said.

"The daughter?"

"Ofelia. I don't know what I would have done." Josiah took a deep breath and settled the Colt back into his holster. "How did you come to be here, to care for Lyle?" Josiah asked.

Pearl wiped the tear from her eye. "I feared you were dead once I heard of your capture by the Comanche."

"Oh." It occurred to Josiah then that the tears were for him. Pearl was relieved to see him. He wasn't sure how he felt about that, so he turned away, saw Scrap Elliot jump off his horse and run toward the house, gun drawn.

"Easy there, Elliot," Josiah yelled out. "Everything is fine here."

"You sure?" Scrap said, his attention quickly drawn to Pearl. It seemed like he couldn't take his eyes off her.

212

"Yes."

"Ma'am." Scrap doffed his hat, swinging it low, overacting the gentlemanly role by more than a tad.

Pearl Fikes smiled, then laughed slightly. "It is good to see you once more, Ranger Elliot."

Scrap looked embarrassed, almost bashful, when he stood back up. He held his tongue and didn't say anything. His manners around women were always precarious and uncertain, as far as Josiah had seen.

"Why don't you take the horses back and tend to them," Josiah said to Scrap.

"Gladly."

Scrap grabbed the reins of both horses and stalked off. Pearl chuckled again, though this time it looked like a nervous reaction. "I've offended him," she said.

"Don't pay any attention to him. He's as sensitive as a baby's skin in the sunshine."

"I should apologize."

"He tries too hard. Trust me, the next time he sees you, all will be forgotten and forgiven."

"If you say so."

Josiah looked past Pearl, inside the house. There was no noise, nothing stirring. He longed to see Lyle but didn't want to wake him.

213

"How did you come to be here?" Josiah asked, his voice soft. "I didn't expect to find you here."

"Juan Carlos came for me. He did not think he could care for the child and was opposed to leaving the boy with strangers in 'Little Mexico.' He and Ofelia know a lot of the same people, but they are very unfamiliar with each other, so coming to get me seemed even more appropriate to Juan Carlos than caring for a child himself. If one can imagine."

Josiah chuckled then. "No, I can't imagine that he'd be a good candidate to watch over Lyle. Where is Juan Carlos? I would like to see my old friend."

"Who knows? You know Juan Carlos. One minute he's here, and the next he's gone. You never know when he's going to show up next."

"It's been months since I've seen him. July, before we ventured into Lost Valley."

"I worry about him. His age will prohibit his adventures one of these days," Pearl said, wistfully.

Josiah silently agreed. But he also knew that Juan Carlos was the kind of man that lived for adventures, and he would most likely die in the middle of one of his great escapades rather than wasting away on a deathbed. "How long have you been here?"

"Since last night. There was no word of your fate. I was prepared to wait as long as it took." Pearl was facing him now, standing less than a foot away. In one easy step that couldn't have been done more gracefully if she had been a professional dancer employed at the Opera House, she snuggled up into Josiah's chest, her arms fully around him in a tight embrace. "I don't know what I would have done if something had happened to you."

Josiah was surprised but didn't resist, didn't pull away. He welcomed her embrace and was immediately intoxicated by her sweet smell and the feel of her body against his. A thousand emotions shot through his entire body. Finding Pearl waiting for him on his porch was the last thing he had ever expected. Molding his body to hers in a moment of welcome and relief was beyond belief.

Pearl cocked her head to Josiah. Her beauty was breathtaking. He kissed her. Kissed her long and hard, like she was his lover and he'd fought through an entire war just to return to her. She responded in kind, the kiss wholly returned.

Questions floated away, the answers unimportant at the moment. The entire world —

past, present, and future — fell away. Feelings began to surface inside of Josiah that he had restrained for a long, long time. And it was then that his body began to respond to his own desire just like his heart had, and he pulled away from Pearl as quickly as she had embraced him.

"I'm sorry," he whispered.

She shook her head. "Don't be."

It was then that Josiah sensed something else, a presence behind him. He turned just in time to see Scrap stalking off again, this time shaking his head in disgust.

Josiah was sure the boy had witnessed the entire moment with Pearl, and he was certain that that would lead to nothing but trouble. Serious trouble.

At his young age, Lyle wasn't old enough to know or understand why his father had been away longer than he was supposed to have been. For all Josiah knew, Lyle had barely missed him, had been unaware of his extended absence since there was a normalcy to it. But Lyle reacted happily when Josiah woke him. The two-year-old — almost three-year-old — boy squealed in delight once the sleep was wiped from his eyes.

"Papa! *Me alegro a verte!*"

Josiah looked at the boy oddly. He didn't understand a word his young son had spoken to him.

"He said he's happy to see you," Pearl said. She was standing at the doorway and must have seen the confused look on Josiah's face.

"I'm going to have to talk to Ofelia."

Lyle jumped into Josiah's arms.

Pearl shrugged. "There are worse things than a boy learning to speak two languages. Especially here."

"It might cause him more trouble than it's worth when he's older." Josiah didn't mean to sound harsh, but his tone must have been harder than he'd intended because Pearl stepped back.

"I'm sorry. He's your son."

"Papa!" Lyle shouted again, not giving Josiah the opportunity to respond or apologize.

Josiah smiled then. "It's good to see you, too, son. It's good to see you again."

"Don't go," Lyle said.

"I'm home now."

The boy shook his head. "Don't go. Missed you."

Night had fallen. Scrap had disappeared. And Josiah had no choice but to see Pearl

Fikes home. He did not take the time to wash the trail off himself, or to settle into being home. There was no way he was going to just thank Pearl and send her on her way . . . but seeing Scrap, realizing that the embrace had been witnessed, had been a public display with them standing on the porch, made Josiah extremely uncomfortable.

The last thing he needed was for Pete Feders to become an enemy. Major John B. Jones, too. One whisper to either man of Pearl Fikes's affection for him would certainly be a nail in the coffin of his career as a Ranger. Though that seemed like an odd thing to be concerned about at the moment. Josiah was also concerned for Pearl. He wasn't sure of her feelings for him, but more importantly, he wasn't sure she could understand his lack of resources to court her properly. There was certainly no question of his desire for her; he most surely wanted to explore their mutual desire for each other as far as it would go. He was sad that it was impossible, that it could never truly ever happen. A relationship with a woman like Pearl Fikes was something beyond a dream for a man like him.

Josiah set out to ready Pearl's buggy. Missy, Scrap's horse, was gone from the stable, and Lady Mead had been properly tended to. He was happy to see Clipper, but the horse didn't show any emotion or gratitude upon seeing Josiah, not that he'd expected any. But Clipper followed Josiah's lead outside and easily took his place, tied to the back of the buggy.

For a November night the air was warm and dry. Any clouds of the day had departed, leaving the sky clear. Interior lights burned brightly in nearly every house and building, casting odd lots of shadows on the dirt street, making it look almost golden.

Josiah pulled the buggy up in front of his house. Pearl was standing there in wait, with Lyle's hand in hers, an odd sight for Josiah to see.

There was a time when he could never have imagined another woman in his life. Josiah had loved Lily fully and completely. But he felt something for Pearl, even though those feelings seemed ill-fated.

He helped Pearl into the buggy, settling Lyle between the two of them on the single seat. The horse, a large black stallion with no hint of white anywhere on its body, responded to Josiah's "giddy-up," and they were on their way.

"I could have waited to return home until morning," Pearl said.

Josiah looked away. "That would have been inappropriate."

"I suppose, in some people's eyes."

"Pearl," Josiah said, his voice exasperated. "There is nothing that I would like more than to be able to court you."

"There is nothing stopping you."

They passed by the governor's mansion. The lights inside were aglow — gaslights instead of coal oil — brighter, hotter, the gold glow reflecting off the street. It was another Greek Revival building set three hundred yards from the Capitol building, bounded by Lavaca, Guadalupe, Tenth, and Eleventh streets. The bricks had been made in Austin, and the pillars were made of pine logs, shipped thirty-three miles southeast, from Bastrop. The big house was a reflection of Texas through and through.

"There is, Pearl, and you know it. Besides your mother never permitting my presence in a proper setting, I have other considerations."

"Peter."

"Yes, Captain Feders. I know of his feelings for you."

"You should let me worry about Peter and Mother."

"If only it were that easy, Pearl, but it's not."

Lyle snuggled in between the two of them. The boy had been especially well behaved since Josiah's return, more than happy to be at his father's side.

For a moment, Josiah let his imagination run with the image, the three of them in the buggy, the day sunny and happy, all of them dressed in finery, everything perfect, full of love. But it was just for a moment, and Josiah knew more than anyone that the idea of them as a family was just a fantasy.

All he had to do was convince Pearl of that.

CHAPTER 20

Pedro, the manservant on the Fikes estate, met Josiah and Pearl at the door.

The house was grand, not far from the governor's mansion in both distance and style — smaller, but still impressive. The deceased Captain Hiram Fikes had spent little time on the estate when he was alive, and Josiah knew little of the history, how the house had come into being and whose money had financed it, but he secretly suspected that the captain had married into money. If that was the case, then the past might be a predictor of his own future, one of the reasons, among many, that he felt incapable of courting Pearl.

Captain Fikes had obviously been uncomfortable with his marriage arrangement, since he'd had a secret relationship with Suzanne del Toro, "Fat Susie," purveyor of soiled doves and a savvy businesswoman of ill repute in Little Mexico, and spent so much time away from the house and estate on official Ranger business.

There was little to convey the captain's unhappiness based on outside appearances. The house was made of brick and had four white columns that held up a gabled roof over a two-storey portico. It looked as if a view had been important, since the grand house looked out over a calm meadow, with a pond nearly in the center of it.

It was by the pond where Josiah had first encountered Pearl the previous spring, had felt an attraction to her even though he was still grieving for his own lost family, and had kissed her more by accident than on purpose, unlike what had just happened. This kiss had been no accident — it was like the long awaited arrival of sunshine after a horrifying storm. He could bearly stand to be near Pearl without touching her in some way or another.

There was acreage to the estate, though Josiah did not know how much. There were two barns full of equipment and a bunk-house for plenty of hands to plant and harvest crops, tend to the horses and other livestock, mostly a nice herd of cattle.

If the estate had been far out in the hill country, it might have qualified for a ranch, albeit a small one, but inside the confines of

Austin proper, Josiah doubted it held that classification.

On his last visit, he had accidentally spied Pearl and Pete Feders in a heated conversation behind one of the barns, and it was there that he witnessed Pearl rejecting Pete's offer of marriage. This return to the estate was uncomfortable for Josiah, especially when he factored in the obvious dislike the Widow Fikes held for him, even though he never could figure out why she disliked him so much.

"It is good to see you again, Ranger Wolfe," Pedro said.

The manservant was an inch or two taller than Josiah and was one of the most refined Mexicans that Josiah had ever encountered. He was dressed in traditional garb, a black frock coat over a highly starched white shirt, black string tie with perfectly equal bows, and flawless black pants void of lint or creases. Pedro looked like a mortician, except that he wore white gloves.

The Mexican spoke without much of an accent, and Josiah had learned previously that the Widow Fikes had sent Pedro back east to some highfalutin college for an education before assigning him permanently to his manservant duties. Pedro essentially ran the house and most all of the business activities on the estate, as far as Josiah knew.

It had been less than a year since the death of her husband, so the Widow Fikes was still officially in mourning, still wearing the heavy dress some women called weeds. Word was, the widow barely left her bed on most days, and when she did, it seemed her goal in life was to make everyone who crossed her path as miserable as she was.

"Yes, it's good to see you again, too," Josiah answered.

"The chance of your survival seemed grim," Pedro said.

Pearl stood silently by Josiah's side. Lyle was sitting in the buggy. A tall windup grandfather clock ticked behind Pedro. Somewhere in the distance a campfire burned on the estate, the smell of fresh cooked steak wafting on the breeze. Probably one of the hands that worked for the Widow Fikes.

Josiah nodded. "I assure you that my survival was in serious question, Pedro. I feel lucky to be standing here on your doorstep."

"Miss Pearl, your mother has been worried about your absence," Pedro said. "She was going to send for you, but I convinced her to allow for more time."

"She noticed I was gone?" Pearl's tone

was sharper than normal, and Josiah recognized and remembered the tension that existed between Pearl and her mother. Pearl favored Captain Fikes in demeanor and attitude, which meant, unfortunately for her mother, that she had a mind of her own.

Josiah looked over his shoulder and checked on Lyle. The boy was sitting stiff as a board in the buggy, just like he had been instructed to do. Satisfied, Josiah turned his attention back to Pearl. "Thank you for looking after Lyle, after all the trouble I've caused you. I don't know how I can ever thank you."

Pearl locked her gaze on his and would not look away. She had an expectant look on her face. "Well," she said, "perhaps you can come for dinner once you get settled at home. Pedro, see that it gets done. We have a party planned for tomorrow. Set another place."

"But your mother . . ." Josiah protested.

"My mother will be on her best behavior. Trust me. It is time we had some life in this house. Being away from it has done me a world of good. Visitors for Mother will be the tonic for what ails her, whether she knows it or not."

"I don't think this is a good idea," Josiah murmured.

Pearl smiled, then stepped away from Josiah and pushed inside the door, her eyes locked on Pedro this time with the same steely, demanding glare she had favored Josiah with.

"I am serious, Pedro. There will be no discussion with my mother — she will not cancel this invitation without my knowledge, do you understand?" Pearl said.

"Yes, Miss Pearl, I do."

Pearl nodded in approval and disappeared behind Pedro, into the flickering shadows of a grand entrance, without another word or glance toward Josiah.

Josiah's mouth went dry.

Pedro exhaled. "I will have the buggy tended to, Ranger Wolfe. There is no need for you to keep your son out in the night air any longer."

"I'll be on my way then."

"I will send word when all of the proper arrangements for this dinner have been made."

"I would rather you didn't."

Pedro cocked his thick black right eyebrow at Josiah. "You do not find Miss Pearl attractive?"

"The fields between us are broad," Josiah said. "Our lives are very different. I'm just a common man, and I really don't know the ways of her world. Or yours for that matter."

"Miss Pearl is more common than you think, Ranger Wolfe."

"There's nothing common about Pearl Fikes," Josiah said.

Pedro chuckled. "Perhaps you are right. But nonetheless, I will expect to see you in attendance at the dinner. I do not wish to encounter Miss Pearl's wrath anytime soon."

Josiah knew that it was of little use to protest. "Thank you, Pedro," he said, turning to leave.

"Ranger Wolfe," Pedro said, in a deep, commanding tone. "You need to watch out for yourself. There are people who care about your well-being . . . as well as your demise."

Before Josiah could respond, Pedro stepped back and closed the door solidly, almost in a slam. It echoed in Josiah's ears like the first beat of a war drum.

The comment created more questions but also confirmed his suspicions that there was more to the events of the last few days than he understood.

He was tempted to go pound on the door and demand an explanation from Pedro, but decided that drawing attention from the

Widow Fikes at such a late hour was probably not the best thing to do.

It was time to go home.

Josiah settled Lyle in front of him in Clipper's saddle and eased away from the big house.

"Papa, I'm sleeping," Lyle said.

Josiah chuckled, his mind immediately drawn away from the confusion that Pedro had created. He had missed Lyle more completely and thoroughly than he could ever have imagined. Being held captive by the two Comanche had most likely caused him to reconsider his own mortality, even though that was an old battle.

Josiah knew how fragile life was.

How could he not after all that he had witnessed in his years as a soldier, lawman, and Ranger? He could not, however, reconcile that knowledge of fragility and duty with a change in occupation, one that offered less danger and a consistent presence in his son's life. The thought of Lyle being left alone in the world, left with strangers, was even more troubling now that Ofelia had been called home.

Juan Carlos had chosen well in bringing Pearl to the house to watch over the child, but it was not her place . . . not now, maybe not ever. It was even more important in the coming days for Josiah to decide about the direction of his life.

If Scrap had been correct, and there was no reason to doubt him, and the governor was ordering a reduction in the size of the companies of the Frontier Battalion, then perhaps it would not be a bad thing if Josiah was one of those men let go. Perhaps it would be the best thing to happen — forcing Josiah to find employment and a life more certain, closer to home.

It was something to consider, but that kind of change would not completely create a safe environment for Lyle to grow up in, and Josiah knew it.

There would always be danger and a threat, as long as Liam O'Reilly was free, on the run, able to turn a town and the law into his own. As long as that was the case, Josiah knew he would always be looking over his shoulder . . . and Lyle's.

CHAPTER 21

The glow from the gaslights in the governor's mansion caught Josiah's attention again, as he rode slowly by.

Gaslights were a relatively new presence in Austin. The newspaper, the *Austin Daily Statesman,* had called the piping of gas to the governor's mansion "a step toward modernization, fraught with peril." And Josiah couldn't have agreed more. A gas leak not only had the potential to silently kill every member of the household, but it could blow the place up, leave it in crumbles, like it had been struck by the most powerful bomb ever used in the War Between the States.

A bat chittered overhead, drawing Josiah's gaze away from the house and back to the moment. Obviously there were some creatures that still showed favor to the city at night. Josiah pulled Lyle closer to him.

The demise of the mansion, and its occupants, was a distant concern for Josiah. It was his own demise that worried him, the echo of Pedro's warning still ringing inside his head, flapping about just like the bat's wings.

The warning could have meant nothing. Or it could have been intentional, an arrow pointed to a deeper meaning, or at someone who truly meant him harm. But who? Pete Feders? The Widow Fikes? Someone else in the ranks of the Frontier Battalion? Scrap? None of them made any sense, unless Pedro was somehow connected to Liam O'Reilly and knew of the outlaw's intent. But that seemed unlikely. The comment was very confusing, and unsettling enough to keep him on high alert — even more so than he already was.

The night air was cool, and Lyle was snuggled up against Josiah. The bat had gone on, searching out whatever insects it could find at that time of night.

The boy's head was cocked to the side, and there was no doubt that Clipper's steady, even pace had lulled him quickly to sleep. Josiah had the reins in his right hand while his left hand and arm gently barred Lyle from moving at all. It would only take a second to sweep his hand to the left and reach the Colt Frontier if he had to.

As good as it was to be home, Josiah felt just as uncertain as he had been when he was on the run from the Comanche brothers, not knowing what was coming, if he would survive one minute to the next.

Those concerns were dimmer now, of course, but this was the first time in recent memory that Josiah had been wholly responsible for Lyle's well-being, and that was such a different kind of survival that Josiah could hardly process the scope of it.

Ofelia was hardly ever more than two feet away from the boy.

It was frightening for Josiah to fully consider that he would have to continue to act as both mother and father to Lyle.

At that moment, Josiah realized how much he had depended on Ofelia and taken for granted that she would always look after Lyle, when in reality, she had no reason to stay other than her own love of the boy. Josiah paid her what he could and made sure she had everything that she needed, within reason. Thankfully, Ofelia didn't require much to make her happy, or to keep her well tended.

Josiah knew it was wrong of him to even have thought that Ofelia would stay with him forever. But he had.

Lost in his own grief, in his own need for

a bit of adventure, for life to continue on, he had let his responsibilities to his son fall to someone outside of his blood family. Ofelia wasn't a stranger, but she also wasn't bound to either of them.

One way or another, Josiah knew that everything he had taken for granted would have to change.

The inside of the house was silent.

The floor creaked when Josiah eased open the front door and stepped inside. Josiah barely knew his way around in the dark in his own house. The creak gave Josiah sudden cause to stop and take a deep breath.

He didn't sense another presence in the house or see anything that would suggest malevolent entry, but there was no use in being foolhardy. As far as he knew, there was still a price on his head, put there by the outlaw Liam O'Reilly, not by any real enforcers of the law. Still, that money would be enough of a pull for those walking on the darker side of life to consider cashing in on the bounty. Whether it could ever be collected was another matter, one that held little to no consequence for Josiah. Some men went after a bounty more for the challenge than the payoff.

He let his eyes adjust to the darkness

inside the house. It only took him a minute to make out the familiar cupboard, wash sink, table, and two chairs that he had brought from his pine cabin in East Texas.

An open interior door led into the room where Lyle's bed sat waiting, the darkness deeper inside the room. It was a sparse house. One so small it probably could have fit inside the foyer of the Fikes estate. And that was one of the rubs that Josiah carried with him . . . still turning over the thought about Pearl's demand that he attend a dinner, and perhaps something more, at the mansion. His house was hardly a house befitting a woman such as Pearl. Somehow, he had to convince her of that.

Josiah made his way to the room and to the small child-sized bed and gently laid Lyle in it. He took off his son's simple leather shoes, unfurled his socks, then covered the boy up with a lightweight blanket.

Lyle was completely asleep, off in a dreamland, bearing little knowledge of his physical location, just that he was safe, or so Josiah hoped, under the watchful eye of his father.

A window hung open just to the left of the bed, and Josiah closed and locked it as quietly as he could.

The window looked out over an alleyway that separated two long rows of houses very much the same size and simple style as Josiah's. The houses stood close to each other, and most shared space for tool sheds, gardens, outhouses, and chicken coops. It could be a noisy area, even more so when the train was moving through. It was like living on top of a thundercloud most of the time.

Lyle hardly moved at the sound of the closing window. There was nothing to see in the alleyway, so Josiah backed out of the room easily, as certain as he could be that the boy was safely tucked into bed.

He lit a coal oil lamp that sat on the table where most of the meals were shared when he was home. Ofelia usually sat on a stool that was tucked in the corner — on her own accord — rarely sitting at the table with Josiah and Lyle. It was like she felt out of place, though Josiah had never considered such a thing until now.

The room immediately came alive in the light.

Josiah flicked his eyes, adjusting again to the brightness. As he'd thought, the room was empty, and he immediately allowed himself to relax. He could hardly believe he was home. It seemed like he had been gone a lifetime, when in fact it had only been a few days.

He took off the gun belt that had once belonged to Charlie Webb, gave its origin very little thought, and set it on the table.

All he wanted to do was pull his boots off, clean himself up the best he could at the moment, have a bite to eat, and sleep under a roof that was familiar and safe.

It looked like he was going to be able to do just that. He had one boot completely off and the other halfway, when he heard footsteps approach outside the door and climb up the porch steps.

Josiah froze for a second, listened for voices, for more than one set of footsteps, then stumbled back over to the table and unholstered the Colt.

The door slowly pushed open, the hinges protesting slightly, the creak drawn out by the deliberateness of the person opening the door.

"If you want to live to take another breath, I would suggest you stop right where you are," Josiah said. He was standing flat-footed now, the six-shooter aimed squarely at the door, the hammer cocked, his finger firmly on the trigger.

The movement of the door stopped.

"Don't shoot, Señor Wolfe. It is me. Juan

Carlos. Juan Carlos Montegné."

Josiah took a deep breath, took his finger off the trigger, and headed for the door. He'd been through way too much in his life to be completely relieved. There was no way to tell if Juan Carlos was totally alone. For all Josiah knew, his friend had a gun to his back, and someone was using their friendship as a ruse.

"Are you alone, Juan Carlos?" Josiah stopped at the door and stood off to the side.

"*Sí, señor.* It is just me."

Josiah wedged the barrel of the Colt into the crack of the door, then swung the door open with all of his might — catching it with his other hand, so it would not slam into the wall and wake up Lyle.

The color had drained from Juan Carlos's face. In the dim light, it was easy to see that Josiah's actions had frightened the old man.

Juan Carlos was only half-Mexican, but his skin was still dark, leathery from years spent under the sun. He had deep wrinkles in his face, crevices that looked like limestone cut by the wind and water. His hair was white as a cloud and just as thick as cotton. He was skin and bones, spindly, like his half brother, Captain Fikes.

"I am serious, señor. I am alone." Juan

Carlos put up his hands.

Josiah swept out of the doorway, his eyes searching for any sign of movement on the street that would indicate Juan Carlos was lying. Satisfied, he grabbed the old man by the shoulder, pulled him inside, and locked the door quickly.

"What is the matter, señor? What have I done?"

"Nothing." Josiah edged over to the window, pushed the curtain back slightly, and checked again to make sure the street was quiet. "It is good to see you, old friend."

Juan Carlos cocked his eyebrow. "How come I do not believe you, *mi amigo?* What has happened since I have left that you do not feel safe in your own home?"

"You don't know?" Josiah asked, pulling back from the window, facing Juan Carlos fully for the first time.

"No, señor, I don't. We have much to talk about."

"Yes, we do," Josiah said. "Yes, we do."

CHAPTER 22

The two men sat facing each other, waiting for a pot of Arbuckle's to come to a boil on the small woodstove in the corner. For a long moment, the two of them said nothing. Josiah was glad for the company, glad to see his friend, and even gladder that Juan Carlos was alone. One more confrontation would have likely done him in. He would have fought to the death to protect his house, and Lyle.

It did not take long for the comforting aroma of the coffee to complete the task of relaxing Josiah. Hopefully any kind of confrontation would wait until another day.

The ride into Austin had been long and finding Pearl standing on his porch an uncomfortable surprise. He wondered what had become of Scrap, but didn't dwell on the boy's whereabouts too much. Scrap had gone off in a hotheaded rage more than once since they had been riding together, and would turn up sooner or later with some wild tale to bestow on Josiah's unwilling ears.

The rest of Josiah's concerns — Pete Feders's luck and accomplishments in Comanche and the fate of the company — were distant at best. Now that he was home, all in one piece, his own life a matter of uncertainty, he wasn't about to venture too far, too soon.

"Do you have news of Ofelia?" Josiah said, getting up from the table to pour two cups of coffee.

"She is well. From what I understand, she is on her way back here," Juan Carlos said.

"Her daughter has recovered?"

Juan Carlos shook his head no. "She is bringing her with her, along with the rest of the family that remained east. There is a place for them in Little Mexico and she wants to be close to your boy."

"She's moving her entire family here?"

"*Sí.* That is what I understand."

Josiah poured the coffee and handed a steaming cup to Juan Carlos. "How do you know this?" he asked. He felt a moment of relief, but knowing that Ofelia was heading back to Austin changed nothing. Josiah knew now that he could not depend on her forever, not any longer.

The old Mexican stared at Josiah and smiled, taking the coffee, refusing to answer the question or reveal his source of knowledge.

"I am more concerned with your adventures," Juan Carlos said, taking a silver flask from his pocket and emptying a healthy finger of whiskey into the coffee.

"I would not call the last few days an adventure."

Juan Carlos had been eyeing Josiah carefully, watching every move he made. "You have a limp. Are you all right?"

"It's just a graze. Happened in Comanche."

Juan Carlos nodded and started to say something, but Josiah cut him off before he could get a word out of his mouth.

"I wish you would have left Pearl out of this," Josiah said.

His tone was hard, harsh. He was in no mood to rehash the events of the last few days at the moment. He was still reeling from being in Pearl's presence, from having her in his house, watching over Lyle, realizing that he had left his son in peril, in the company of strangers.

"I had no choice, señor. What was I to do? Take the boy with me? You were missing. I thought you were a dead man."

242

Josiah glared at Juan Carlos. "Lyle doesn't belong with Pearl."

"Do not be angry at me. I was fearful. Pearl is my niece. I know her heart, how she longs for . . ." Juan Carlos stopped talking, drew his thin mouth tight, and looked away from Josiah.

"Where'd you have to go that was so important?" Josiah asked, changing the subject.

Again, a wise smile returned to Juan Carlos's weathered face. "You should not be so angry about Pearl's presence. She is quite taken with you. *¿No estás listo para el amor?*"

"You know I don't speak Mexican."

"Perhaps it is time you learned."

Josiah shrugged his shoulders. "I know enough to understand the floors that Pearl and I walk on are completely different. She is accustomed to a palace, not a simple house like this. I cannot give her the life she is accustomed to."

Juan Carlos laughed. "Then *you are* ready for love?"

Josiah's face turned red as he sat down at the table. After a long pause, he said, "I know you had no other choice but to leave Lyle with her. But please, don't involve Pearl in my life again."

"If that is your wish, *mi amigo,* then I will abide by it."

"It is my wish."

Silence settled between the two men, and they both allowed it to continue. The night outside was quiet now that it was fully dark. There was still a liveliness to Austin, but the activity of rowdy cowboys looking for a good time with drink and women was blocks away. Another world away, really, and that was just the way Josiah liked it. He only wished that he was farther away, out in the hills somewhere, or even better, home in East Texas, where the only rowdy occurrence that presented any hint of concern was the hunters that came out at night — foxes and coyotes mostly. But that was not to be — still, the street outside of the house was reasonably quiet, void of travelers at that time of night.

All Josiah could hear was the steady breath of his son sleeping comfortably in the other room, and that was enough for him. He took a sip of the Arbuckle's and set the mug of coffee on the table.

"What of your travels, Juan Carlos? The last I saw of you was in that motte south of Dallas."

Juan Carlos eyed Josiah carefully, then nodded. "I met up with an old friend, and

244

headed south to the Nueces Strip."

"A testy place, even for you, my friend," Josiah said.

"I like it there."

"The place is full of bandits and cattle thieves."

Juan Carlos laughed. "Why do you think I was there?"

"I never know with you. Tell me of the mission, of your friend then." Josiah wanted nothing more than to hear something else other than his own troubles, his own past.

"Ah, my amigo, señor, is a friend to us both, though you do not know it yet."

"And who would that be?"

"McNelly. Leander McNelly," Juan Carlos said.

Josiah was not surprised to hear the name. Once Richard Coke was elected to governor in 1873, he created the now financially troubled Frontier Battalion, but he also designated a special force of Rangers, financed mostly by ranchers, to quell the thievery and troubles along the Nueces Strip.

Captain John B. Jones, the commander of the Frontier Battalion, and potential suitor of Pearl Fikes, had recommended Josiah speak to McNelly after the Lost Valley incident that occurred the previous summer, about Josiah potentially taking up with the Special Forces, but Josiah declined, sure that the work along the strip would be even more dangerous than what the Battalion faced. He chose to stay within riding distance of Lyle at the time, and it looked like that had been a good decision.

"McNelly, uh?" Josiah said. "Why am I not surprised? I have always thought you would make a competent spy, Juan Carlos. Is that your mission?"

"You ask more questions than I can give answers to, señor, but I have done plenty of work for the captain that requires my tongue and appearance. Cortina is a fierce adversary and is committed to keeping his business pure and alive."

"So Cortina is riled up in the south and the Comanche are fighting their last fight in the north?"

Juan Cortina had a long history of riling up Texas landowners near the border, most notably near Brownsville, where Cortina had maintained control over the town for a while, until he was ousted in 1859 by a group of men calling themselves the Brownsville Tigers and the early Texas Rangers, headed up by Rip Ford. Once the War Between the States started, Cortina gave up the attacks and went into politics, shoring up Mexico's side with the Confederacy. Once the war was over, Cortina fell out of favor and went back to stealing cattle, which obviously, was still going well for him.

"I have been in Dewitt County, señor, along with forty men including Captain McNelly."

"The Sutton-Taylor feud?"

Juan Carlos nodded. "The trial is over."

"Where is McNelly off to now?"

"You must not speak of this . . . McNelly is ill, señor. I fear his time on this earth is short. *Que Dios bendiga su alma.* May God bless his soul." Juan Carlos tapped his forehead, then his chest, making the sign of the cross.

Josiah had never seen Juan Carlos make any reference to a religion and was surprised by the show of it. "I was surprised when I met McNelly the first time."

Juan Carlos nodded. "He is a short, wiry, tubercular man."

"Consumption has most certainly taken its toll on him."

"*Sí,* that is why his family moved to Texas in the first place."

"He is ill again?"

"Still," Juan Carlos said. "I think he is all worn out from watching over the feud."

"So he's back to Burton?"

"To the cotton farm, *sí*."

"That leaves you free, then?" Josiah asked.

"I was never captured. Just serving a role, honoring my brother's legacy."

"I miss Captain Fikes, but I cannot imagine your loss."

"We have all lost something. *Y vamos a perder otra vez, sí tenemos la suerte.* And we will lose again, if we are fortunate . . ."

". . . To live long enough," Josiah finished the sentence. "Captain Fikes used to say that."

"*Sí,* he did." Silence filled the room again. Only it did not last as long as the last time. Juan Carlos stiffened, fidgeted in his chair. "I came back in hopes that all was well with you, *mi amigo.*"

"And so it is," Josiah said.

"But I have to ask you to leave again."

Josiah stood up. His coffee cup was empty. "I can't leave. Not until I hear from Captain Feders. If then. They are cutting the size of the companies, and I fear I may be released from the Rangers."

"For some reason, I do not believe that you see that as a bad thing."

"You are right, my friend. Lyle needs me."

"Captain McNelly needs you."

"What do you mean?"

"I asked that you accompany me. I am

sorry, señor."

"Where?" Josiah's jaw clenched, but he would not release his anger on his friend.

"To Mexico."

"Why in the blue devil would I want to go to Mexico?"

"To stop Liam O'Reilly. *El Tejón.*"

"The Badger."

"*Sí,*" Juan Carlos said, standing up, facing Josiah, looking him squarely in the eye. "I know of his bounty on your head. Have been offered it myself. You will never be safe as long as he lives."

"Why is he in Mexico?"

"To negotiate an alliance with Juan Cortina. If that happens, you are surely a dead man, Josiah Wolfe, and there is nothing I can do to save you."

CHAPTER 23

Josiah stood at the door and watched Juan Carlos disappear into the darkness. He was troubled by what he had learned from his friend. In no way, shape, or form did Josiah expect to be ready to leave for Mexico anytime soon. It would take two days at the least — to which Juan Carlos had reluctantly agreed — to make arrangements for Lyle's care and safety, as well as prepare for the journey.

Juan Carlos had warned Josiah that each minute Liam O'Reilly lived as a free man was one more minute that both he and Lyle lived in the shadow of certain death. It was a warning Josiah was well aware of, took note of, but did not acknowledge vocally. Surely this was not the warning Pedro had meant to give . . . How would he know?

Fear in his own voice was not something Josiah wanted to hear, and he knew it would be there if he spoke. Juan Carlos would not look down on him, but still, Josiah had learned a long time ago that fear was worse than any kind of unseen sickness he had ever encountered. Once it was set free, it was deadly.

There was plenty to fear. Outlaws had came for Lyle once before, knew the boy was Josiah's weak spot, and there was nothing stopping them from plotting and acting on a better-thought-out second attempt.

There was no question that Josiah understood the danger he was in in Austin, but at this late hour there was nothing he could do about any of it. Tomorrow would have to come first.

Josiah closed the door to the house and stood just inside, resting his back against the door.

He could still smell the coffee he'd shared with Juan Carlos, hear Lyle breathing in the next room. Somewhere in the distance a dog — not a coyote — barked lazily, once every minute or so, like it was bored, not alarmed. A train might shake the house in the middle of the night as it made its run through Austin and then on north, but for now, everything seemed quiet, like it should, in its place.

That realization didn't calm Josiah. His mind was running furiously, like a pig that had slipped loose of the butcher, its neck just barely nicked. His whole body ached, including both new wounds and old. He felt sick and tired — the previous days had finally caught up with him, and now he had to think of leaving again.

His stomach lurched, and for the first time in a long time, he honestly didn't know what he was going to do.

There was a time in his life when he'd found comfort on difficult days in the bed next to his wife, Lily, snuggled together in warmth, passion, and acceptance — but now, nearly three years after her death, he could barely hear her voice or see her face in his memory.

No matter how hard he had tried to keep Lily alive in his mind, her image kept fading away, slipping just out of his grasp, almost like she had never existed in the first place.

Lyle favored Lily, had her hair and her button nose. Sometimes, Josiah was sure Lyle had inherited Lily's eyes, too, soft blue, the color of a pale summer day, but mostly he thought that it was just wishful thinking, hoping that Lily, maybe in some form or another, could watch him through their son's eyes, watch out for all of them like an angel. But Josiah, in the wake of Lily's death, was reluctant to believe in a greater life after death, or the existence of power, spirit, or hope. Lyle had Lyle's eyes. Lily couldn't see him any more than he could see her.

Loneliness enveloped Josiah then, adding to his physical pain, but he pushed away his grief as best he could, settling in for the night.

His senses were like exposed nerves.

Every sound seemed loud and dangerous. The creaking and settling of the house sounded like a series of odd unmatched footsteps, and the wind carried voices from far away — all plotting against him.

He knew he was letting his fear get to him, that he was overwhelmed.

He chided himself, screamed silently in his mind at his own weaknesses, because he had surely been in worse situations than being home alone with a sleeping two-year-old boy in the next room.

War and capture by the Comanche had been more uncertain — but then he never totally feared for his survival. He knew that the right opportunity would present itself so he could escape the Indians, or conquer the Northern Aggressors, and return home.

Now he was not so sure of victory — or what to do next.

He moved through the house quietly, each

step taken like he was inches away from the enemy, fearful that he would wake Lyle.

Safe, he continued outside to the privy. Before stepping inside, he reached down and slid his Bowie out of his belt, then threw open the door, expecting Big Shirt or Liam O'Reilly to be staring back at him, his own Winchester in one of their hands.

It would only take one shot at close range to end everything. Josiah wasn't taking any undue chances. Those voices on the wind might just be real.

There was nothing inside the privy except the normal stink after a warm day.

At any other time, Josiah would have laughed out loud at himself. But he didn't. He took Juan Carlos's warning seriously, knew firsthand what O'Reilly and the Comanche were capable of.

The city would not fend them off. Probably the opposite. Most likely, they had rat holes that they shared with other outlaws, escape routes throughout all of Austin, where they could flee, unseen. Josiah was sure of it.

His business complete, Josiah stepped back outside and stopped to make sure everything in the surrounding area remained as it should. His fingers tingled.

The sky was clear, the stars staring innocently down at him. The bored dog continued to bark at its regular interval. Way off in the distance, piano music tinkled upward into the air out of a saloon. The world continued on while Josiah was fighting with shadows and threats that were not real — at the moment.

From where he was standing, all Josiah could see was one roof after another, a line of houses in all four directions; no mountains in the distance, no piney forests, no broad vistas, just human life up close.

He felt like a bull locked in a stall so tight that he couldn't move or breathe. He had to wonder again if making the move from Seerville to Austin had been worth it. If the risk and the sacrifice would give Lyle a better life after all or if he was just fooling himself.

Neither of them was any safer in the city than they had been in the country. Maybe less so.

Right now, he felt like a fool, defeated. And he knew he couldn't let that feeling last . . . or he would drop his guard, overreact, and end up a dead man. Defeat — giving up — was just as much a poison as fear was, and Josiah knew it.

Shaking off the negative blanket of thought, Josiah eased back into the house.

He checked on Lyle, who had not moved, then set about bringing darkness to the small house. Once the last hurricane lamp was extinguished, he stood in the center of the house and let his eyes adjust to the fullness of night.

He did not know the shadows very well in the little house, had spent little time there — and when he had been there, Ofelia was in charge.

Scrap was right, she was more like his wife than a wet nurse. Josiah wondered if Ofelia felt that way. She had never implied that she minded the way things were — they both had agreed that they would know when the day came to change things.

Maybe it was time, Josiah thought.

He headed into the room where Lyle was sleeping and checked on the boy one last time. He was lost in dreamland, eyes pinched shut, the thin blanket gripped in his tiny hand.

Josiah's bed was on the other side of the room — in actuality only a few feet away from Lyle's bed. He pulled off his clothes, not thinking a thing about it, letting them fall to the floor.

It wasn't until he was completely out of the clothes that he realized — remembered — that the clothes didn't belong to him.

They were Charlie Webb's clothes.

He bundled up the shirt and pants and set them next to the bed gently, thinking that he had to save them from harm, they did not belong to him, they were on loan. Someday he would take the opportunity to return them to Charlie's widow.

Billie Webb had been kind and generous to him, and as he settled into bed, he stared up through the window at the moon and wondered if she was all right, safe from harm. He wondered what would become of her and her newborn baby. She was not that much different than he was now. Alone in the world with more responsibility than she should have had to handle. But something told Josiah that Billie could handle whatever came her way. Like him, she had no choice.

With images of Billie weighing heavily in his mind, Josiah quickly drifted off to sleep.

He sat straight up at the first sound.

The moon had fallen from the sky, and the room was totally black now. It was the middle of the night, silent beyond the sound that had woken him up. Any dream that may have pulled at Josiah slipped away, out of his grasp and memory, just like the images of Lily. He hadn't been dreaming of her, he was sure of it — knew how that felt when he woke; like there was a hole in his chest and fire in his loins.

Out of instinct, his hand went to the empty side of the bed, always — still — checking for Lily to be there. The waste of time and motion could have proven costly since the thump that had woken him up in the first place happened again, only this time it was louder.

Josiah reached to the floor for the Colt Frontier, eased the hammer back, and aimed the barrel toward the door, all the while listening carefully for the next sound.

It only took a couple of heartbeats before the next thud came. Somebody was on the front porch.

As he eased out of bed, Lyle stirred. Josiah stopped, caught his breath, then slid past the boy's bed and out into the front room. He hugged the wall and saw a shadow move across the window.

Two heavy footsteps stopped just outside the door.

The heavy knock on the door surprised Josiah. He wasn't expecting it. He was expecting somebody to kick in the door and rush in, guns blazing.

"You in there, Wolfe!"

Josiah recognized the voice just as Lyle started to scream, startled out of his sleep in the middle of the night by the loud knock on the door. In a flash, Josiah went from protector, ready to kill, to angry as a bull — ready to kill.

"Come on, Wolfe. Wake up!" It was Scrap Elliot. And he was obviously as drunk as a cowboy fresh off the trail.

CHAPTER 24

Josiah lit a lamp, washing the house in a quick, bright light, then swung open the front door. He did not hesitate like he had with Juan Carlos, unsure and fearful that the Mexican was not alone. He didn't care if Scrap wasn't alone — didn't care if the late night rousing was a trick and Scrap was O'Reilly's ploy. The Colt was still in his hand, any fear lost, replaced with anger, close enough to erupt into an urge to kill. He couldn't remember being so mad.

Scrap was leaning on the jamb, trying to hold himself up, smiling crookedly at Josiah. He smelled like he'd washed every part of his body in whiskey for the last week. He was pickled.

Lyle screamed at the top of his lungs from his bed.

"Get in here." Josiah grabbed Scrap's shirt collar and pulled him inside.

Scrap stumbled inside the door, crashing

to the floor with a whoop, holler, and cackle. Lyle screamed even louder. Josiah looked out the door, up and down the street, and didn't see hide nor hair of any living creature except Scrap's blue roan mare, Missy, who was standing nervously in front of the house.

The damned horse wasn't even tied to the post. A clue to how drunk Scrap really was. He never mistreated his horse, or any horse for that matter. Leaving an animal to fend for itself was a greater sin than killing a man in Scrap Elliot's book.

Josiah rushed out of the house and quickly tied Missy to the hitching post.

He was aware of everything around him, still not certain that Scrap hadn't been tricked into leading someone to the house. He had never seen Scrap so drunk, but mostly he was aware that his son was inside the house, screaming at the top of his lungs, afraid and unsure of what was happening. Ofelia was not there to calm the boy down. She would have had Lyle in her arms at the first whimper — now he was alone.

A light filled a neighbor's house two houses down, and Josiah hurried back inside his own house, closing the door as gently as his anger would allow, but it was still a slam, and Lyle reacted in kind by screaming even louder.

Without saying a word, Josiah trudged past Scrap, who was on all fours, trying to pull himself up into a standing position. It looked like the floor beneath Scrap was made of ice for all the falling over he did. Seeing Scrap in such a state might have been funny in the right setting, but as it was, there was nothing funny about being awakened in the middle of the night by a drunken clown.

Lyle was standing up in his bed, tears rolling off his red cheeks, arms stretched out to Josiah as he made his way into the room.

"Ofelia, Ofelia! *¿Dónde estás?*" the boy screamed.

Josiah swept Lyle up into his arms, unsure of what he'd just said — which made Josiah even angrier. Added to everything else, the fact that Lyle had peed himself made Josiah certain he was going to explode into a rage at any second.

"Where is Ofelia, Papa?" Lyle asked, trying to catch his breath, his chest lurching heavily in between every syllable.

"She is away."

"Gone, gone?" Lyle wiped his face with his shirtsleeve, finally calming down, though tears still dripped out of both of his eyes.

Josiah shook his head no. "She'll be back soon."

Lyle whimpered, then looked over his shoulder. "Who that?" he said, pointing to Scrap, who had yet to make it up on two feet.

Josiah exhaled heavily. "A friend."

"He's funny."

"Yes. Hysterical." Josiah took another deep breath, then set about finding a set of fresh nightclothes for Lyle.

It didn't take long to clean the boy up. By the time he was finished and had Lyle back in bed, Josiah found Scrap sprawled out on the floor, snoring like a newborn baby himself.

The sun beamed through the bedroom window, warming Josiah's face. He woke up slowly, surprised that it was fully daylight outside. Lyle was sitting on the side of Josiah's bed staring at him, smiling.

"What are you doing?" Josiah asked in a soft voice, wiping his eyes the rest of the way open.

"Nuttin'."

Josiah smiled back at Lyle, and pulled him to him, giving him a big, hearty hug. Lyle giggled and tried to worm free, but Josiah wouldn't let him go.

"Hungry, Papa."

"Okay, okay."

Josiah let loose of the boy and watched him scramble out of the room.

For a moment, the world felt like everything was right. He was home, had slept in his own bed, and Lyle was safe and sound. But it only took him a second to realize that everything was not right . . . that the days to come were going to be just as dangerous and uncertain as the days past.

Josiah expected to find Scrap Elliot still sleeping off his drunken state in the middle of the floor, but Scrap was nowhere to be seen. He was gone.

Lyle was sitting at the table, staring into an empty coffee cup. "Hungry, Papa."

"All right, all right."

Josiah wasn't inept when it came to cooking. He cooked most of his own meals on the trail, and he had been served up a fine morning meal by Ofelia more times than he could count. So Josiah set about getting the woodstove fed, then tried to decide what to feed Lyle.

Scrap's whereabouts would have to wait.

It didn't take long for Josiah to find all of Ofelia's food storage and wares, and he was soon in the midst of making a batter for johnnycakes.

It was amazing to Josiah how quickly life for him had changed. One day he was hiding in a barn, fleeing a bogus bounty, then the next day he's in the kitchen taking the place of a Mexican wet nurse, caring for his young son. He was glad that his fellow Rangers weren't anywhere near to witness the transition.

Thankfully, Lyle was of an age where he could communicate and practice the art of discipline. The boy sat patiently, waiting for his meal, never taking his eyes off of Josiah.

Finally, Josiah set a plate full of johnny-cakes and eggs in front of Lyle.

"What that?" the boy asked.

"Breakfast."

Lyle shook his head no.

Josiah nodded his head. "Yes, it is," he said, making firm eye contact with Lyle.

Tears started to well up in Lyle's eyes, and at that very moment, Josiah knew his realization the night before, that things had to change in his life, couldn't be more true — or more urgent.

When a knock sounded at the door, Josiah was reasonably confident that it was Scrap, come to finish what was left of breakfast.

The Colt Frontier was atop the cupboard on the same wall as the door, loaded, ready, and out of Lyle's reach. Still, Josiah wasn't taking any chances; he peered out the window before going to the door.

Lyle was sitting in the middle of the floor, playing with a locomotive carved simply out of wood.

Josiah was surprised that the person at the door wasn't Scrap. It was Pedro Martinez, the manservant from the Fikes estate. He went to the door then and opened it.

"You're not the person I expected to see on my doorstep this morning," Josiah said.

Pedro was standing stiffly outside the door, holding a package wrapped in thick plain brown paper with the name "WATSON & WILLS FINE TAILORS" stamped on the side.

"Good morning, I hope the day finds you well, Ranger Wolfe," Pedro said. He didn't smile or change his facial expression at all. He was stone-faced, all business.

Josiah eyed the package curiously but said nothing. "I'm fine, thanks." He looked over his shoulder to check on Lyle. The boy seemed to show no interest in Pedro.

"Miss Pearl has sent me to see you this fine morning."

"I suspected as much."

"She requests your presence this evening at six. Dinner will be served at seven."

"I had forgotten all about the invitation. Are you sure it's tonight?"

"Yes, Ranger Wolfe. I can inform Miss Pearl that this is an inopportune time for you, if you would like."

Josiah stared at Pedro and didn't respond. He had no idea where Scrap was, when Ofelia would actually return, and when she did, if she would be capable and willing to watch over Lyle — or if he even wanted Ofelia to watch over the boy every minute of the day, like he had in the past. Risking Ofelia's absence again was not something he wanted to experience. And then there was the journey to Mexico with Juan Carlos to prepare for. For all he knew, the Mexican would just show up and expect Josiah to be ready to go at a moment's notice — they had not set a specific time, other than Josiah's protest that he needed time to prepare. A dinner at the Fikes estate was the last thing Josiah was prepared to deal with at the moment.

"I was told to bring you this, as well," Pedro said, pushing the package toward Josiah.

"What is it?"

"A gift."

Josiah looked at Pedro oddly, accepted the package, then pulled a piece of the paper back enough to get an idea of what was inside. The tear revealed black fabric, and a button. It was a shirt, at the very least. "I can't accept this."

"Please, Ranger Wolfe. I insist."

"You?"

"Yes, me. I do not want you to feel out of place. It is as much for Miss Pearl as it is for you. Now, please, will you honor Miss Pearl with the pleasure of your company this evening?"

Josiah hesitated, stared upward, then said, "I'll do my best to be there."

"Good." Pedro nodded, then backed off the porch, mounted a horse, and rode off in the direction of the governor's mansion.

The horse looked familiar, like a chestnut mare that Josiah had saved the life of in the spring — named after Captain Fikes's lover, Suzanne del Toro — Fat Susie. Surely, it couldn't be the same horse. The Widow Fikes had ordered that horse killed — and Josiah had thought for certain it was safe in the livery. Perhaps Pedro had rescued it.

Josiah shook his head and walked back inside the house. Lyle barely paid him any mind, until Josiah set the package down on the table and started to unwrap it. To his great surprise, there was more than a shirt in the package — there was a fully equipped, formal suit: frock coat, pants, shirt, suspend-

268

ers, tie, and even a pair of shoes.

A note inside instructed Josiah to stop by the tailors in the afternoon to make sure the garments fit properly.

"What that, Papa?" Lyle asked.

"Trouble," Josiah answered. "Nothing but trouble."

CHAPTER 25

Josiah found Scrap in the livery a half a block from his house.

Scrap was cleaning out Missy's stall, arranging a clean coating of straw on the floor. He looked up as Josiah stopped at the gate, said nothing, and went back to finessing the straw with a pitchfork.

"I expected to find you still sleeping on the floor," Josiah said. There was a hearty tone in his voice.

Scrap's skin was as white as his eyes — if you could see the white in them, since the color was obscured by a series of hard red streaks — and his jaw was set hard. It was obvious that Scrap Elliot was in the midst of one heck of a hangover, and it was all Josiah could do not to bust up laughing.

Lyle stood by Josiah's side, holding his hand, kicking at the straw, unaware of what was going on, not caring.

"Had things to do," Scrap said. He set the

270

pitchfork in the corner of the stall, but didn't hook it up against anything, and it fell to the floor with a soft thud. Scrap grimaced, as if the little sound had hurt his head.

Josiah couldn't restrain himself any longer and started laughing.

"What in tarnation is so funny, Wolfe? Can't you see I ain't in the best of shape. I got me a ferocious achin' in the head."

"That's what's so funny." Lyle looked up at Josiah and then laughed, too. Josiah looked down at Lyle, put his index finger to his lips and said, "Shoosh. Mr. Scrap isn't feeling well," then started laughing again.

Scrap grabbed a brush and clenched it so hard his fingers turned red. His face was red now, too. The hangover had quickly been replaced by anger or embarrassment, Josiah wasn't sure which.

"Ain't funny, Wolfe," Scrap said.

"Okay, okay, you're right."

Missy snorted loudly, kicked back her right leg a bit, and Lyle thought that was funny, too, so he kept laughing.

The sound of his son's laughter was honey to Josiah's ears, and he smiled broadly. It had been a long stretch of one bad day after the next recently, and there hadn't been a stitch of laughter to be found anywhere this side of Comanche, Texas.

Josiah looked over to the next stall and saw that Lady Mead had already been tended to. Beyond the palomino mare was Josiah's Appaloosa, Clipper.

The sight of the horse filled Josiah's heart and took his memory back a few days — back to the attack of the Indians at the San Saba River. It seemed less an attack than a trap, and Red Overmeyer had paid dearly for Josiah's failure to see the trap — with his life. Suddenly, Josiah's mood changed, and he gripped Lyle's hand a little harder, getting his son's attention. "Okay, no more laughing."

"How come, Papa?" Lyle asked.

"It's just time." Josiah nodded, and Lyle copied his movement, nodding back with a big smile on his face.

"Thanks for taking care of the horses," Josiah said to Scrap in his normal tone, squaring his shoulders.

"That palomino is a fine horse. Needs some steady care, but she could be a beauty," Scrap said.

"She's been left to her own devices for a little while."

"What are you gonna do with her?" Scrap asked, relaxing, taking the brush to Missy's back.

"Take her back when I can. I'll be glad to be on my saddle the next time, but I'll kind of hate to part with the mare. She could be a good horse."

"You think that's a good idea?"

"What? Not keeping her?"

"Taking her back to Comanche?"

"It's the right thing to do," Josiah said.

Scrap shrugged, kept brushing, and didn't respond any further. He seemed easily lost in the task, glad that Josiah was not laughing at him any longer.

The stalls were just inside two tall doors that were standing wide open. Bright sunlight beamed into the livery, making all of the straw look like gold strands lying on top of the hard dirt floor. From where Josiah was standing, he could see clear blue skies, a reprieve from the dreariness of typical gray November skies. It looked to be a fine day, warm enough for just a long-sleeved shirt and no jacket.

The railroad was about thirty yards to the north of the large barn, and a whistle in the distance announced the coming thunder of steel and steam. It was the early train, one of two freights a day. The sound and rumble would be deafening. At least for Josiah.

Lyle started jumping up and down, squealing. He loved trains.

273

"Settle down there, boy," Josiah said.

"Train's a-comin'! Train's a-comin'!"

"I can hear that. Now, settle down."

There was another noise that had captured Josiah's attention. Only this one was closer — still distant — but closer. It sounded like yells, screams, hoots and hollers. He cocked his head, making sure he wasn't hearing things.

The mob sounded about as far away as Congress Avenue.

"Train!" Lyle said, jumping up and down, pulling on Josiah's hand toward the door.

"Hush now," Josiah said, sternly.

Scrap stopped his chores and looked up. "Sounds like a hangin' comin' along with that train. Ain't none that I know of. How about you, Wolfe?"

Josiah shook his head no. "How would I know?" He looked down at Lyle and gave him a gentle tug. "I said stop."

The tone in Josiah's voice got Lyle's attention. He pursed his lips together tight, stiffened, and exhaled. "All right."

"That's not what you say, is it?"

Lyle looked up at Josiah curiously. "Yes?"

"Yes, what?"

"Yes, sir."

No one said anything for a long minute. Josiah nodded his approval, then listened

274

closer, his curiosity growing at the rising noise from a couple of blocks over.

Scrap walked out of the stall and stood next to Josiah. "Little hard on the boy, ain't you?"

"He's got to learn manners sooner or later."

"You mean ones in English?"

Josiah shot Scrap an angry look; his blue eyes blazed hard as the railroad tracks. Scrap looked away and offered no apology for expressing his opinion about Lyle being raised by a Mexican.

Ofelia had never found herself in Scrap's good graces, and Josiah was certain she never would. Still, there was a point to be made, and Josiah knew it, was seeing it with his own eyes. He just didn't know what to do about it.

The ground began to rumble under Josiah's feet as the train grew closer. Lyle could barely contain himself, but it was obvious, with the restrained look on his tiny face, that he was trying with all of his might.

Just then a man went running past the open doors of the livery.

Scrap pushed past Josiah and ran out the door, coming to a stop. "Hey there, fella."

Josiah and Lyle joined Scrap, as much out of curiosity as dread, as to what Scrap was going to do next.

The man, short and bald, a butcher's apron still wrapped around his waist, stopped at Scrap's yell.

"What you want there, man?" The man turned to face Scrap and Josiah. His German accent was thick, and the apron and his hands were bloody. Something had stopped him right in the middle of carving his pork.

"What's going on? You know?" Scrap asked.

The bald man nodded. "Rangers is coming into town. Word is they is draggin' a Comanche behind them in ropes. Gonna take it right up to Governor Coke. That I got to see!" he said, turning, running off as fast as his portly body would allow.

Josiah and Scrap looked at each other, said nothing, and started to run after the man. It didn't take Josiah but about three steps into the run before he realized that Lyle had pulled away from him.

The little boy was standing where Josiah left him, looking in the opposite direction, looking at the coming train. The big locomotive was slowing down, blowing off steam, the brakes squealing, the ground shaking hard.

Lyle was set to break into a run toward

the train . . . and Josiah knew that with the graze, the wound on his leg, the boy might be more than a match for him. He lunged toward Lyle, missing him just before he lit out.

Lyle ran as fast as he could toward the train, clapping his hands, laughing, never looking back.

"Lyle! Stop!" Josiah screamed.

It took all the energy Josiah had to catch up with Lyle, reaching out for him like he was about to dive off a big cliff and unaware of the drought-ridden creek bed awaiting him at the bottom.

Josiah scooped Lyle up into his arms, his heart beating rapidly, about three feet from the railroad tracks.

He could hardly scold the boy — he was the one who'd gone off and left him. Still, the thought of Lyle running toward the train, being pulled under the wheels just by the pure force of their energy, was something Josiah could not bear to imagine. How could he live with himself if he let something happen to Lyle? Sickness had taken Lily and his three daughters. Negligence would be too much to take. He was sure of it.

The train skidded past, sparks flying from the wheels, smoke rolling off the track from metal on metal, and then the steam. The horn blasted, pushing away any thought, any fear from Josiah's mind.

Lyle clapped and screamed with excitement, and Josiah just let him, held him as tight as he could, tears welling in his eyes. He ignored Scrap, who had stopped, motioning for Josiah to join him.

The butcher disappeared around the corner, and the steam and smoke from the train enveloped Josiah and Lyle. For a long moment, Josiah wasn't sure if either one of them were dead or alive. They were just lost in a fog — hot and sulfur-like — the sun beaming overhead, distant and unreachable.

CHAPTER 26

Congress Avenue was lined three-deep with people. It was like the Fourth of July had arrived on winter's doorstep, bringing enough excitement to pull every November-weary resident out of the shops, saloons, and normal routines of the day, to the side of the road to see what was coming. Not that the weather was inclement — the sky was as blue as an exotic jewel — it was just surprising to see life as it generally was come to such a halting stop in the center of the capital city.

The crowd was reasonably quiet, necks craning, whispers passing among friends and strangers, shoes curiously rustling on the boardwalk.

It was such an event that it had even drawn the presence of Blanche Dumont, one of Austin's most well-known madams, keeper and arbiter of a prosperous house of ill-mannered ladies, pushing her way to the street for a better view of the rumored Comanche. She reminded Josiah of Suzanne del Toro, another former keeper of soiled doves. Blanche had taken over the girls that worked the Paradise Hotel after Suzanne was murdered. Josiah had never returned there — and hoped he would never have to.

Blanche Dumont rarely left the confines of her house, so seeing her out in public was akin to seeing a rattlesnake stand on its tail and dance of its own accord.

The crowd parted in a wide V as Blanche made her way through the crowd. It was hard to miss her since Blanche was wearing white from head to toe; lace, velvet, and feathers adorning her expensive dress and hat. She looked like a swan making its way out to the center of a pond.

Josiah turned his attention to the street, his interest in Blanche Dumont less than most people's. He didn't know her, had never had an encounter with her, or with any of her girls. He'd been to the cathouse district all right, but only the one visited mostly by Mexicans — Little Mexico — to a house called *El Paradiso,* not to the finer, more expensive houses run by Blanche Dumont.

Those memories in Little Mexico were not pleasant, and his curiosity was so piqued by the sudden arrival of a Comanche on the main street in Austin that he could have cared less whether Blanche Dumont was now walking among the very women and men whose lives her business serviced and routinely affected in a negative manner.

Josiah held tightly to Lyle's hand. The temptation to carry him was great, but the boy was nearly three years old. Regardless of how Josiah felt — fear still coursing through his veins at even the thought of losing Lyle to the wheels of the train — he would not treat his son like a baby.

He had lost sight of Scrap and could barely see over the crowd and into the street.

There was nothing to see at that moment.

He could only hope he knew who the Ranger was, who the Comanche was — he just didn't know why they would be in Austin, heading down Congress toward the capitol building, drawing everyone out to see.

"Been pulled out here on account of nothin'," a man standing next to Josiah said. His teeth were yellow, and he smelled of cows and beer.

Josiah didn't respond, just pushed forward toward the street, making sure Lyle was close to him.

"Why on earth would a Ranger bring a

281

savage heathen into our town?" one woman said to another as Josiah passed by.

It was a quiet statement, almost a whisper. The woman was dressed properly, but plainly — at least in comparison to Blanche Dumont — in a simple dress that fell all the way to the ground and was dark brown in color. She wore no hat, her long hair was piled on top of her head, and the dress bound her so tight at the waist that the woman's pursed lips made her look like she was going to explode at any moment. From the appearance of things, she had been in the midst of a dress buying excursion when the excitement had pulled her out of the store.

At first, Josiah thought the woman was talking to him.

He was thick into the crowd now, shoulder to shoulder. It wasn't until another woman answered that he realized he wasn't being spoken to directly.

The woman responded, "To scare us. That's what I think. So the Rangers will get more money from the governor."

Josiah pushed on, dragging Lyle with him, constantly looking down to make sure the boy was all right.

The first woman posed a good question, Josiah thought. One he didn't know the answer to. Though he didn't agree with the second woman, he would be interested in seeing what the real reason was for bringing the Indian into Austin.

It took some doing, but Josiah and Lyle made it to the edge of the crowd and could finally see up and down the street.

Scrap Elliot was standing in the middle of the road all by himself, with a big, silly grin on his face. "Hey, Wolfe, looka there, it's B. D. Donley," he said, pointing south.

The last time Josiah had seen B. D. Donley, Pete Feders had ordered him and two other Rangers to head north out of Comanche to go after Liam O'Reilly.

The other two Rangers, Karl Larson and Slim James, boys Josiah didn't know well, were still riding with Donley — the three of them rode abreast, easing down the street like they were leading a parade.

The Indian was bound behind them with a rope leading from each horse and wrapped around his hands, trailing after Donley's tall black steed, a scrappy-looking stallion.

Much to Josiah's disappointment, Liam O'Reilly was nowhere to be seen.

The trio of Rangers had obviously failed to capture the Badger but had succeeded in bringing in his Comanche sidekick, the one Josiah had called Big Shirt.

Donley had wanted to scalp Little Shirt in the middle of the street upon his arrival in Comanche, so Josiah was surprised that he had let Big Shirt live upon capture and hadn't just brought in a scalp and left it at that.

Instead, Ranger Donley had created an event that was likely to draw attention all the way up to the capitol building, if it hadn't already.

Big Shirt looked weary, stumbling after the horse, trying to keep pace. The knees were torn out of his pants, and blood could be seen on his skin, even from where Josiah stood. Still, the Indian had a scowl on his face, feeding the Anglo fear of Comanche with a full dose, even though it wasn't needed.

Josiah pulled Lyle as close to him as he could.

The little boy had little or no inherent fear of Indians like Josiah had at his age — and beyond.

Any Indian, Comanche or otherwise, that might have been seen in Austin was either a "friendly" or a half-breed, both anxious to fit in and not be noticed. Hostilities with Indians occurred in the outlying communities, and usually all that made it into the city was the news of an attack, or tall tales, perpetrated by liars and men wanting to make more of themselves than they really were.

When Josiah was a boy, especially in East Texas, the tales of the abduction of Cynthia Ann Parker were fresh, used to control a child and instill fear. Josiah had not told Lyle those stories, or of the time in his own life when he'd had a face-to-face confrontation with a Comanche in the woods, was knocked unconscious, and lost his father's favored long gun to the savage.

Encouraging a healthy fear in Lyle was not something Josiah had thought about until that very moment, when he locked gazes with Big Shirt, who was staring directly at the boy.

"Get over here," Josiah said to Scrap, ordering him out of the middle of the street.

"Why?"

"What makes you think you want to be part of this?"

"I'm a Ranger, ain't I?"

"At the moment," Josiah said, a familiar unwavering tone in his voice that he used when he was in charge.

Scrap stared at Josiah, then kicked the toe of his boot into the dirt. "Dang it." He walked over to Josiah, who was about a foot out from the crowd. Scrap knew the tone by now.

"This is going to be big trouble, mark my word," Josiah said. "You don't want to be associated with Donley and his antics."

Scrap shrugged and turned toward the approaching trio.

Lyle looked up and tugged on Scrap's sleeve. "*Hola,* Mr. Scrap."

"Can't you speak English like a real Texan, Lyle?"

Lyle nodded, then looked away.

Josiah quickly intervened before Scrap could continue on. "Not here, Elliot."

Scrap started to say something, but he obviously thought better of it and turned around, his back to Josiah and Lyle, facing the crowd.

Josiah pulled Lyle next to him and patted him on top of the head. Lyle smiled upward at Josiah, then stuck his tongue out at Scrap.

CHAPTER 27

B. D. Donley looked a lot taller than he really was sitting on top of his unkempt black stallion. He was a head shorter than Josiah and had thick black hair that was usually coated too heavily with pomade. His voice was scratchy and weak, his face pocked and bumpy like a dry creek bed, and his eyes were nearly black, too, always shifting around at one thing or another. Josiah hadn't trusted the man from the first day they'd met, and that sentiment still held true.

Donley brought the other two Rangers to a stop upon recognition of Josiah and Scrap. Karl Larson and Slim James were less known to Josiah, since his time with the Battalion had been varied from the start, but both men immediately offered a quick hello to Scrap Elliot.

"Hey there, boys," Scrap said. "Looks like the huntin' was good."

287

Karl Larson was a big boulder of a man, his arms as big as anvils and his chest barrel-shaped. His clothes were covered with trail dust; even his bushy blond mustache looked to have bits of dirt in it. "Was a good ting you wasn't with us, there, Scrap," Larson said, easing back in his saddle, firing a load of tobacco spit back at Big Shirt.

"Why's that?" Scrap asked.

Slim James chimed in before Larson could answer. " 'Cause you and Donley would've had a brawl about whether to bring the Comanch back alive." Slim was true to his name, tall and lanky, arms about as thick as broomsticks, but like Scrap, he had a gift with horses. The two of them raced whenever the opportunity to play showed itself back at the Ranger camp.

"Ain't no doubt about that," Scrap said.

Big Shirt fell to his knees, offering nothing but a sigh of exhaustion and a muted groan of pain.

"Good to see you made it back to Austin, Wolfe," Donley said, dancing his horse forward a bit, tossing a glare over his shoulder that could only mean one thing: for the two Rangers to shut their mouths. His teeth were crooked and tobacco brown. "I surely thought them folks from Comanche would track you down and hang you with your toes to the ground like they did John Wesley Hardin's kin."

Josiah could feel every eye of Austin burning into his neck. The crowd across the way was just as thick as the one he'd pushed through to get to the street. It was amazing how silent the crowd was — they were listening to every word spoken. Somewhere, a crow cawed in the distance.

"I did nothing wrong," Josiah said. His voice was even and his gaze hard. He had no desire to look away from Donley's snickering grin and accusatory glare. He would just as soon knock the man from his horse, but he restrained himself for his own sake, and Lyle's.

"Killed a deputy from what I understand. You'll have to account for that, Wolfe."

"I'm aware of my deeds, Donley, and their cause. Captain Feders saw fit to send me back to Austin, and you out to capture or kill Liam O'Reilly. Tell me the Irishman's dead and buried and we haven't much more to talk about."

Donley shook his head no. "I have only the Comanch here to show for my troubles — and to prove that the savages still intend to bestow fear upon us all. Do you hear that, fine citizens?" he yelled, doffing his hat in a

289

wave, raising his butt up off the saddle, nearly standing up. "Let loose, this savage will slit your throat, steal your scalp, and eat your kidneys for dinner." He licked his lips.

The crowd recoiled.

Donley was enjoying himself, and Josiah was certain that the Ranger was up to something — something no good, since he was making such a show of Big Shirt's presence.

There was an audible gasp from the crowd. A symphony of feet rustled backwards behind Josiah.

"That's enough, Donley. You've riled these fine people enough. What is your intention?" Josiah asked.

"I aim to speak directly to Governor Coke himself."

"On Feders's orders, or your own accord?"

"On accord of all the Rangers," Donley said, puffing his chest.

Josiah held his doubt tight in his throat, only allowing it to escape as a deep baritone groan. He was sure there was more to the man's ploy than making a case for all of the Rangers to retain their status and pay, but he had no choice but to take the man's word and let things play out as they would.

"Come with us, and see for yourself,

Wolfe. Or are you too busy playing wet nurse instead of acting like a Ranger?"

Josiah's doubt fell away as anger flashed up his spine. "Watch yourself, man."

Donley smirked then said, "Come on, fellas, the governor's waiting. He surely knows we're coming by now."

Both Larson and James nodded. They seemed fully in line with Donley's intent, sitting up straight in their saddles, ready to follow.

They started to move away slowly, Donley finally breaking eye contact with Josiah.

Josiah stepped back, his own intention clear: that he wasn't going to join in on Donley's game. There was no way Josiah was going to bust into the capitol with a Comanche in tow. He had enough trouble to consider.

Larson slowed and spoke directly to Scrap. "What about you, Elliot? Comin' along?"

Scrap glanced over at Josiah, trying to show no emotion one way or the other. "Nah, I think I'll hang back."

"Suit yourself, but you'll be missin' a spectacle," Larson said.

"I've had my fair share of those, thanks," Scrap answered.

Josiah was relieved but said nothing. He

would wait until the trio was out of earshot to tell Scrap he thought he'd made a wise decision.

The uncomfortable feeling in the pit of Josiah's stomach did not fade as Donley pulled ahead. He still had to face Big Shirt.

Big Shirt had heaved himself up off his knees once he realized that Donley was on the move again. It looked like the Indian had spent plenty of time facedown in the dirt as it was.

"I'll kill you, Josiah Wolfe," Big Shirt scowled, "if it's the last thing I do."

Josiah stood his ground, let his eyes and stance say everything that needed to be said: *I know that, and I'll be ready when the time comes.* He slipped his hand down to his gun and let it rest softly on the grip.

Lyle tucked himself behind Josiah's legs, hanging on tightly to his pants. Now was not the time to discourage fear, and Josiah knew it.

After Big Shirt passed, and Josiah breathed a sigh of relief, and was about to ease back into the crowd, then B. D. Donley brought the black stallion to a quick stop. He looked over his shoulder. "Hey, Wolfe, I have something that belongs to you." He reached down to a scabbard and pulled a familiar Winchester '73 out of it. "This is yours, if I ain't mistaken."

Josiah nodded. "It is." He started for Donley, but stopped once he realized that Lyle was still attached to his leg. "You go stand with Mr. Scrap while I go get my rifle."

"Do I have to?" Lyle asked.

"Yes." The farther away from Big Shirt he kept his son, the better it was for them all.

Lyle let go of Josiah's leg. "All right."

"What do you say?"

Lyle looked up at Josiah, confusion on his little face until he realized what his father wanted from him. "Yes, sir."

"That's more like it."

There was smoke rising from the chimney of his house, and for a moment, Josiah was confused and concerned — until he saw Ofelia walk out on the porch as they approached.

It only took Lyle, who was sitting in front of Josiah in the saddle, a second to realize that it was Ofelia he saw, too.

" 'Felia, 'Felia, *hola, hola!*" Lyle yelled, waving madly.

Josiah was afraid the boy was going to jump off of Clipper's back right then and there. He pulled him closer, tighter.

Lyle looked up at Josiah, scrunching his

forehead. "Go, Papa, go faster."

Ofelia waved back, a wide smile growing on her face as she recognized Josiah on his own horse, Lyle cupped in the saddle.

"You can wait," Josiah said.

"Don't want to. Missed 'Felia."

"I'm sure you did."

Lyle squirmed in the saddle, and Josiah finally gave in, urging Clipper to move along a little faster. Scrap wasn't that far behind them, and Josiah didn't need to turn around to know what kind of look was on Scrap's disapproving face.

There was no question that Scrap's views were right, that Josiah needed to live without Ofelia — but to be honest, having his trusted rifle back in his possession and seeing Ofelia on his porch were moments akin to stumbling on a vein of gold right in the middle of Austin. It was about as much happiness as he could take.

He wasn't sure how he was going to live without Ofelia, and he hoped, for the moment, he wouldn't have to. He hoped they could work something out that suited them both — a solution that would never leave Lyle in the hands of strangers again.

Josiah brought Clipper to a stop, and before he could get a grip on Lyle, the boy had already slipped out of the saddle and jumped into Ofelia's waiting arms.

"Allí está mi niño," Ofelia said. "There's my boy."

Lyle buried his face in Ofelia's neck, telling her over and over again how much he had missed her. *"Allí está mi* Ofelia," he answered.

Tears welled up in Ofelia's deep brown eyes. She was short, squat, about as tall as she was big around, and was dressed simply, as always, in a brightly colored cotton dress she'd sewed together herself. This one was yellow, and looked even brighter in contrast to her smooth dark brown skin in the beaming sunshine.

"It is good to see you," Ofelia said to Josiah, still clutching Lyle tightly. "I feared I would never see you again."

"It is good to see you, too, Ofelia. I'm glad to be home," Josiah answered, sliding off Clipper. "And I'm glad you're home, too." He looked at her questioningly, waiting for an answer.

Ofelia nodded her head. *"Sí,* I am glad to be home, *señor."*

"Bueno! Bueno!" Lyle clapped his hands and giggled loud enough to overcome Scrap Elliot's grunt of disapproval at the whole scene.

CHAPTER 28

Josiah stood at the end of the lane staring at the house. It glowed in the darkness like a giant honeycomb bathed in bright sunlight.

Every lamp in the large mansion was filled and lit on the highest turn. Torches stood burning under the portico, lighting the entire front of the house. Shadows made from darting insects decorated the front of the house, as the bugs sought out heat on the cool November night.

For Josiah it was hard not to feel a tandem kinship with the insects. He understood the desire of a mere moth drawn to the torches and light in every window, curious, in need of warmth, sustenance, and the hope of a life beyond the darkness. The hesitant human being that he really was ached to turn and go home.

All of the light did little to excite him. The dinner at the Fikes estate was obviously a bigger affair than he had anticipated or thought about, but he should not have been surprised.

The smell of burning hardwood drifted up out of the chimneys and mixed with the unmistakable smell of beef roasting on a spit. Music from a fine piano eased out of the house, a soft ballad sung by a sweet female voice floating carelessly on an unseen breeze. Josiah didn't have to wonder who was singing. He knew it was Pearl, entertaining a house full of guests, waiting for his arrival.

Leaving was on his mind more than staying. But the light held him in sway, and he knew he was drawn to Pearl in a way he did not understand, even though he was smart enough to know that she was a flame that could leave him wounded or worse.

An impressive collection of buggies, coaches, and wagons sat in front of the house, some manned by drivers sitting, waiting, lazily holding their spots, enjoying a smoke or a nip of whiskey to stave off the boredom and coolness of the night.

Even the horses seemed to be entranced by the easy mood that hung in the air. They stood, mostly with their heads down, feasting on the gift of hay provided by the Fikes estate, the best from anywhere around.

Wispy clouds barely obscured the moon

as it rose up behind the house, casting even more shadows on the ground in front of Josiah. The entire world suddenly looked unfamiliar to him. His stomach bound itself up in knots, and he knew he was on the verge of walking into a house where he knew nothing of the rules or ways.

Manners were a medium concern, needed less on a twenty-acre farm in East Texas than in a mansion blocks away from the Capitol building.

Now he was frozen in fear for his lack of them, among other things.

He had nearly been stricken with the same statue-like fright when he was getting ready to leave Lyle with Ofelia for the dinner, but Ofelia would not hear of him not going once he told her of the event.

She'd promised him that she was not leaving the house or Austin again anytime soon. Beyond that, nothing had been settled between them. Time had slowed, and they both seemed glad to have a sense of normalcy return to their lives.

Standing now at the end of the lane, life for Josiah was anything but normal. He was fully prepared to turn and leave, forgo the dinner and Pearl's invitation all at once, regardless of the implications, when he heard another buggy drawing up behind him on the lane.

He turned to see Juan Carlos driving toward him in a fancy buggy. He was alone. It was not a sight Josiah was accustomed to seeing, Juan Carlos out and about in plain sight for anyone to see, heading toward a big event.

"Whoa, there," Juan Carlos said, bringing the horse and buggy to a stop. "I thought that was you, Señor Wolfe. Are your feet stuck in the mud?"

"Just thinking," Josiah said.

"You'll be fine in there. Pearl will see to it, I promise."

Josiah eyed Juan Carlos carefully. "What are you doing here?"

"Earning my keep."

Josiah chuckled. "You're taking orders from the Widow Fikes? I never thought I'd see the day."

A wise smile crossed Juan Carlos's face. "Pedro and I are old friends. I help out when the need arises, when there is something to accomplish."

"Here? What would that be?"

"If I were known as the captain's brother I would be well suited to sit at the table and rub elbows with the likes of you. Next to my beautiful niece, where I should be. As I'm not known as blood kin to anyone in that house, and have no desire to be, I'm well suited to serve and remain unseen even though I breathe the same air in the same room. I can listen."

Josiah nodded. "For what?"

"Information that may help us on our journey," Juan Carlos said.

Josiah took a deep breath. "I don't think now is a good time for me to leave. Feders told me to wait until I spoke to him before doing anything."

"That problem will resolve itself soon."

"What do you mean?"

"Trust me, Señor Wolfe."

"Lyle needs me," Josiah said, sternly.

"Lyle needs a father who is alive. We will leave before daybreak. Enjoy the party, Señor Wolfe." Juan Carlos flipped the reins in his leathery hand, and the horse, to which Josiah had paid little attention, responded and the buggy tore off toward the house.

If the ground had been hard and dusty, Josiah would have been covered from head to toe in dirt.

Josiah did not have to knock at the door. Pedro opened it widely as Josiah walked stiffly under the portico.

The manservant was decked out head to toe in the finest black suit Josiah had ever

300

seen, more perfect than the last time or any other time they had met. Pedro stood squarely in the middle of the doorway, an angry look crossing his face as he took in the sight of Josiah.

"You are late, Ranger Wolfe," Pedro said.

"I have a son. He needed to be tended to before I left," Josiah said.

He had not dressed in the suit that was given to him the day before with instructions to attend the tailor for a fitting. Instead, he wore his own clothes, his Sunday best that he saved for weddings and funerals.

Regular churchgoing was not something Josiah took into consideration, so it had been a while since the suit had seen the light of day. As it was, he was dressed in a black broadcloth frock coat and a vest to match, with his father's gold watch tucked neatly in the pocket. His boots were wiped fresh of muck, and his black pants were a little tight. The last time he'd donned the suit was the day he'd laid Lily to rest in the family plot back on the farm in Seerville.

He wore his everyday hat, the brown felt Stetson, since it was the only hat he owned and he thought little of the prospect of buying a new one just for a fancy dinner invitation at the estate. Of course, he could have worn the hat that was sent to him . . . but he wanted nothing to do with wearing clothes that did not belong to him.

Comfort was a just cause as far as he was concerned, but he also felt he needed Pearl . . . and Pedro . . . to realize that he was what he was: a simple man with a simple life. A fine suit of clothes could not change who he was underneath, no matter how much the clothes cost or how well they fit.

"But you chose not to wear the fine suit?" Pedro said.

"The package is on my horse. I hope you can return it."

"If I must," Pedro snipped.

"You must," Josiah said.

"As you wish, Ranger Wolfe," Pedro said, stepping back and allowing Josiah entry into the house.

Josiah sucked in a large gulp of air and walked into the house, right past the snarling Pedro, without saying another word.

CHAPTER 29

As soon as she saw Josiah walk through the door, Pearl stopped singing. The light around her was bright, as the Fikes home had, at just about the same time as the governor's mansion, been equipped with gas lighting.

Standing just inside the door, Josiah was tempted to shield his eyes, the lighting was so intense — but he resisted. He didn't want to imply a salute, or a matter of weakness or discomfort of any kind.

A crystal chandelier, with icy-looking teardrops suspended from brass hoops, hung over the shiny black piano just inside the parlor. Pearl stood beside the piano, wearing a long yellow dress with a high collar. The dress almost matched the color of her hair, which was piled on top of her head, bound with lace and ribbons. She looked like a spring flower in a field of black coats and fancy velvet and satin dresses that were not nearly as beautiful and glowing as she was.

Every man and woman in the room turned toward Josiah to see what had distracted Pearl, what had. stopped the angelic voice from filling up the house. They seemed disappointed at the sight of him, a simple, unknown man in a simple suit of clothes, not distinguished in the least.

Josiah couldn't have felt more self-aware at that very moment, especially when he recognized many of the luminaries of Austin's high society, as well as Governor Richard Coke, with his wife, Mary, close at hand, standing in the center of the parlor.

Coke was a tall man, bald on top with dark hair on both sides of his head, offset by a neatly trimmed six-inch beard. He had been a district court judge ten years prior, but was ultimately removed because the military governor at the time thought Coke was "an impediment to Reconstruction." It was an apt judgment, since Coke's recent election as governor was widely seen as the end of Reconstruction in Texas. He was not without his foes, especially of late as he struggled to balance the budget — which included cutting the Frontier Battalion down in size.

Coke eyed Josiah carefully, then turned

his attention away, drawn by a question from an unknown man to his right.

Standing around and beyond the governor was an assemblage of men Josiah did not know, but who he assumed were members of Coke's political party, administration, and inner circle. There were at least twenty people stuffed into the parlor, and a few others lingered outside in the grand foyer.

Josiah did recognize Rory Farnsworth, the local sheriff, with whom Josiah had had some dealings in the past. And to his surprise, Major John B. Jones was also in attendance, standing in the center of three lovely young women in the corner, just to the left of the piano. A large, wavy fern almost obscured the major. Once Jones looked up and saw that the distraction was only a meager sergeant, he quickly turned his attention back to the fawning and giggling women.

Jones had taken a liking to Pearl earlier in the spring, at the time of her father's death, or so Josiah thought, but she obviously was not the center of the major's attention at the moment. He had a reputation as a man with a different woman of favor in every town he entered, leaving behind a broken heart or a waiting woman in his wake. At forty, Jones was still a bachelor, with a reputation bordering on being a cad. The competition for Pearl's affection looked to have been pared, but for some reason, Josiah wasn't lightened by the prospect, though he would have been disappointed to see Pearl fall under the spell of Jones's apparent charms.

A Negro sat at the piano, waiting for Pearl to resume singing. He was dressed identically to Pedro — formal, in a black suit, starched white high-collared shirt, with a black string tie — only the Negro wore white gloves, as if his brown hands were not allowed to touch the white keys of the piano.

Josiah had never seen the Negro before and didn't know his name, but he was sure the Fikes house employed more people than he could count or know of.

Pearl motioned for the Negro man to start playing again, then whispered something in his ear. The Negro looked to Josiah, smiled brightly, and nodded.

A soft tinkling immediately filled the room, happy music, not a ballad, as Pearl made her way through the crowd toward Josiah.

Everyone parted, allowing her eager exit from the piano, very much in the manner that the crowd had parted earlier in the day for Blanche Dumont — who was missing from the elite gathering, but who surely knew some of the members in attendance intimately.

Josiah stood stiffly, unsure of what to do other than wait for Pearl. He did not want to greet Pearl in front of everyone. He wasn't sure he knew how. A handshake, a kiss on the cheek, or a bow?

To make matters worse, not only had Pearl's attention and action been drawn to him, but so had the Widow Fikes's.

She was sitting on an Empire sofa framed in an exotic wood, probably mahogany. The back crest was undulating in style, and the upholstery was a soft brown color, beige, with thin beaded pleats. The sofa sat under a portrait of a very much younger Mrs. Fikes, who was never a beauty like her daughter, but had obviously come readily equipped with a regal air; she looked like a princess of a foreign land waiting on a servant to feed her.

The portrait was surrounded by thick red draperies that hung all the way from the twelve-foot ceiling to the floor. The widow was not as tall and thin as Pearl, but rotund, or at least she appeared to be since she still dressed in widow's weeds — a thick, ruffled black dress, a lacy hat with the veil pulled back, and tightly bound boots — that made her look very big, like a big old laying hen with her feathers all puffed up in defense. She bore no other color but black from head to toe, a continued show of mourning.

The widow curled her lip in distaste as she met Josiah's gaze, recognizing him. He did the same. He looked away, then, back to Pearl, who was nearly in front of him.

"I thought you weren't coming," Pearl said.

Josiah's throat was parched, like it had closed up in fear. "I had to get Lyle settled. Ofelia returned or I would not have been able to come." He stood still, hands plastered to his side. It seemed the most appropriate hello he could conjure.

"You could have brought him," Pearl said. "We got along just fine."

Pearl stared at Josiah, her deep blue eyes penetrating his. He was tempted to turn and leave, but he had made it this far, it was too late to back out now. Besides, staring back at Pearl, Josiah became less aware of the rest of the room and the eyes still targeted on them. It was like they were the only two people in the world. A surge of energy compelled him to reach for her, at least touch her hand, but again he resisted, unsure if it was the right and proper thing

to do, if a public touch was socially accept-
able.

"Lyle is not ready for this," Josiah said.
He wanted to add that he wasn't either . . .
but let the words die before they left his
mouth.

"I suppose you are right. I am glad to hear
of Ofelia's return. Juan Carlos has told me
of her importance to you."

Josiah nodded, heard a rustling behind
Pearl. "Why am I here?" he whispered.

"Because I wanted you to be comfortable
in this house."

Before Josiah could answer, before he
could tell Pearl that he doubted that he
could ever be comfortable in a house so big,
proper, and unknown, Pedro stepped out of
the parlor, chimed a silver triangle, and announced that dinner was ready to be served.

The chair at the head of the table sat vacant.
The dining table was long, easily seating
the thirty or so guests. Josiah had never seen
a table so long, or one so full of food and
adornments. The aromas were hard to
decipher, the mix a feast of beef, roast
turkey, vegetables, salads, puddings, and
things Josiah had no idea the names of.

The vegetables were still fresh from the
recent harvest, and the breads were so warm

that the yeasty smell almost overwhelmed all of the other aromas in the cavernous room.

A log blazed gently in a fireplace big enough to store three or four good-sized sheep.

Three chandeliers hung over the table, one right after the other, hanging high from the ceiling. Candles lit the table in a perfect sequence of candelabras forged of pure gold. Each place setting had three plates, a bowl, a glass made of crystal, and more silverware than Josiah had ever seen or knew what to do with.

He chastised himself again for being there. It felt like he had just walked into a camp of Indians, unaware of the language, the mores, which way to move without offending his hosts and sending them into a fit of rage.

The crowd had intervened, separating Pearl and Josiah, as they made their way out of the parlor. He stood, now, lost in another moment of uncertainty.

The Widow Fikes sat on one side of the empty chair, and Pearl sat across from her mother, directly on the other side of the table. A massive centerpiece nearly blocked their view of each other. Pearl sat blank-faced, staring into the flame of one of the low candles on the candelabra. For some reason her expression and demeanor had changed once the crowd had separated her from Josiah and she had taken her seat.

A murmur of voices echoed off the plaster walls, bouncing down from the ceiling as the guests made their way to their spots. It seemed most everyone knew where to sit, except him.

Governor Coke headed for the chair next to the Widow Fikes, his wife, Mary, comfortably on his arm. Almost as if on command, or from an unseen finger snap, servants appeared out of nowhere, easing the chairs out for the women of the major dignitaries.

Josiah was not surprised to see Juan Carlos, decked out in finer clothes than he had ever seen him wear, ease the chair out for the governor's wife. The woman, tall and proud, almost royal, smiled at Juan Carlos as she sat down.

Juan Carlos stayed true to the expectations of servitude and showed no emotion, though Josiah was almost certain he saw him quickly whisper something in the woman's ear as he pulled away from her. Mary Coke smiled, then looked down to her lap as Juan Carlos made his way to the next woman.

Major Jones headed toward the empty seat

next to Pearl, and Josiah held his breath.

Jones still seemed more interested in a young brunette girl who sat two seats down from Pearl. The brunette must have caught Jones's eye, an inviting look maybe drawing him away from Pearl. He immediately sat down next to the girl, after she was properly seated, and resumed his conversation with her, almost ignoring Pearl. He did offer a quick nod to her, which Pearl ignored, then turned away.

Josiah was still unsure where to sit, next to Pearl or somewhere else? When he looked to Pearl for guidance, she looked away. It almost looked like she had tears welling in her eyes.

Before Josiah could move his feet in a step toward Pearl, he felt a hand softly touch his shoulder.

"Here is your seat, sir," Juan Carlos said, urging Josiah to a chair about midway in the table.

Josiah turned and started to protest, but the look on Juan Carlos's face warned him off. He did as he was instructed, taking the chair, sitting immediately. The only way he could see Pearl was if he leaned forward and looked down past the plates of the guests in between them. Even he knew that would be rude, so he just sat, hands in his lap, staring straight across the table at one of the most beautiful roast turkeys he had ever seen. His stomach growled, reminding him he was hungry.

To Josiah's relief, Rory Farnsworth sat down next to him.

Farnsworth was a sprightly man of medium height, who always wore a finely waxed mustache. He was younger than Josiah, making the sheriff not quite thirty years old. He had attended some fancy college out east, and he was always happy to spout on about the lessons he learned about the law there, and how he put his knowledge to practice on a daily basis.

Truth be told, the Farnsworth family was heavily connected in the political arena. His father, Myron, was a banker and was seated, along with Farnsworth's mother, to the left of the sheriff. Rory was unmarried, a bachelor in the social circle, always on the lookout for a girl with wifely aspirations. Surely he'd tried to woo Pearl . . . maybe been rebuffed, maybe not, Josiah did not know, and didn't care to presume, or know, such a thing.

"Good to see you, Wolfe," Farnsworth said, offering Josiah a firm handshake.

Josiah shook the man's hand. "Good to see you, too, Sheriff."

The two men had worked together before Josiah's venture into Lost Valley over the previous summer, when Suzanne del Toro had been murdered by her own brother, who had wanted nothing more than the business that Suzanne ran — a sad story of greed. After the brother was killed, Blanche Dumont filled the vacuum.

"You can call me Rory here." Farnsworth smiled and set about making himself comfortable, unfolding a cloth napkin and placing it in his lap.

Like a child, Josiah watched Farnsworth's every move and aped him as closely as possible.

"Thanks, Rory," Josiah said.

"Kind of surprised to see you here, Wolfe."

"Why's that?"

"You're . . . um, not usually at these kind of things."

"I'm a friend of the family."

"I know you rode with the captain, but that's a different thing."

"I suppose it is."

More chairs scooted out and in, the noise of the settling guests still a bit loud. The piano player was still at work, too. The tune he played was softer, background music, a song Josiah did not recognize but could still hear. He pulled himself forward and mustered a quick look down the table. The seat next to Pearl was still empty . . . and she looked just as distraught as she had previously.

"That was quite the spectacle today your Rangers put on, wasn't it?" Farnsworth said.

"Um, what? Oh, you mean the Comanche Donley escorted into town?"

"Yes. Darn near scared the daylights out of the entire city. Most of our fine citizens have never seen an Indian close up."

"I'm not sure that was Donley's intent. Scaring them, I mean." Josiah was still not sure what Donley's true intent was, other than to make a spectacle of himself — a matter at which the Ranger excelled.

"It most certainly was his intent to scare everyone. Didn't you follow him down to the square?"

"Where?"

"The Capitol. He walked that savage right up to the governor's office." Farnsworth lowered his voice at that point, realizing that Governor Coke was clearly in earshot of their conversation. "The governor relieved the Ranger and his two partners of duty right then and there."

"What happened to the Indian?" Josiah asked.

"You haven't heard?"

315

"No. Tell me he hasn't escaped."

"Hardly," Farnsworth said. "The Rangers — or ex-Rangers — still have custody of him, claiming ownership. They are putting him on display at the Opera House tomorrow at noon. Two bits a person. Can you imagine paying good money to see a Comanche shackled and snarling?"

"No," Josiah said, looking away from Farnsworth. "I can't." He was not surprised in the end at Donley's ploy. Making money off an Indian was a distasteful thought, but Donley had always seemed to be involved in money transactions in one form or another. When Scrap raced Missy, Donley was the first one to collect the bets, and the winnings and losses.

Josiah chewed on the information he'd just learned from Rory Farnsworth and started to wonder about the broader consequences of Donley's action. But in reality all he cared about was the fact that he had persuaded Scrap not to have anything to do with Donley's charade. Scrap would surely be on the bad end of the stick if he'd joined up with the other Rangers as they presented Big Shirt to the governor.

The crowd grew silent as one more person made their way into the dining hall, drawing Josiah's attention away from his thoughts and hunger.

Captain Pete Feders walked into the room, head up, a stoic look on his scarred face, dressed in a semblance of clothes that looked like a uniform but bore no epaulets, tassels, or medals. There was not one speck of dirt to be seen on the man's clothes. Even his boots shined like a mirror.

Feders walked right behind Josiah, and made no acknowledgment of his presence.

The captain had his eyes on one thing: Pearl. He sat down immediately next to her, said something into her ear that only she could hear, then took her hand softly into his.

Pearl quickly yanked her hand away from Feders's grasp, and glared across the table at her mother, whose demeanor had changed from bored ambivalence to bemused contentment, once Pete Feders strutted into the dining hall and took his place next to Pearl.

The mystery of the empty chair was solved, and Josiah was not the least bit surprised to learn whom it had been saved for.

CHAPTER 30

Josiah stared at the plate full of food. He had lost his appetite even though it was the prettiest plate of food he had ever seen. His senses were overwhelmed. The smells wafting up from the table were like nothing he had ever experienced before — vegetables lathered in butter and unknown spices, more kinds of breads than Josiah knew existed, deep red wine in crystal glasses instead of beer or coffee in tin mugs, and beefsteak cooked to perfection, emitting a familiar but refined aroma, one that would never be found at a campsite. Still, he could not bring himself to eat.

"What's the matter, Wolfe?" Rory Farnsworth said.

"Nothing."

"Sure, and President Grant is your long lost uncle."

"Might be."

"You'd be sittin' up at the head of the

table if that was the case."

Josiah glanced toward Pearl, though he couldn't see her clearly, just her tight profile. "It'd take more than that for me to be sitting up there."

"Yes sir, looks to me like you'd have to be a captain in the Rangers, a man of fine stature instead of . . ."

"Instead of what, Farnsworth? An uneducated man like myself? A meager sergeant with little to show for his life?"

Josiah had seen how Farnsworth looked at him on arrival, judging him head to toe, knowing his clothes were the best he had but nowhere near the best that could be bought. His pants were so tight at the waist he could hardy breathe when he sat down. But still, he did not regret his decision to return the suit of perfect clothes to Pedro. He might have fit in and been more comfortable with his appearance, but he wouldn't have known how to move or who he really was.

Rory Farnsworth's face turned red as the bowl of pickled beets that sat in front of him. "I didn't mean anything, Wolfe. I just meant . . ."

Josiah cut him off again. "I know what you meant."

The sheriff pushed his chair back, the beef

on his plate half-eaten. "I need some fresh air," he said, standing up, wiping his mouth with the white cloth napkin, and throwing it on the plate.

Josiah watched Rory Farnsworth exit the dining hall. He felt bad but not too bad. He liked Farnsworth and was glad to have had his help in the past, but there was never any doubt that the two men were separated by the worlds they both walked in, just like Josiah and Pearl were.

The misunderstanding was another perfect example of why Josiah felt he shouldn't be sitting in Fikes's house at all. He should be home with Lyle, or out on the trail with Juan Carlos, bringing Liam O'Reilly to justice. After a brief touch of the gun on his hip, the Frontier Colt, he was reminded of Billie Webb, and he wondered about her fate, and the baby's. He hoped they were safe.

Farnsworth's father looked across the empty seat at Josiah with a questioning, then judgmental, look.

Josiah shrugged his shoulders and started to pick at his food with a heavy silver fork, ignoring the banker and his snobbish glare. He figured he might as well not let the food go to waste. The way things were going he'd never be invited back to the house again.

Not that he minded.

The meat tasted like nothing that had ever crossed his tongue. The steak seemed to melt in his mouth before he could finish chewing. Surely, the cow was butchered just prior to cooking. The taste of the meat was a quick addiction.

Polite chatter surrounded him, but now that he had started eating, everything, including Pearl and Pete Feders, faded from his view or concern.

He ate the whole steak without stopping, without being concerned about his manners, whether he was using the proper fork or not. When he looked up, he realized a few people were staring at him. He smiled back at them and picked up the fine crystal glass that was filled with the deep red wine and drank it all down in one gulp. He wiped his mouth and let the smile stay on his face.

"More wine, Señor Wolfe?" a familiar voice said from behind Josiah.

Josiah smiled even more broadly. "Why certainly, Juan Carlos. I don't mind if I do."

"As you wish, Señor Wolfe." Juan Carlos poured a fresh glass of wine from a dark brown bottle. "You need to pace yourself," he whispered in Josiah's ear, after filling the glass, disappearing before Josiah could protest.

He had captured almost everyone's attention, including that of the governor, who was looking his way with disdain.

Josiah raised the glass of wine to the governor, then downed it, too, like it was a shot of whiskey instead of fine wine.

He was instantly warm from head to toe, but it was a different feeling than he'd felt the few times he had drank whiskey or beer. He liked the wine. It was sweet, and he wanted more. Alcohol was not a vice of his, and whether he had any tolerance for wine was unknown to Josiah.

Before he could flag down Juan Carlos, who was on the other side of the table, filling a glass for the governor's wife, Pete Feders stood up and banged a silver spoon on the side of an empty crystal glass.

The chatter stopped immediately; everyone's attention had been forcefully garnered, including Josiah's. He was not drunk, though one more glass of wine would surely take him to that unknown place. He still had his wits about him. Dread settled suddenly in his stomach.

"I have an announcement to make," Pete Feders said.

Pearl rustled in her seat.

"I have asked Mrs. Fikes for Pearl's hand in marriage, and she has obliged and given

322

me permission," Feders continued.

The room erupted in applause. Josiah didn't clap. His mouth went dry.

Feders smiled. "Now if only Pearl will say yes." He bent down on one knee and started to say something . . . but was stopped by Pearl, who bolted out of her chair and ran out of the room, sobbing uncontrollably.

The night air felt good against Josiah's face. He had mixed in with the crowd as they all sought to leave the dining hall and was standing under the portico, leaning against a tall pillar, trying to regain confidence in his feet.

At first, the guests had been shocked at Pearl's immediate exit from the room. They all just sat silently, staring at the befuddled Pete Feders and Widow Fikes.

Pete dashed out of the room after Pearl, and Mrs. Fikes feigned a hand on her forehead and promptly fainted in her chair, tumbling to the floor like a boulder pushed off a steep cliff. That was everyone's cue to vacate the house. The social page of the *Statesman* was going to have a lot to report the next day to those in Austin who cared about such things.

Carriages and buggies came and went, picking up their charges as quickly and comfortably as possible. It looked like a parade in front of the house, or like the last time Josiah had spent any time there, which was for Captain Fikes's funeral. The latter was probably more apt, a parade being far too happy an event to reflect the state of the faces of those promptly leaving the grounds.

There were times when Josiah wished for a vice like tobacco. It would make passing the time a little easier. As it was, he was beginning to feel more like himself, the fuzzy effect of the wine clearing away. It was time to go home, to leave all the unfinished business at the Fikes estate to work itself out on its own.

Now that Feders had clearly stated his intentions publicly, there was no question that he would not relent until Pearl accepted his proposal. Josiah knew that. Josiah wasn't sure why he was even there in the first place, other than showing gratitude to Pearl for watching over Lyle. He wished that was all there was to it. It was hard not to be attracted to a woman as beautiful as Pearl Fikes.

He took a breath and took a step away from the pillar, steadying himself, but stopped when he saw Pete Feders emerge out of the darkness, walking right toward him.

324

CHAPTER 31

Josiah could smell alcohol on Feders's breath when he spoke. "What are you doing here, Wolfe? You come to taunt me?"

"I'm just leaving, Captain." Josiah had to restrain himself not to call him Pete. That would have surely brought out the worst in Feders. It was obvious that it wouldn't take much to provoke the man to a fistfight. His face was red with rage and embarrassment.

"You saw what happened inside? With Pearl?" Feders asked.

Josiah nodded. "I'm sorry, Captain."

"Sure you are, Wolfe. I know you carry a torch for Pearl." Feders gripped both of his hands, then let them fall to his side in tightly balled fists.

Josiah stepped back, putting up both of his own hands, flat out, as if to fend, or warn, off an impending attack. He didn't want to fight Feders here — or anywhere for that matter. "I have only become acquainted with Pearl Fikes since we returned to Austin in the spring with Captain Fikes's body. I'm in no position to court a woman like Pearl. You know that. I have a son to raise, and I have chosen my life as a Ranger. That leaves me little time to seek stature or a fortune, one that would entice a woman already of means. Besides that, I don't know that I can ever love another woman like I did my boy's mother."

It was an unusually open confession for Josiah, but he knew he needed to disarm Feders, convince him that a fight wouldn't solve anything, wouldn't make Pearl accept his marriage proposal, or make what had just happened in the dining hall disappear from everyone's mind.

Feders glared at Josiah, his teeth clenched hard, then he drew a deep breath and looked away quickly. "I'm not sure I believe you."

"That's your right." Josiah drew a deep breath of his own, preparing to take a chance. "You've known me for a long time, Pete. I've never double-crossed you or anybody else before, why would I start now?"

Feders narrowed his eyes. "There aren't too many women in this world that are as beautiful and smart as Pearl Fikes. She is a gracious prize. One worth losing everything to gain, or dying for, as far as I am concerned."

Josiah wasn't going to agree or disagree. "Maybe you're tryin' too hard, Pete."

Feders exhaled loudly, then kicked the dirt, sending a heavy clump sailing into the darkness, soiling the shine on his boot. "I lose sight of myself every time I get within a mile of her."

"I felt that way about Lily. I just had to give her some room. If you smother the sunlight from a bluebonnet, it's not going to bloom, now is it?"

"I suppose not."

Silence fell between the two men. They had a history together. Time spent riding together as Rangers before the Frontier Battalion was formed, and after, both of them devoted to Hiram Fikes. He'd known Feders while Lily and the girls were alive, when the whole world for Josiah existed on a small piece of acreage in East Texas.

He ached to return to that little piece of Heaven every minute he was out riding with Fikes and Feders — still did as far as that went.

Josiah and Feders had never been friends, but he trusted his back to Pete then — and he had ever since he joined up with the

Frontier Battalion. It had only been recently — ever since Pete took on being a captain — that Josiah began to doubt the man, or at least doubted his leadership capabilities. Pete led by his mood, not his brain like Captain Fikes had. That changed everything.

"I have some news for you, Wolfe," Feders said. "You have been resolved of any wrongdoing or crime in Comanche. I want you to know that. I want you to know what I did for you, putting my neck on the line and saving yours from the rope. Those folks got a taste of revenge when they hung John Wesley Hardin's kin, and you're just a lucky man we showed up when we did or we wouldn't be having this conversation. Your belly wouldn't be full of good wine and beefsteak."

Josiah didn't show the sigh of relief he felt upon hearing the news and the fact that Feders had seemed to finally stand down.

The wine had made Josiah a little unruly inside the house, but he had not lost a lick of his senses when it came to seeing a fight heading his way.

"I appreciate that, Captain," Josiah said, noting the stiff difference in Feders's stance and tone.

"I'm sure you do. That was a fine mess

you created."

"I was just trying to stay alive."

Feders let his fists fall open. "I probably wouldn't go that way again for some time, if I were you."

Josiah agreed silently with a nod. "How'd you know to find me in Comanche in the first place?" It was not a question that had occurred to Josiah previously, but when he thought about the arrival of Feders and the company in Comanche as lucky, the timing seemed almost too perfect. The release made him feel emboldened enough to ask.

"Where else would you have been, Wolfe?" There was a crack in Feders's voice, and he looked away, then back directly at Josiah with a hard, accusatory glare. "What are you suggesting?"

"Nothing. Just asking a question." Josiah felt odd, like he had just verbally attacked his father, with no reason, no cause for suspicion, just curiosity. Pete's reaction only made matters worse, but all things considered, Josiah chose not to pursue the question any further.

"I regret the loss of Red Overmeyer. He was a good man," Josiah said, changing the subject. "I failed him."

"Maybe. Maybe not." Feders was still stiff, but he appeared to relax a bit. He drew a deep breath and took a step back, away from Josiah.

"What do you mean?"

"I had some concerns about Overmeyer's allegiance. He was always a little mysterious and unpredictable when it came to Indians," Feders said.

Josiah was curious and uncertain about Feders's doubt regarding Red. It was the first he'd heard tell of any question of the man's character. There was never any doubt in Josiah's mind that Overmeyer was a fine Ranger, any more than Pete was a fine captain — albeit unpredictable. Now he was starting to doubt everything he'd ever believed.

"He stood and fought with us in Lost Valley against the Comanche and Kiowa," Josiah said. "I'm not sure that you're making sense to me, Captain."

"He was out scouting at the start. It never crossed your mind that the whole troop went down in that valley and the mass of savages suddenly appeared out of nowhere? He gave the all clear to Jones, if I am not mistaken."

"Jones led us into the valley. It was his decision." Josiah was getting defensive, and a little annoyed. Feders was not at the Lost Valley fight; he had stayed back at the

Ranger camp along the Red River because of a conflict with Major Jones. Josiah didn't think much about it at the time.

"A scout worth his salt would have figured out it was a trap," Feders said with a snarl.

"What are you saying? That Red Overmeyer was a spy for the Indians?" Josiah asked, incredulous. "That he intentionally sent innocent men to their deaths? I saw a man die in the worst way, captured and mutilated by the Kiowa like he was nothing more than a rabbit. I spent time with Overmeyer; he never gave me one reason to question his desire to be a Ranger."

There was, though, perhaps some truth to what Feders was saying — at least enough to hear him out.

It was always obvious that Overmeyer had spent plenty of time among the Indians — mostly friendlies on the plains. But being a spy just didn't make sense — or Josiah didn't want to believe it. He had trusted Red Overmeyer.

What would there have been to gain by betraying his fellow Rangers in the Lost Valley? Nothing that Josiah could see. Still, there was no question that Overmeyer's past was dim. He could have known some of the Indians or, at the very least, known how to trade with them.

"Maybe he was a spy for the Indians," Feders said. "Or maybe he was a spy for Liam O'Reilly. Perhaps he intended to give you up all along. Collect O'Reilly's bounty for himself. Maybe those two Comanche and him had a deal. You ever think of that?"

Josiah felt the air go out of his chest.

He had questioned how the Indians knew his name, how they knew he was going to be out along the San Sabine scouting with just Scrap and Overmeyer and no troop to back them up.

"If what you're saying is true, then the Comanches would have had a reason to see Red Overmeyer dead," Josiah said, coming to a conclusion he didn't like, but was starting to make sense in a roundabout kind of way.

He still didn't feel absolved of Overmeyer's death. He wasn't sure he ever would.

Feders nodded. "They were going to keep the bounty on your head for themselves."

"Which kind of explains why they left Elliot to live on the tree."

"It could. Killing a traitor and a competitor was one thing. Killing a Ranger was totally another. Not that I believe for a second that those two Comanche didn't have it in them to slit Elliot's throat. I think they had orders not to draw any more attention to themselves than necessary, since they rode right into Comanche with no worry about riling the town. It's you that O'Reilly was after. Still is, as far as that goes."

"My aim is to take care of that right away," Josiah said, squaring his shoulders, preparing to head to the barn to retrieve Clipper and go home.

"We're not done yet, Wolfe," Feders said, sternly.

"What else is there?"

"You do realize that you've been relieved from the Battalion?"

"I beg your pardon?"

"Are you not off on a journey with Juan Carlos at the request of Captain McNelly?"

"Yes, but . . ."

"You're one of McNelly's men now, Wolfe. Our association is formally over as of this moment. You have no reason to be here or in my company ever again. Is that clear, Wolfe? We are done. Any problem you have with Liam O'Reilly is now yours and yours alone."

Feders didn't give Josiah a second to protest, to question anything about what came next, nothing. He spun on the heel of his boot and walked straight into the Fikes mansion like he already owned the place, slamming the door solidly behind him.

Josiah stood motionless, feeling like he had just been sucker punched by an old adversary — knowing full well he should have seen *something* coming.

The lights in the mansion began to go out one by one, window by window. The glow that had been so bright and welcoming earlier was now quickly becoming cold and dark, the entrance barred, forbidden, and the night uncertain and full of unfamiliar shadows.

CHAPTER 32

A torch stood burning outside of the barn.

The orange flame was waning, but a steady stream of thin black smoke spiraled upward. Shadows played on the wall of the barn; a slow dance of unknown images since there was little breeze. A towering live oak stood near the entrance of the barn, offering a canopy of shade in the hot summers to the stable of fine horses the Fikes place continued to house.

Josiah had been in the barn before, in the spring, after returning the captain's body to the family. There was a bunkhouse attached to the back of the barn, fully equipped with an area set aside for baths and cleaning up after a long day's work. But Josiah had no desire for a bath, or a moment of ease. All he wanted was to get as far away from the estate as possible, as fast as he could. He wanted to go home and sleep in his own bed one more night before leaving with Juan Carlos.

He hoped to never return to the estate. Without the presence of Captain Fikes, it was a foreign country whose citizens spoke with angry and unknown tongues — with the exception of Pearl.

The light from the torch was bright enough to see clearly inside the barn, to the stall that housed Clipper.

When Josiah walked inside, the horse looked up, flipped his ears in recognition, then went back to eating a mouthful of first-class oats that half filled a narrow trough. It seemed they both were going to get their belly filled with tasty food one last time before hitting the trail again.

"Better enjoy that, old friend," Josiah said, entering the stable. His saddle was not in sight. Surely it was in the tack room.

Clipper snorted and looked up again, but past Josiah, out into the darkness, deep into the barn. His ears pricked up, getting Josiah's immediate attention.

He'd learned to trust the horse's announcements a long time ago. They'd saved his hide more than once.

"What is it, fella?" Josiah whispered, rubbing the Appaloosa's sturdy neck with one hand, unlatching the snap on his holster with the other.

He sure did miss wearing the swivel rig that he used with the Peacemaker he'd lost to Little Shirt, but he had gotten as used to Charlie Webb's Colt Frontier and its holster as he could.

He eased the Colt out of the holster, then stepped quickly and quietly against the wall, into a deep shadow. There was no use taking any chances. Not once he heard footsteps coming his way.

Feders might have changed his mind about a last-minute fistfight . . . Or it could have been someone else, a foe set on him by Liam O'Reilly, come to collect in an unsuspected place. They'd think he'd have his guard down here, and trailing him to the big to-do at the Fikes estate wouldn't have taken much effort. He wasn't safe anywhere, not even in Austin, and he couldn't forget that. Not for one second — or he'd end up a dead man.

It was beginning to become tiring, looking over his shoulder all the time. The journey with Juan Carlos couldn't come soon enough. Being a frightened rabbit was no way to live.

Josiah put his thumb on the hammer and eased his finger onto the trigger of the Colt.

He could see a figure emerging out of the darkness, and his eyes fixed on it, just like

Clipper's were.

The night was silent, cool temperatures sending every living creature searching out a bit of warmth left over from the day. A lone cricket rubbed its legs together somewhere in the barn, but nothing answered back. Rats and mice might have been watching from a distance, but Josiah doubted it. His presence had sent them scattering. Too bad that only worked on rodents.

He put as much pressure on the trigger as he could, raising the gun up from his waist. Fanning a shot was something he only did in practice. He had never faced a man, or Indian, with that kind of action, nor did he ever think he would. If he was to take a shot, he wanted it to be sure. A kill with one bullet was always his aim. He only killed if he had to . . . and always replayed the event more times than he could count afterward, his soul aching for a better solution than dealing a man sudden death. Bill Clarmont's death still played heavily on his mind.

The figure held a steady pace, entering the barn unconcerned with being seen.

It only took Josiah a second to recognize Pearl. Seeing her again made his throat dry up all over, and his chest lurched, like his body was warning him to leave as soon as he could, before it was too late, before he did or said something he might regret.

"Josiah, is that you?"

He slid the Colt back into the holster and walked out of the stall, stopping at the gate. "Yes, it's me."

Pearl was standing just inside the open double barn doors, the torch burning behind her, silhouetting her body so that all of her features were hard to see. But it was obvious she had shed her formal dress after running out of the dining hall. Now she was wearing a simple white linen dress, her feet bare, her silky yellow hair falling over her shoulders.

"Are you alone?" Pearl whispered.

"I am," Josiah said.

Pearl did not hesitate then, and ran to Josiah, wrapping her arms around him, pulling him close without hesitation or invitation.

Josiah stiffened and held his hands at his side, for a moment. He wasn't expecting her to rush to him.

Pearl buried her face in his chest, and held him tight, like they had not seen each other in years. Her pain was obvious and disconcerting.

Josiah could tell she had been crying for a long time.

"I'm sorry," Pearl said.

Josiah exhaled, looked up into the darkness of the rafters, then let his eyes wander all around the barn. The last thing he needed was for Feders to walk in and find Pearl Fikes wrapped around him in an embrace — even if he hadn't initiated it. He knew how it would look after what Feders had just said to him.

"Is something wrong?" Pearl angled her face up at Josiah. She looked like an angel with a broken heart. The torch made her hair look even more golden, her skin alabaster, and her blue eyes twinkled with wetness.

He had not welcomed her touch, or returned the warmth and press she offered him. It was hard not to. Her skin was soft, velvet, and made his fingers burn with the want of more of her touch . . . but he resisted.

"No," Josiah said, stepping back away from her a couple of steps, pulling from her embrace, determined to jump on Clipper as quickly as he could and ride away as fast as he could. "I was just leaving."

Clipper snorted, pawed at the straw, then returned to eating the oats luxuriously. Josiah stood back a foot or two from Pearl, unmoving.

Pearl wiped the tears from her eyes. For a brief second, Josiah thought he saw a flash of anger cross her face but decided it must have been a shadow when she looked at him square on.

"You're angry with me, aren't you?" Pearl asked.

"Why would I be angry with you?"

"Peter. I didn't know he was going to be here. My mother arranged for him to be at the dinner without my knowledge."

"She was the reason I didn't want to accept your invitation in the first place," Josiah said.

"I know. I thought I could handle her. But she is dead set on me marrying Peter Feders."

Josiah nodded his head. "He's a fine man, Pearl. You could do worse than being courted by a man like Pete. I've seen his courage and bravery more times than I can count."

"You surely can't mean that, Josiah."

"I owe him my neck."

Pearl took a step toward him then. "He'll never have my heart."

Josiah looked away. He could see the outline of her body, the curves and the mystery of it, because of the dancing flame behind her. Heat begin to rise from his toes

— the coolness of the night hardly a concern now that she was near.

"I will never, ever marry Peter Feders, Josiah. You know that as well as I do — and you know why. I don't care what trick my mother tries to play on me, what social obligation she tries to enforce, he is not the man for me."

A flowery scent hit Josiah's nostrils — springtime perfume, but he couldn't pinpoint the fragrance, it wasn't something he had ever encountered before. It mixed with his own musky smell, and the voice in the back of his head screamed at him to get out of the barn and run away from Pearl Fikes as quick as he could — before he lost control of all of his senses, control of parts of himself that he had forced to lie dormant for a long, long time.

"I'm sorry to hear that, Pearl."

"Don't be." She stopped within inch of him, looked up with fully open eyes, and tilted her head toward him. "I'm not something that can be easily broken," she said, staring into his eyes. "I've been lost before. Married before. You know that. I'm not lost now. I'm right where I want to be."

"You're sure?"

"Yes," Pearl whispered.

Josiah slipped his arm around her waist

and pulled her to him. He couldn't resist her eyes, her acceptance and desire, any longer.

Their lips met in a hard hunger, more so than when they'd kissed on the porch of his home. Now they were alone, their desires growing and bordering on release.

Pearl arched into Josiah's body, and at that very moment, he knew he couldn't stop himself, couldn't hold back any longer, couldn't control for one more second the desire he felt for her.

They made their way into the darkness of an empty stall, their hands searching each other's body knowingly, confidently, not shyly — unbuttoning a shirt, tugging at a dress to feel more skin, each touch more comforting and familiar as they settled onto a soft bed of straw, never losing sight of the look in each other's eyes, a deep blue ocean broken by a small island where they both sought refuge after a long, long, journey.

CHAPTER 33

The sun was just breaking over the cloud-less horizon, warm, fuzzy yellow light slowly eating upward into the grayness of night. Somewhere in the distance, a robin began to chirp, not singing like in spring, but calling out for another of its kind. It only took a second for an answer to come back, farther away, but familiar — then the closest robin rejoiced, breaking into a song that was meant to announce its existence and location.

Morning was coming on gently, but Josiah was in no hurry to see the day fully arrive. He wanted time to stop, wanted to live in the private world he and Pearl had created over the past few hours, and live there for the rest of his life.

It was a world with no past or future, no responsibilities or consequences. It just was — of the moment — of need, desire, fulfillment, touch, and the rush of power rising

344

deep from their loins and hearts. They were like animals, unleashed and unashamed of anything that was brought on by instinct. Their bodies had smashed together, then molded to each other. After that, discovery and pleasure were the only things that mattered.

Love and longing were not mentioned. Their physical attraction had long since been judged as mutual — there was no indecision getting in the way of their need to touch and be touched. They both had trudged through a long, lonely desert. Whatever lay ahead for them, individually and together, was buried deep, for the moment, in the recesses of their minds that held out hope for ecstasy. Reality was completely out of reach.

There would be time enough for expectations, for the world to have its say about what had happened between them. Time for regret, if it came, or embarrassment or shame, for that matter.

But that time was not now.

Josiah wanted to stay joined as one with Pearl for as long as he could, feel her welcoming warmth — take pleasure in her heavy breath, committing it solidly to memory in case he was ever sentenced, by himself or another, to that lonely desert again.

"I really have to go," Josiah whispered.

Pearl opened her eyes and stared at him. They were face-to-face, Josiah gently on top of her, hesitating to move. She shook her head. "No." Her arms around his waist, she pulled him tighter against her.

Josiah buried his face in her neck, tempted to stay longer, wanting nothing more than to add another moment to their night. He pulled back though. Pearl whimpered as he did, closing her eyes, looking away. Sadness was interrupting their world. It was hard telling what emotion would come next — from either one of them.

He stood up slowly.

Pearl lay naked on a quickly made heap of horse blankets, her hair sprawled out underneath her head, her body perfect. She was more beautiful than he could have ever imagined. Even more so when she opened her eyes again — the sadness gone, replaced with need, begging him one last time to stay.

Josiah never wanted to forget how Pearl looked at the moment — longing for him to stay, to come back to her. The image would make the miles he had to travel a little easier, he thought.

"What if you never come back?" Pearl

asked in a husky whisper.

Josiah exhaled deeply. "Then we'll both be glad we had this night."

"Don't go."

"I have to. Nobody I care about is safe as long as Liam O'Reilly is a free man. That includes you. He seems to have eyes everywhere." Josiah found his long johns and began to put them on.

Pearl sat up, pulling straw from her hair, covering herself with one of the blankets.

The air was cool but not cold. Light was creeping its way into the barn, and Pearl glowed like a mythical creature, or Penelope on that last day before Odysseus set out for Troy.

Josiah's mother had loved the Greek stories, and they had read them together when Josiah was in his early teens. He hadn't thought about that for a long time, and the memory made him warm and glad that he had a comparison to make, a story to latch on to, though that journey was a long one. Josiah hoped to return a lot sooner than his fictional counterpart.

"Can't you leave that man's fate to Juan Carlos?" Pearl said.

"Even if I could, I wouldn't. Juan Carlos is spry, wise, and skillful for his years, but I fear he's no match for O'Reilly. Especially if he has already matched up with Cortina. That is a well-fortified hornet's nest. Juan Carlos can't go it alone. It would be suicide — and I would carry his death on my shoulders for the rest of my life and still have to look over my shoulder. And yours."

Worry crossed Pearl's face. "Juan Carlos has more ways about him than you're aware of."

Josiah chuckled. "More ways than I want to know. Is it a family trait? These hidden skills?"

Pearl's face reddened with blush. "Perhaps. I have my own secrets."

"I'm sure you do."

"Please reconsider, Josiah." Pearl said, her face and tone serious.

"McNelly requested I go. I have to."

"McNelly?"

Josiah found his socks and pants and nodded his head yes. "I'm not riding with the Frontier Battalion any longer. Pete Feders is no longer my captain. I'm not sure how that got arranged, but I am glad of it now."

Pearl's eyes grew narrow. She started to say something, then held her tongue.

Silence fell between them for a long moment. The robin drew closer, singing from the live oak just outside the door.

"I think it's best." Josiah slipped a suspender over his shoulder.

"You will be gone longer, farther away," Pearl finally said.

"McNelly is at his ranch for the winter. This is a special assignment, one I would have leapt at if it hadn't come my way with the release from the Battalion. We have to stop O'Reilly."

"He feels the same about you." Pearl stood for a long second, her search for clothes stopped, as she let the blanket fall away. It was one last sly attempt to derail Josiah's departure. But it was, regrettably, too late for that.

"You're sure a sight to behold," Josiah said.

"I won't ask you to stay again. Not this time."

Josiah looked away. "I would stay if I could. There would be too many complications. Too many lives left at risk."

Pearl walked to him then and slid her arms around his waist. "Promise me you'll come back."

"I will do everything in my power to make it back here. There's nothing more I'd like than to see you in a proper bed."

"Being improper?" A smile curled across Pearl's lips.

Josiah didn't answer her. He kissed her

349

deeply, closed his eyes, and let himself reenter their special world one last time.

Josiah didn't look back as he left. He knew Pearl would be standing in the shadows watching him go, her eyes still begging him to stay. He didn't want to see that or take the risk of being seen.

He had eased Clipper out the back of the barn, taking an unseen exit from the Fikes estate.

The sun was nearly up over the horizon, and every man and woman who worked in the mansion was already up, or would be soon. The day had begun, and though he had gotten hardly any sleep, just a doze now and then, afraid he would miss one second of being with Pearl, Josiah felt invigorated, and oddly at peace with how the whole night had turned out.

The road was nearly a trail, one that led into town over a steep hill and through a healthy grove of oaks and maples. A creek cut through at the dip, with pecan trees and junipers as thick as he had ever seen them.

He had traveled this trail before, but only at night, his senses lost in confusion as he had sought an escape from the estate, when he wanted to be as far away as he could be. That seemed like so long ago — he was a different man on the same trail.

He felt alive now, fully himself, surprised at how much life had changed in a matter of a few short months. Facing reality would come sooner rather than later, but for the moment, he still wanted to bask in the joy and pleasure of the previous night.

Clipper was moving along at an easy trot, the light certain now and the trail clear. The horse seemed to sense Josiah's mood and mirrored it thoroughly and implicitly until the Appaloosa heard something ahead and stiffened, piquing his ears.

Josiah heard the same thing as the horse, at about the same time. He pulled back on the reins, bringing Clipper to a stop, his hand automatically easing onto the grip of the Colt.

It only took a second for the rider to appear, pushing full out. To Josiah's relief, it was Scrap Elliot.

Clipper relaxed as Josiah loosened his hold on the reins. They both sat there waiting.

Scrap saw Josiah just as soon as he cleared a bend in the trail, braking Missy, the blue roan mare, hard, but gentle. "There you are," he said.

"What are you up to, Scrap?"

Scrap looked at Josiah oddly, not accustomed to the happiness in his voice.

"Come to gather you up, that's all."

"I'm on my way home now."

"Best hurry that up."

Josiah furrowed his brow, noticing the sweat on Scrap's forehead, the full complement of bullets in his belt, and the stuffed saddlebag tied over the saddle. "Where's the trouble?"

"Ain't none yet, but Juan Carlos is madder than a hot pepper at your absence."

"What do you know about Juan Carlos?"

"Tarnation, Wolfe. I'm goin' with you. I'm one of McNelly's boys now, too."

CHAPTER 34

The noise from the hustle and bustle of Austin reached them long before they left the trail. Morning had fully broken, the edge of the sun a quarter of a hot red plate on the horizon.

Clouds that looked like narrow fingers stretched out overhead, the soft light coating the underside with warm tinges of pink. It was hard to tell if the sky was angry or happy. The combination of colors was confusing, especially against the sky that seemed to suck up the hues like a sponge. In some places it was blue, mostly off in the distance, to the west, and in others it was almost pure white, void of any perceptible weather or attitude.

The sky over Austin itself turned from pink to fire red, the color of a warning flag, but that did not deter Josiah. He pushed Clipper as hard as he could, rushing home, riding as fast as he could — just so he could leave again.

Scrap and Missy had no trouble keeping up, and there was no question that on a good day, the roan mare could outrun Clipper by a fast mile. Today was not that day though. There was no need for Scrap to make haste any more than he already was; the boy had already done his duty.

The thought of the boy riding along to the border with him and Juan Carlos was both an aggravation and a comfort to Josiah. He was glad Scrap was still a Ranger, even gladder that he hadn't followed after Donley and fallen into bad graces with Governor Coke, but it felt like there was a rope tied to Josiah that always ended up being looped around Scrap. It was something to get used to, and mostly, Josiah didn't want to be partnered with anyone, especially a hothead like Scrap Elliot. He liked riding alone or with the boys of the company, not just one man.

Little puffs of dust flew up behind the two horses each time a hoof landed heavily on the ground. There was no need to worry about hiding their destination, but Josiah was tense anyway, constantly looking for the next ambush, sure that O'Reilly would kill him sooner rather than later.

Regardless of Juan Carlos's knowledge of

the Irishman's trek to the border and potential union with Cortina, there were enemies to be on the lookout for right in the heart of Austin.

How far O'Reilly's shadow and orders fell was never in question. The scoundrel had picked up right where Charlie Langdon had left off, creating a gang of followers who, for some reason, were more than happy to do his bidding.

There was no doubt O'Reilly was capable of meanness and madness, violent acts that would make even the most experienced Ranger wince and look away, but it had never appeared to Josiah that the Irishman had the gift of persuasion — other than with a six-shooter and a knife. There had to be more to the man's power than he knew.

The trail narrowed through another thick grove of trees, and Josiah continued to lead the way.

Buildings on the outskirts of the city were easily within a half a mile's ride, in sudden view once they broke out of the trees. Josiah was not planning on slowing down until he reached the house he called home, but he was surprised to see a familiar horse standing idle in the middle of the trail about fifty yards up.

Juan Carlos was waiting, sitting on his

nameless chestnut stallion, a hard look on his face.

Josiah pushed Clipper a little harder, rushing to Juan Carlos, then eased the Appaloosa back, coming to a quick stop. Scrap followed suit and stopped Missy beside Josiah, with a concerned look on his face.

"Whoa, there, Clipper," Josiah said, patting the horse's sweaty neck. "I expected to find you at the house," he said to Juan Carlos.

"I am here."

"I can see that. Something is wrong." Josiah squinted knowingly, it wasn't a question.

"*Sí,* there is. Two men are watching the house, waiting for your return. They are well armed and unfamiliar. I am sure they do not intend to look out for your best interests."

Josiah felt a burning sensation in his chest. "I was afraid that might happen." He flipped the reins, but Juan Carlos eased his horse in front of Clipper, gently grabbing the bridle, not allowing Josiah to pass.

"You cannot go home, señor. They will kill you and your son."

"They will anyway. I have to protect him."

A slight smile slipped across Juan Carlos's leathery brown face. "Señor Lyle is not

356

there. Nor is Ofelia."

"Where are they?"

"Safe in Little Mexico."

"You're sure?"

"That's the first place they'll look," Scrap interjected. "Everybody knows Wolfe favors Mexicans." He waited a second, then nodded. "No offense to you, Juan Carlos," he added.

Scrap's tone was conciliatory, which was as uncommon as a pure white hawk flying overhead. The gesture surprised Josiah, but he didn't care at the moment to find out what had changed between the two men. Perhaps it had something to do with McNelly, or maybe not.

"If those men go after *el niño,* they will not leave there alive." The look in Juan Carlos's eye was as unmistakable as the certainty in his voice.

Scrap just shrugged. "We're gonna have to have our eyes peeled then." He looked at the sky, then said, "It'd be easier to travel at night, but I got a feelin' there's bad weather comin' along. Pink skies ain't for fairy tales. Saw a tornado once in the afternoon after seein' a mornin' sky like this one here."

"You cannot go home, Señor Josiah. I have packed as much of your gear into my bags as I could."

Josiah exhaled loudly. "If you think it's best."

"I do."

"I would have liked to have seen Lyle before I left."

A gentle, knowing look crossed Juan Carlos's face. "It is a good thing you did not come home last night, señor. There may have been more trouble than we could have handled. Leaving this way has, perhaps, saved some shooting and fear that the boy would remember. Trust me, this way is better." He paused, then allowed himself to smile, broadly. "Did you enjoy yourself?"

Josiah felt his face flush. It was most certainly the color of the sky, but he said nothing, gave no indication of what had happened or would happen. Juan Carlos knew somehow, though. That wasn't a big surprise.

"Yeah, Wolfe, come to think of it, what in tarnation was you doin' out so late at the Fikes place?"

"That's none of your business, now, is it?" Josiah snapped.

Juan Carlos started to laugh. It was a tiny laugh just in the bottom of his throat at first, then it dropped to his thin, almost invisible belly, and he laughed deeper.

"What did I say?" Scrap said.

"Nothing," Juan Carlos said in between laughs. "I just have not seen Señor Josiah look so young and foolish in a very long time. It is a nice thing to see."

"If you say so." A perplexed look crossed Scrap's face. It didn't appear that he found anything funny about the situation.

"Thank you, Juan Carlos, you're a true friend," Josiah said, the note of sarcasm in his voice high — which of course, made Juan Carlos laugh even harder.

"I think we had better go," Scrap said. "Are you comin', old man, or are you gonna sit here hee-hawin' all day, drawin' all kinds of notice right to us?"

"Usted tiene el humor de una chiva," Juan Carlos said to Scrap, grabbing his stomach, forcing himself to stop laughing.

"What did he say, Wolfe?"

"How in the heck would I know?"

"You live with a Mexican."

"That doesn't mean I speak Mexican."

"He called me a name, didn't he?"

Josiah rolled his eyes. "Don't get your feathers all in a ruffle, Elliot, I'm sure he didn't call you any names, did you, Juan Carlos?"

"I said you have the humor of a goat," Juan Carlos said, trying to catch his breath.

For some reason, Josiah found that funny,

and he started to laugh, too. Juan Carlos joined him, leaving Scrap to sit on Missy with his arms crossed, a petulant look on his face, unsure of what to do next — fight or flee.

CHAPTER 35

Austin disappeared behind the trio as they headed south, and the hill country rose up to greet them.

It was a long ride to the Nueces Strip, and since Juan Carlos was in the lead, with no specific and unspoken orders from Captain Leander McNelly, Josiah found himself in the odd position of following, unaware of what their true destination was or, for that matter, what their true mission was, other than to stop the unlikely union between Liam O'Reilly and Juan Cortina, if they could.

The Strip, a broad area between the Nueces River and the Rio Grande, was home to more than its fair share of ruthless outlaws, not only Cortina, but John King Fisher, too.

Wild longhorns roamed the countryside and locally brought only about two dollars a head at market, but the long trek up to

Abilene raised the price to forty dollars a head, making cattle hunting and rustling an extremely lucrative occupation. Brand doctors abounded, and if they were caught out in the brush, they were hanged on the spot. In a city, at the stockyards, the branders were most often sent off to prison if they were foolish enough to show their faces.

Josiah was well aware of the potential for Liam O'Reilly to grow his band of outlaws into a full-fledged outfit with corrupt fingers stretching all over the state of Texas, if he was successful in the Strip.

O'Reilly had already demonstrated that power in Waco and Comanche, though he'd eventually lost influence in both towns. Not only was he a cold-blooded killer, but the Irishman was also an astute businessman who had a talent for wrangling the local power, taking control of entire towns. Obviously ambition was part of the outlaw's makeup, too.

Cortina was an interesting choice for O'Reilly to try and side with. He had served in the Mexican War at a very young age, quickly becoming a folk hero to the people of Mexico. In the late 1850s, Cortina was outraged by the treatment of poor Mexicans living in Brownsville, gathered up eighty men, and took control of the town. It was called the First Cortina War. The people of Brownsville revolted, creating a militia of their own called the Brownsville Tigers. It wasn't long before the Texas Rangers showed up, and later with Colonel Robert E. Lee, commander of the Eighth Military District, the army showed up, too. Cortina was defeated and driven back into Mexico.

When Texas seceded from the Union and joined in the fight with the War Between the States, Cortina invaded Zapata County, starting the Second Cortina War, siding with the Union. He was defeated by Captain Santos Benavides and, once again, was driven back into Mexico. But Cortina continued making trouble, on both sides of the border, offering aid to the Union since Benavides was a Confederate. Cortina eventually became a general in the Mexican Army, and after the end of the War Between the States, he was considered a Union criminal of Texas, even though a pardon had been presented, but failed in the legislature.

It was only natural that the fortunes being made in cattle would catch Cortina's attention. He knew the Nueces Strip better than anyone. It was rumored by everyone that he had a large faction of rustlers that stole from the ranches and rounded up the wild longhorn as well. But recently, the ranchers had started to make some noise about the rustling and had been heard all the way in Austin. Cortina was becoming more and more powerful, more and more brazen, and the ranchers were losing a lot of cattle that weren't being shipped up north.

To Josiah, it sounded like Liam O'Reilly needed Juan Cortina far more than Cortina needed O'Reilly — but then again, what did he know of the ways of outlaws? Maybe there was a deal hatched with skills that O'Reilly held that Josiah was unaware of. That was entirely possible, making the charge to stop O'Reilly a larger matter.

But for Josiah, the nuances of the relationship didn't really matter. The trip to the Nueces Strip was personal for him.

He wanted to see the Irishman dead and buried.

They eased their pace as Onion Creek came into view. The uplands stretched out before them, and the ground was dry, eerily similar to the San Saba, but lacking in alkali and biting flies.

Mesquites were sparse, junipers were healthy, and off in the distance, the creek was lined with cypress, sycamore, and pecan trees. Josiah's hunger kicked in, as well as his instinct, and he knew the spot would be a good place to hunt for white-tailed deer or fox squirrels.

The trees were mostly bare, and there was little bird life. On a perfect day there would be all kinds of songbirds singing and fluttering about, but the roiling sky overhead and a steady wind had driven away any signs of life, leaving the trees in silence.

The red sky of the morning had turned to an angry black in the west. Wind was starting to kick up, and the smell of a fierce rain was too strong to ignore.

The storm clouds reminded Josiah of Comanche, of Billie Webb. No matter what had happened since his return to Austin, even last night in Pearl's arms, he could not get the girl out of his mind. He worried about her welfare and was certain that that was the only reason her memory would not leave him alone.

"There is a shelter not far from here, an overhang that will protect us from the weather," Juan Carlos said.

Josiah looked at the limestone toward the outcroppings, and for a moment held the memory of Lost Valley, of being trapped under a similar outcropping by an angry band of Kiowa. It was not a good memory.

Scrap had nearly gotten them killed, and there was a question whether or not the boy's impetuousness had caused the knife attack that left Josiah wounded. The scar was still tender, but he had decided long ago not to blame Scrap. Still, the outcropping made him nervous.

"Is there a way out?" Josiah asked, forcing his thoughts back into the moment. Not losing sight of where they were when there were men who wanted to see them dead — or Josiah at least — was extremely important.

They were riding three abreast at a slow pace. Scrap shot Josiah an angry look because of the question but held his tongue. The Lost Valley fight was still a rub between Josiah and Scrap, neither of them daring to bring up the subject.

Juan Carlos nodded. "There is. To the best of my knowledge, we have not been followed. But that does not mean someone is not waiting for us."

"That makes me feel better," Josiah said.

"Just the truth," Juan Carlos answered. "What is the matter, Elliot?"

"Nothin'."

"We've been in a situation like this before," Josiah said.

"That's not what I was thinkin' about, Wolfe," Scrap said. "I was thinkin' it's a long ride to the Strip, and this ain't startin' out so well."

Juan Carlos shook his head and picked up his pace, leading his horse a little to the south as he climbed down toward the creek bed.

The blackness in the sky had nearly reached them, and Josiah felt the first raindrop hit his face. A lightning strike burst out of the sky a good distance away, hot white fingers hungrily reaching for the earth. Thunder rumbled a few seconds later, giving Clipper a noticeable start.

"Why do you say that?" Josiah asked, reining the horse back, quickly calming him.

"Just like usual, I'm bringin' up the rear, and I ain't got a clue as to what's goin' on."

Josiah eyed Scrap, raising an eyebrow in frustration. "We trust you with our backs, isn't that enough?" With that, he kneed Clipper, catching up quickly with Juan Carlos, leaving Scrap to think about what he'd just said.

Another clap of thunder spurred Scrap and Missy to join Josiah and Juan Carlos under the overhang.

The fire was small, and on occasion, Juan Carlos flapped his hat over it, dispelling the rise of smoke so they wouldn't draw any attention to their location. The storm was fully overhead now, and the trio was safely tucked under the overhang. It was dry and cool next to the limestone, nearly like being in a cave, except there was a sheer wall, facing southwest, that helped keep most of the wind and rain away from the three men.

Juan Carlos had a full complement of jerky for the long ride, and there'd been time to get some fresh water for a pot of coffee. The aroma of Arbuckle's filled the air, along with the smell of some johnny-cakes frying in a small skillet.

The horses were not so lucky, tied to a line just outside the overhang. Still, there were some tall sycamores that helped to protect them from the weather.

"We're gonna lose half a day's ride," Scrap said.

"That is not my worry," Juan Carlos answered, staring out into the storm, at nothing in particular.

"What is?" Josiah asked. He was sitting with his back propped up against the wall, his Winchester at his side, cleaning the Colt Frontier.

"It will be much easier for us to be tracked when we leave." Juan Carlos walked to the very edge of the overhang, stuck his hand out, made it into a cup, and let it fill with water that was draining off from above. "If

O'Reilly has already met up with Cortina, their plans made, then he will know we are coming."

"How would he know that?" Scrap asked.

Juan Carlos shook his head. "I do not know. O'Reilly has eyes everywhere. I think he will be on the lookout for us, either way. The Badger is wary of everything and everyone."

"The only way he would know we are coming is if those eyes were Ranger eyes," Josiah said.

"Perhaps." Juan Carlos drank the water from his cupped hand, then angled over to the fire, standing over it for some warmth. "That is not entirely out of the realm of possibility, but I have not been able to discover who those eyes belong to, if that is true."

"Well don't look at me. I ain't no rat," Scrap said.

Josiah stopped cleaning the Colt and put it away . . . within reach. "If we thought that, you'd be a dead rat."

"No worry," Juan Carlos said. "I have ways of finding these things out. I have my own set of eyes in places Cortina or O'Reilly would not suspect."

CHAPTER 36

Fort Clark stood on the horizon, a twenty-acre complex of wood frame and limestone buildings, some still under construction. The fort had originated in 1852 as a guard post for the San Antonio–El Paso Road. When Texas seceded from the Union, the fort was taken over by the Second Texas Mounted Rifles and used as a hospital. Josiah knew some men who'd served with that outfit, or at least they'd claimed to, but for himself, this was his first visit to Clark and the outlying town of Brackett. The construction was a result of a rebuilding project after years of overuse and neglect.

The trio of men stood with their horses lined nose to nose at the crest of a thousand-foot rise. As they looked west, it seemed like they could see forever as dusk started to settle into night before them.

The ride had been long, hard, and fast, the three of them fair enough horsemen to keep up with one another and make solid time. Almost four days had passed, constantly on the lookout for an ambush, for trackers, for a posse of O'Reilly's men on their tail — but there had been nothing, not one single threat.

The ride to Fort Clark had been almost too easy as far as Josiah was concerned.

"More to worry about here," Juan Carlos said, looking explicitly at Scrap, who was in the middle. "Kickapoo. Lipan Apache. Rustlers. Outlaws. Some Comanche. *Bandidos* crossing back and forth across the river selling off stolen cattle. It is *una tierra hostil,* a hostile land. Cortina knows every rock, every bad man's heart, and every good man's weakness within a thousand miles. You cannot let your fears get the best of you, or we could all die."

"I can handle myself," Scrap said.

Juan Carlos gripped the reins tighter, holding his horse steady. "Watch yourself in the fort, if we have need to make a visit. Colonel Mackenzie employs a fine group of Negro Seminole scouts. We may have need of their services."

"I ain't no slouch," Scrap said.

"I know how you feel about Mexicans. *Usted no puede ocultar su perjuicio.*"

Josiah sat on Clipper on the other side of

Scrap, listening, looking over the land in front of him, barely paying attention to the two men's conversation.

His eyes were fixed on the town of Brackett, the lamps starting to burn inside the houses, the residents preparing for the coming night. He let his thoughts wander to Lyle, then Pearl, hoping their safety and comfort were not a concern, knowing that there was nothing he could do, so far away, other than look out for himself, Scrap, and Juan Carlos and accomplish his own mission as well as the one Captain McNelly had set for them: Stop Liam O'Reilly at any cost.

"You know I can't speak Mexican," Scrap protested.

"It is just as well," Juan Carlos said.

"You have a plan?" Josiah asked.

Juan Carlos nodded. "We will stay in town."

Josiah stared at the old Mexican, questioning him with his eyes first. "If O'Reilly or Cortina have men here, they will be on the lookout for us. They'll know we're here if what you say is true."

"That is the plan," Juan Carlos said. "Cortina will find it very interesting that I have ridden into Brackett with two Rangers."

"He knows you?"

Juan Carlos smiled. "Of course he knows me."

"Well, that's the stupidest thing I ever heard of," Scrap said.

"Do you think that the three of us are going to sneak up on O'Reilly, or Cortina in the land that he calls home? That is *estupidez*. Foolish, as you say."

"You really want them to know we're here?" Scrap continued.

Juan Carlos nodded. "We are safe in Brackett. It is once we leave the protection of the fort that we will be in danger. The men there will not cast a shadow on us."

"And your plan extends beyond that?" Josiah asked.

"*Sí.*"

"That's good enough for me," Josiah said.

"Well, it ain't for me," Scrap said.

"Fine," Josiah said. "Stay here."

Brackett was the Kinney County seat, and the jail sat right across the street from the county courthouse. Like in Fort Clark, the buildings in Brackett were made of ash-layered limestone and were of recent construction.

There was a quarry, not far out of town, that supplied all of the limestone. The towering mountains and deep canyons supplied an unlimited source of materials to accommodate the growth of Brackett and the rebuilding of Fort Clark.

Juan Carlos tied his horse to the hitching post in front of the jail. It was a small building, single level, about eight hundred square feet at the most, nothing like the county jail in Austin. The jail was as nice-looking a building as Josiah had ever seen for housing outlaws.

"Wait here. The sheriff is *un viejo amigo,* an old friend. I want to say *hola,* let him know we are here," Juan Carlos said.

Josiah nodded, stayed in his saddle, and watched Juan Carlos disappear inside the building.

Scrap grunted, then fished into a pocket and pulled out a quirlie he'd pre-rolled and lit it. The air immediately smelled of tobacco, and though Josiah did not smoke, the smell was a comfort to him. It meant they were in a moment of relief and relaxation.

Light burned brightly from inside, and Josiah wondered if there were gas lamps in the jail like there were in the Fikes estate. The glow was intense, almost white, as it cut through the windows and into the darkness outside. It was easy to see moving shadows through the window next to the door and hear loud, welcoming voices. The curtains were drawn so he could not see any one man in particular, just their outlines. There was more than one man.

"I feel like a sittin' duck," Scrap said, exhaling a lung full of smoke.

"You're going to have to trust Juan Carlos."

"Not likely to happen anytime soon."

"Then why did you come?"

"Orders. I want to keep on bein' a Ranger."

"Obviously Juan Carlos has McNelly's trust."

Scrap shrugged. "Don't matter. I'll do what I'm told, you know that, Wolfe. But I ain't gonna take no orders from a Mexican or a half-breed Indian, especially a half-breed Negro Indian. Nobody said they were equal to a Ranger, now did they?"

Josiah shook his head no. "Juan Carlos works for himself as far as I know. I don't know what his relationship with McNelly is, but I figure they've known each other for a long time. Can't see McNelly sending anyone on a special assignment without trusting him."

"So you're sayin' Juan Carlos is a spy?"

"Maybe."

"Well, I ain't takin' orders from no spy."

Josiah said nothing in response to Scrap's announcement. There was no use arguing with the thick-headed boy. He took a deep breath and looked up to the sky. It looked the same as the night sky that covered the ceiling of Austin, even though they were two hundred miles from home.

There were some men who could navigate by the night sky, knew the stories about warriors doing battle above them with great beasts like bears and lions, but Josiah didn't know any of those stories.

He knew the Big Dipper when he saw it, the Little Dipper, too, but beyond that the night sky was a mystery to him. Just like the streets of Brackett, which were mostly quiet now. He had no idea where he was at.

The street a couple of blocks over, however, held a line of saloons and hotels, and Josiah supposed the nightly entertainment was just starting there, especially considering the fort wasn't that far out of town, offering bored and well-moneyed soldiers plenty of opportunities to while away the time and spend their monthly allotments.

"I don't imagine you'll have to take orders from anybody, except for maybe me," Josiah finally said. "You're a fine shot, Elliot, and one of the best horsemen I've ever met. I just wish you had as much talent with your mouth as you do your trigger finger."

"Well, thanks," Scrap said. "I think."

The door to the jail opened, and Juan Carlos walked outside, a smile on his face. He stopped, hitched up his pants like he was prone to do since he was so skinny, and was about to say something to Josiah when the first shot rang out.

Juan Carlos didn't have time to react.

The bullet, which came from behind Josiah and Scrap, caught the Mexican solidly in the shoulder, knocking him back against the hard wall of the jail.

The second shot dropped Juan Carlos to his knees.

He fell flat on his face before Josiah or Scrap could reach for their guns and return fire.

CHAPTER 37

Scrap spun around and fired blindly into the darkness, quickly emptying his six-shooter.

Josiah jumped off Clipper and began shooting, too, hesitating only a second after seeing a shadow move along the roof of the two-storey courthouse across the street.

With his free hand, Josiah grabbed his Winchester out of the scabbard, readying himself to take aim when he ran out of bullets. He knew there was little chance of hitting anything, but like Scrap, he emptied his gun. He holstered it, and aimed the rifle upward, drawing a breath, gathering his thoughts, before pulling the trigger.

The light from the jail became even brighter as the door swung open and footsteps rushed out behind Josiah.

He looked over his shoulder, saw two men take up positions behind the limestone columns that held up the jail's roof. They had rifles and joined in the shoot-out without any questions or direction. Josiah assumed it was the sheriff of Kinney County and a deputy, roused by the gunfire and come to help.

Scrap continued shooting, so Josiah dropped back, his concern less about his own safety than that of Juan Carlos.

The Mexican hadn't moved a muscle that Josiah could tell — it was hard to say whether he was dead or alive.

Josiah crouched down next to Juan Carlos, just as a bullet pinged off the dirt about a foot from the Mexican's head. He was going to see if he could find a pulse, see if Juan Carlos was still alive, but now all he wanted to do was get his friend out of harm's way, regardless.

"There's more than one," Scrap yelled out as he slid off Missy, then smacked her on the rump, sending her out of the line of fire.

The blue roan mare tore off down the street like there was a trophy and a huge payout involved in the run. Gunshots didn't spook that horse one bit.

Josiah whistled and Clipper quickly followed after Scrap's horse.

Scrap found a spot between the jail and a barn that probably held the sheriff's horses, and started firing upward to the roofline of the courthouse where Josiah had seen the shadows move.

Josiah grabbed Juan Carlos by the wrists and started to drag him back into the darkness created by the overhang of the jail's roof.

A bullet hit the dirt a couple of inches to the left of Josiah's boot. That motivated him to struggle even harder to move Juan Carlos as quickly as he could.

He left any concern of hurting Juan Carlos behind. He pushed his legs as deep and as fast as he could, yanking the man's limp body behind him into the darkness as fast as he could. He came to a stop next to the jail, on the opposite side of the building from Scrap, securely in the shadows, hidden from the shooters on the roof — or at least he hoped so.

There were still shots being exchanged, but it was more a volley now than a shootout and a shower of bullets. It seemed like there was only one gun on top of the courthouse taking shots at them. Josiah didn't know if one of the shooters had been taken out, or if they had escaped and were planning an attack from another hidden spot.

It didn't take long for Josiah's eyes to adjust to the darkness.

There were no windows on this side of the jail, and whatever lay beyond was of little concern. All that mattered was that the building helped hide him and Juan Carlos.

Josiah quickly felt Juan Carlos's neck, searching for a pulse. He found a faint but steady rhythm that gave him immediate hope that his friend had a chance of surviving. He was more than glad the Mexican was still alive.

Juan Carlos groaned, then his eyes flickered open.

"Take it easy there, friend," Josiah said.

"I underestimated O'Reilly," Juan Carlos whispered. His voice was weak and cracking with pain.

"Don't worry about it. Save your strength. Where'd they hit you?"

"In the shoulder," Juan Carlos coughed weakly, clutching his stomach at the same time, "and in the belly."

Josiah exhaled, knowing full well the gut shot might yet prove to be fatal. "Hang on."

"If I don't make it," Juan Carlos said, "find a scout in the fort by the name of Dixie Jim. He will know what to do without me. He will take you into the Strip where you need to go to find Cortina."

"It doesn't matter."

Juan Carlos licked his dry lips, his eyes

wide open, the pain he was feeling certain. He struggled to say something but couldn't find — or say — the words.

Josiah looked over his shoulder for a source of water. He thought he could see the outline of a well and water pump just behind the jail. He started to get up and go find out, but Juan Carlos reached up and pulled him back.

"You have to know that Pearl's fate and heart are in your hands," Juan Carlos said so softly now that Josiah had to lean down next to his mouth to hear him speak.

Josiah pulled back. "What do you mean?"

"She is *mucho* valuable. The man who marries her stands to become wealthy beyond belief. You must know that."

Josiah had assumed as much, knew that Pearl's station in life was way beyond his own — and he thought then, as he did now, that giving into his strongest desire was a mistake for him . . . and her, but he couldn't help himself. There was no time for regret now.

"You are in the way," Juan Carlos whispered. "And I can't help you."

"In the way of what?" Although Josiah knew the answer to that question — at least he thought he did. He was in Pete Feders's way. Especially now, considering what had happened before he left Austin.

It made no sense to Josiah why Juan Carlos was bringing up the subject, other than his own fondness and love for his niece. There was no question Pearl was the apple of Juan Carlos's eye, the only reason, now that his half brother was dead, that he tolerated the Widow Fikes. As far as Josiah knew, Pearl was the only living relative that Juan Carlos had.

"If you love her, you have to save her . . . Save her from him . . ." Juan Carlos whispered. His eyes fluttered, he licked his lips deeply again, and then lost consciousness before he could finish the sentence.

Josiah's heart sank at the sight and at the thought of losing Juan Carlos. He wanted to scream out: *Save her from what? From who?* But he knew better than to draw the bullets to him. If there was any hope of keeping his friend alive, of saving *him,* then he had to get him help, fast, and not get him shot again.

The gunfire had awakened Brackett. A small crowd had gathered about a block south of the jail. A torch burned brightly, showing the faces of a curious crowd, probably drawn out of the nearest saloon.

The shooting had stopped, though it

remained to be seen if this was a good thing or not. There hadn't been a shot fired in the last five minutes.

Josiah eased away from Juan Carlos, over to the column where one of the men from the sheriff's office had perched.

"I need to get help for Juan Carlos," Josiah said.

Sweat was running down the man's face. It was hard to make out many of his features in the dark, but there was a glint of light reflecting off the star on his chest.

"Doc's got a place a half block over. Once it's safe, I'll send word to get him down here. How bad is Juan Carlos?"

"Gut-shot and took another to the shoulder," Josiah answered.

"Damn."

"I don't know how much longer he's going to last."

"Your partner over there is a keen shot," the man said.

"Elliot's pretty good. You think he got the shooter?"

"Hard to say." The man looked away from Josiah, up to the top of the courthouse. He wasn't wearing a hat, and it was easy to see wisps of thin, white hair, balding on top. "I'm Bill Gamit, Kinney County sheriff, by the way. I've known Juan Carlos for as long as I can remember. He's a good man to have on your side."

"Good to meet you, Sheriff."

"Call me Bill."

Josiah nodded. The man had a gentle but firm voice and a twinkle in his eye. He immediately put Josiah at ease.

"Luke, take yourself up to the roof up there. It's been quiet for a little too long. Take Ranger Wolfe's partner with you," Bill Gamit said to the other man, behind the opposite column.

The man, obviously a deputy since he wore a silver star on his chest, too, nodded, then disappeared into the shadows, off in Scrap's direction.

Josiah wanted to protest that Scrap wasn't his partner, just a fellow Ranger, but he let it go. For all intents and purposes, Scrap *was* his partner on this mission, whether he liked it or not.

"You got any idea who might be shooting at Juan Carlos?" Gamit asked.

"My guess is O'Reilly's in on it. I questioned whether Juan Carlos was making a mistake coming into town so boldly," Josiah said. "But if you've known him for a long time, then you know how he is."

Gamit nodded. "O'Reilly? That's odd. I heard scuttlebutt about some Irish outlaw

385

hookin' up with Cortina, but if that's the case, you're in the wrong place, mister."

"Why's that?"

"Well, if Cortina was close by, I would know it. Last I heard he was about two hundred miles from here, holed up in a little spot outside of Nuevo Laredo."

"Then why did Juan Carlos bring us here?" Josiah said, suddenly exasperated.

"Beats me," Sheriff Gamit said. "You'll have to ask him. If you can."

Chapter 38

"We didn't see anything," Scrap said as he came inside the sheriff's office. "Nothin' up there but roof and some empty cartridges."

Juan Carlos was lying on a cot in a cell, unconscious. Sheriff Gamit and the doctor were inside looking after him. Josiah had been standing at the door of the jail, anxiously awaiting Scrap's return.

"How's the Mexican doin'?" Scrap asked.

"Not good," Josiah said.

"What're we gonna do?"

Josiah shrugged. He didn't have a clue at the moment. "Depends on what happens to Juan Carlos I 'spect."

The deputy who had joined Scrap eased by him, then made his way into the cell where Juan Carlos was, to speak to the sheriff. The deputy was a young man, probably no more than twenty years old, skinny as a nail and tall as a pine tree. His gun hung low on his hip, and it looked like the weight of it could tip him over. He murmured something unintelligible in Gamit's ear, then stood back from the cot respectfully, standing with his arms behind his back.

"That there is Luke. Sheriff Gamit is his granddaddy," Scrap said.

Josiah nodded. That made sense.

The sheriff walked out of the cell, a grim look on his face. "You fellas can stay here tonight if you'd like. Doc says it's touch and go for ole Juan Carlos. Might make it through the night, might not. He's got to get those bullets out of him if he can. Not sure he can survive that. He ain't goin' to Laredo anytime soon, though, so you best be thinkin' of a plan for yourself."

"Damn," Josiah said. "Thanks, Sheriff, I think staying here is a good idea. We don't know our way around town, and hard telling who's got a lookout for us. Seems to me we might end up worse off than our friend here if we leave now."

"That's what I was thinkin'," the sheriff said. "I'll send Luke out to get you some grub. There's an empty cell in the back with a double bunk and a pump just outside the back door. Can't offer you a place to take a bath, but you can clean up a little bit and rest assured you're safe for the night."

Josiah took his hat off. "We sure do appreciate that, Sheriff Gamit."

"Bill."

"All right, Bill," Josiah said, allowing himself to smile for the first time since they'd arrived in Brackett.

The lights were out, and the doctor had long since gone, his task of taking the bullets out of Juan Carlos successfully completed. There was nothing to do but wait and see how things turned out for the Mexican. The doctor gave him a fifty-fifty chance of surviving the night. Not the best odds in the world, but not the worst either.

Josiah was lying on the top bunk, on his back, eyes wide open, staring at the ceiling, listening to every little sound inside the jail and beyond. His trigger finger lay inches away from the Colt Frontier.

It didn't matter that they were in the jail, he didn't feel a bit safe. Somebody knew they were in town. Somebody wanted Juan Carlos dead. And that somebody certainly knew they were still inside the jail. They'd gotten away without leaving a trace of who they were, or who had sent them.

"You awake up there, Wolfe?" Scrap asked, his voice low.

"Yeah, I'm awake. Can't sleep a wink, I

don't think."

"Me either. What do you think the Mexican was up to bringing us here?"

"Don't know, really. The sheriff said Juan Carlos stopped in just as a courtesy, letting him know we were in town. Nothing more than that."

"That don't make a lot of sense to me," Scrap said.

"Me, either, but you've been around Juan Carlos enough. He rarely tells you anything, and he never tells you everything."

"Surprises me you trust him."

"He saved my life once."

"Guess you're even, and I'm one up on him."

"If he lives."

Both men grew quiet then, the thought of losing Juan Carlos troubling — at least to Josiah.

"What are we gonna do now?" Scrap finally asked. It didn't take a loud voice to carry inside the limestone cell, and it was cool, too. Just about right for a thin blanket.

"Juan Carlos told me to look up a man named Dixie Jim. He's a scout at the fort. It's the only reason I can think of why we're here. Maybe this Dixie Jim fella knows the spots around Laredo better than Juan Carlos and can take us in so we can find

O'Reilly and do what needs doing."

"I ain't real comfortable bein' around half-breeds."

"You can always stay here," Josiah said, his voice firm as was befitting the sergeant he was. Scrap didn't answer, so Josiah assumed the message had come across loud and clear. "Good, that's the last I expect to hear about that subject."

"I ain't gonna trust him."

"Nobody said you had to."

The rising sun quickly warmed the jail cell. Harsh light beamed through the window across from the bunks and bounced off the nearly white walls, rousing Josiah awake long before he was ready.

He had been lost in a dream, one with dead people who could speak and living people who couldn't. No matter how hard he tried to stay asleep so he could remember what the dead people said, he couldn't hold on to their words. His mother was there. A soldier that had died next to him in Georgia during the war, a bullet hole squarely in the center of his forehead, the blood caked and old, dirt on his hands, like he had crawled through the earth, out of his grave, just to speak to Josiah in his dreams. Josiah couldn't even remember the man's name.

Pearl was there, too. And Juan Carlos was standing on a hill alone, with storm clouds gathering behind him.

It was futile trying to stay asleep, so Josiah sat up in the bunk, wiping the night away, taking a deep breath, trying as hard as he could to see his mother again in his mind's eye. There was no use in that, either. He couldn't hang on to the image of his mother, her eyes open, life in them, words coming out of her mouth. All he could remember about her now was seeing her lying in the coffin he'd built with his own hands.

He didn't try to apply any meaning to dreams, and for a moment, now that he was awake, he had to get his bearings and remember where he was and why.

First thing he did after putting his feet on the ground and seeing Scrap still sleeping away in the other bunk, was go out and check on Juan Carlos.

It didn't look like Juan Carlos had moved from the last time Josiah had seen him. The Mexican was asleep, or so Josiah assumed, a blanket up to his neck.

Luke was sitting behind a desk in the office section of the jail, and the smell of coffee permeated the room. A pot sat on top of a Franklin stove in the corner.

"There's coffee there for you, Ranger

Wolfe," Luke said.

Josiah was standing at the cell door, looking in at his friend. "Thanks," he said.

"Sheriff'll be in in a little while."

"I imagine we'll be gone by then."

"Headin' out to the fort?"

Josiah nodded yes. "I think we are."

"Your friend ain't goin' anywheres soon," Roy said. "Doc worked on him hard, told me to keep his lips wet with whiskey all night. Ain't heard a peep out of the fella, though. He's a tough one."

"That he is. A good friend, too."

"He and my grandpa go back a long ways. Used to come through town ever once in a while with another Ranger, a short little wiry man who was always up for a game of faro down at the saloon."

"That'd be Captain Fikes," Josiah said. "He was killed last spring."

"Heard about that. Glad they hanged the man that did it."

"Me, too."

Josiah poured himself a cup of coffee and offered the pot to Luke.

"No, thanks, I don't touch that stuff. Never acquired the taste for it or tobacco."

"I like a cup of coffee now and again, myself." Josiah took a sip. "For not drinking

393

it, you sure know how to make a good pot of it."

"Sheriff gets cranky if it's too thick. I learn quick."

Josiah exhaled. He was glad Juan Carlos was still alive, but knew he and Scrap needed to get moving on, so he turned and started to walk back to the cell he'd spent the night in.

"You gonna meet up with those other Rangers?" Roy asked.

Josiah stopped in his tracks and turned around. "What other Rangers?"

"About ten of them rode in yesterday afternoon, 'bout three or four hours before Juan Carlos came through the door."

"They stopped here?" Josiah asked. He could feel his entire body tensing up.

"Nope, rode right on by."

"Why didn't you tell me this before now?"

"I figured you knew. Rangers bein' Rangers and all."

"Did you get a good look at them, know who was leading them?"

"Sure did. A man I never saw before. He had a big ugly scar on his forehead and a hard, angry look in his eyes."

"I was afraid you were going to say that," Josiah said.

CHAPTER 39

The gate to Fort Clark stood wide open. As Josiah and Scrap strode through on their respective horses, it looked to Josiah like most all of the buildings had risen up out of the limestone ground and shaped themselves accordingly, with windows and fancy wood doors.

The buildings were the same sandy yellowish color as the ground, and there was hardly a tree or stretch of green vegetation to be seen inside the fort.

A mockingbird sat on the nearest rooftop, spouting a mixture of hawk calls and bluebird and sparrow songs.

"Used to have one of them birds that lived in a scrub tree next to our house when I was a young'un," Scrap said. "Drove me crazy then, but I kind of like listenin' to 'em, now. They remind me of home."

"That can't be all bad then," Josiah answered, his eyes searching for familiar signs in the fort. Being on army ground provoked old memories for him, too, but he was not as fond of his military memories as Scrap was of his bird memories.

Josiah eased Clipper to a slow trot and pointed the horse toward the open door of a building that Josiah was almost sure held the duty sergeant. Scrap followed right alongside him, not questioning him at all. It was still morning, the drills over, and the fort was relatively quiet. A few men looked up as Josiah and Scrap entered, but the men didn't seem the least bit concerned about their presence. Fort Clark was a long way from the troubles with the Comanche and Kiowa up north at the Red River. Still, Josiah found the openness of the fort a little curious.

"Bad thing is," Scrap said, "you can't never go home when it ain't there no more, but you know how that goes."

"I do," Josiah said, bringing Clipper to a stop in front of another clean, recently constructed limestone building. "Wherever Lyle is, is home for me now."

Scrap smirked. "Last I heard he was down in Little Mexico forgettin' how to speak English."

"He's safe there," Josiah said, his voice hard and void of any emotion.

The mockingbird fluttered off, the white on its wings flapping like thin rags spiraling off in the wind.

"Stay here," Josiah said as he tied Clipper to the hitching post. "If you speak to anyone, make sure and say 'yes, sir' and 'no, sir.'"

"I ain't no child, Wolfe."

"You're no soldier either. This is their world. Respect it."

Scrap scrunched up his mouth and fought back saying the first thing that came to mind. "Yes, sir."

Josiah shook his head and walked inside the building.

The duty sergeant, a middle-aged man with thick black hair, a fair complexion, and a hairless face, looked up from some serious writing. There were scads of papers scattered all across the desk.

"What can I do for you?" There was a lilt to the man's voice, Irish or Scot, Josiah wasn't sure which.

"I'm looking for a man named Dixie Jim."

The sergeant set down the pen he was writing with and looked at Josiah curiously, cocking a thick black eyebrow. "Dixie Jim, you say? You're sure about that?"

"I am," Josiah said.

"Well then, ya might find him out there

cleanin' the stables. He's a horseman when he shows up. Likes to take more than a nip now and again. Can't blame a man for that. Especially one like Dixie Jim."

Josiah shrugged. "Don't know the man myself."

"Well, don't say I didn't tell you so, but 'tisn't too reliable."

"Thanks, I'll keep that in mind," Josiah said. He turned to go, but hesitated, then turned back. "There hasn't been a troop of Rangers come through here in the last day or two, has there?"

Josiah had yet to figure out what Feders was doing in this part of the country — Roy's description of a captain with a well-defined scar had to be Pete.

It was entirely possible that the company was involved in McNelly's plan to stop Cortina and O'Reilly, but something just didn't feel right. Especially with Juan Carlos getting shot and taken out of the picture. Surely the two things couldn't be linked, but they sure seemed to be . . . somehow. The presence of the Ranger company helped explain why Juan Carlos had brought them to Brackett. He had to know he was on Feders's tail. Josiah found it interesting that Feders was on O'Reilly's tail, unless he had been sent by Major Jones to make sure the union with Cortina could never be formally bound. But why would Jones send another company, when McNelly wanted the small troop — Josiah, Scrap, and Juan Carlos — to act in secret? Unless there was more that Juan Carlos was unable to tell him.

The sergeant shook his head no to Josiah's question about Feders's company. "Not that I can say. I haven't seen any Rangers come through, but I was off duty for a few days, spent a little time in Brackett blowin' off a wee bit of stream, myself, if you know what I mean."

Josiah smiled. "I know what you mean. Thanks."

The answer didn't help him relax and didn't clear anything up. At the very least, he would have thought that Feders would have stopped at the fort to resupply the boys, get them freshened up for the ride to Laredo — if that's where they were heading. But the fact there had been no sign of them added to the uncomfortable gnaw that was growing in Josiah's stomach and didn't promise to go away anytime soon.

The stable was easy to find, it was down the road about a hundred yards, on the opposite side from the duty sergeant's office.

"Wait here," Josiah said to Scrap as he slid

off the saddle and planted his feet solidly on the ground.

"Why do I always have to wait?"

Josiah didn't answer Scrap, he just plodded off inside the stable, a large wood-frame barn capable of holding at least a hundred horses. Just inside, he stopped to look around, to see if there was anyone moving about. There was a new smell to some of the wood, but the rafters were full of swallow's nests made of mud, empty now since winter was coming on. For the most part, the barn looked empty, until he heard a loud snore rumble out of one of the tack rooms.

He went to investigate and found a Negro settled in the corner, lying on a bed of straw, sleeping away even though it was nearing noon.

"Excuse me," Josiah said, standing at the door.

The man continued to snore.

Josiah walked into the room and kicked the man's boot. "Excuse me, are you Dixie Jim?" He asked louder this time.

The man roused, rolled off his side, opened his eyes, then sprang up, reaching for his gun — which wasn't there since he didn't have a gun belt on. It was only then that Josiah noticed that he only had one foot. A crutch was propped up in the corner.

"Whoa," Josiah said, throwing up both hands like he was getting held up. "I don't mean you any harm. Juan Carlos sent me."

The man was about half a head shorter than Josiah and maybe ten years older, it was hard to tell, but there was white starting to mix in his wavy black hair. His skin was ten times darker than any Mexican Josiah had ever seen, and he assumed the man was one of the Negro-Seminole scouts that worked out of Fort Clark. His face, with a bold straight nose and blue eyes, was more Indian than Negro. The clothes the man wore were little more than rags. It looked like he had lost his foot just above the ankle, and his pant leg was tied in a knot, just barely raking the ground when he moved.

"Are you Dixie Jim?" Josiah asked, again.

The man nodded, realizing that he didn't have a gun. He slapped his hand to his side, gave Josiah a snarl, then hopped over to get his crutch. "I am. What you want? Ain't you got no manners seeing a man sleeping, you leave him alone?"

The room smelled like Josiah had walked inside a whiskey barrel. "Sorry about that, I'm in a bit of a hurry."

"You say Juan Carlos sent you? You a

friend?"

"I am. We're on a mission for Captain Mc-Nelly."

"Don't know no McNelly. Where's Juan Carlos?"

"He was shot in town. When we left him, he wasn't doing so good, couldn't continue on with us. The last words he spoke to me were about you. I'm hoping you can help me."

The crutch securely under his arm, Dixie Jim stared at Josiah with focused uncertainty. "Was supposed to be waiting for Juan Carlos. Got tired of waiting, I did. You a drinkin' man? What's your name?"

"Josiah. Josiah Wolfe."

Dixie Jim nodded, recognition lighting his eyes, and said, "Ah, you want me to help you track that Badger, that's what they call him, eh? Liam O'Reilly. I'm no killer, are you?"

"I am if I have to be."

CHAPTER 40

With the horses refreshed and the saddle-bags restocked for another two-hundred-mile journey, Josiah, Scrap, and Dixie Jim made their way out of Fort Clark near evening.

The sun was setting off to the west, the sky promising to be clear of clouds or weather. Unlike the first morning out of Austin, there were no hints of red, no warnings that they were going to be traveling in any kind of inhospitable weather. Just the opposite, in fact. The world seemed quiet and comfortable, ready for night to fall and allow a bit of rest to those whose work was done for the day.

Josiah understood the need to ride at night, but he wasn't crazy about the idea. If Juan Carlos had been leading the way, that would have been different, but he wasn't.

There was no way to know whether the Mexican was alive or dead, and Josiah hadn't worked up enough trust in Dixie Jim to wholly go along with the plan without some silent reservations — which he'd keep to himself for a while, watching the ground and the trail as closely as he could, employing his own tracking skills, such as they were.

They made their way along Las Moras Creek at a steady pace, and not long into the ride they passed a barren tree with about a hundred or so vultures that had come in to roost for the night. The sky was gray, and the tree was an old sycamore with white, peeling bark that made it look half-dead, or like bones sticking up high out of the soft, swampy ground.

The big black birds didn't make a sound, nor did they seem the least bit disturbed by the travelers' presence — they just watched the trio pass by, a few of the redheaded vultures bobbing their heads and blasting the ground with splats of white liquid excrement, flapping their six-foot wings casually.

"Nasty old birds, those buzzards. Friends on the wind, and food at night if you're hungry enough," Dixie Jim said. "Rather burn that meat so it don't stink so bad on my tongue."

"Good to know," Josiah said.

He'd made a deal with Dixie Jim, promising to carry three bottles of whiskey and dole it out in bits at a time — after they made camp. In return, the scout promised to get them where they needed to go, by the safest, fastest way possible, and that meant a lot of traveling at night. Josiah had to do everything in his power to trust Dixie Jim, and withholding whiskey from the man was a good start. Scrap had to keep his mouth shut for two hundred miles. One task was going to be easier than the other.

Dixie Jim was in the lead, riding a small Indian paint mare and carrying very little with him. No rifle, his crutch instead stuffed into the scabbard. He only bore a gun on his hip, an old war model Colt with a little rust growing on the outside of the barrel. As far as Josiah was concerned, the gun was more for show than actual use.

Scrap brought up the rear, once again, with Josiah riding comfortably in the middle of the trio.

Josiah was glad to be on the trail, glad to be away from Brackett and the fort, but uncertain of how things were going to work out. If there was a larger plan that he had been unaware of when they set out from Austin, then the details had been left behind in the mind of Juan Carlos.

It was possible that Juan Carlos and Pete

Feders knew of each other's presence and movement toward Laredo to put an end to Liam O'Reilly's freedom once and for all.

Feders had spent a lot of time riding with Captain Hiram Fikes, which, of course, meant he had spent a lot of time riding with Juan Carlos — who was never far from his half brother's side while he was alive.

Juan Carlos knew Pete Feders better, or knew more about him, than anybody, including Josiah himself — at least, as far as Josiah knew.

Regardless, Josiah was determined to use Dixie Jim's skills to ferret out Liam O'Reilly, then formulate a plan once they found him. It was not how Josiah liked to operate, but he was too far from home to turn back, and too close to Laredo not to finish the mission he'd been assigned by Captain Mc-Nelly, even though the charge itself had come through indirect channels.

If Feders was near, then they'd cross paths and go from there.

The Las Moras was in an easy mood since it was November. The water was still as a mirror, reflecting the first star of the evening as it appeared in the darkening eastern sky. Spring rains were long since a memory.

The creek still offered hope of a fish or two, if the need arose along the way — so that was an encouraging thought as far as Josiah was concerned. Chewing on jerky got old real fast.

"Keep it quiet, there, boys. Might be eyes on us even in the night. Apache or Kickapoo might mistake you for Lieutenant John Bullis or Colonel Mackenzie," Dixie Jim said. "They'd love nuttin' more than to rile the tribe with a scalp or two, regardless of us bein' army or not."

Josiah knew that Bullis was the commander of the scouts and knew the lieutenant was well respected by all of the Negro-Seminoles, but he had never met the man to personally know his character.

Mackenzie was a character in and of himself, since he had led raids into Mexico, punishing renegade Indians for the theft of cattle and other crimes they'd committed. Both men were reviled and hated by the Indians, and the shadows of their deeds fell over all white men, linking them with the rage that continued to fuel all of the tribes of Indians that were trying to hold on to the land in South Texas, and the Strip, as their own.

Scrap eased Missy up alongside Josiah so both of their horses were neck to neck, trotting along at an easy gait.

"Seems to me the only one of us that's

gonna alert the savages to our presence is that one there," Scrap said in a whisper.

"Heard that there, young one," Dixie Jim said. "You'd be best to carry a rifle and not a bout of foolishness with your tongue, sayin' things you know nothin' about. I may like the taste of whiskey, but this land speaks to me in ways you can never understand. The land owns me. You hear?"

"I don't hear nothin,' " Scrap said.

"That there is exactly my point."

With most of their traveling done at night, the following two days were spent resting in the shadows of canyons, sometimes in well-used caves that Dixie Jim seemed to know where to find in the places they were staying, like he knew in a town where a hotel was, without asking. Other times they camped under ledges of rock so high it would take the legs of a lizard to climb to the top. But they never camped out in the open, never burned a fire big enough to reveal their location.

Dixie Jim rarely slept, or if he did, he did so away from Josiah and Scrap. Once camp had been made, Dixie Jim would wander off, surprisingly silent with his one foot and crutch, urging both men to rest. He would be the watch, offering no break for himself, or a shift for Josiah and Scrap.

There had been no signs of any Lipan Apache, Feders and the nine other Rangers, or Liam O'Reilly. They had not seen or heard anyone, and the lack of confrontation was a relief to Josiah, but he was starting to question his trust in Dixie Jim. They could be anywhere as far as Josiah knew — riding in circles in the middle of nowhere. All of the wild longhorns, circling buzzards, and hawks looked the same to him.

It was late in the afternoon, and rest had come, though fitfully, for Josiah. They were safe from the beaming sun in one of the caves that Dixie Jim knew, a hole in the wall of a thousand-foot mountain. It was cool inside and light enough to see your own two feet, the ground nothing but soft red dirt, the air dry and still. There was no depth to the cave, no long tunnel deep into the ground or the mountain. It was a wide open mouth of rock that bore no life other than an insect here or there, waiting in the shadows for the Rangers to drop a crumb of food.

Josiah was heating the coffeepot. Scrap had wandered outside to get a breath of fresh air and relieve himself. He had a frustrated look on his face when he returned to the cave.

"I'm gettin' tired of waitin' around for that half-breed," Scrap said. "Ain't nothin' like it was with Red Overmeyer out and about."

The mention of Red stopped Josiah, almost caused his heart to skip a beat. He still felt responsible for the man's death.

Josiah looked up at Scrap, offered him a cup of Arbuckle's. "Did Feders ever mention to you that he doubted Red Overmeyer's allegiance to the Rangers?"

"What do you mean allegiance?"

"Feders seemed to think that Red was more loyal to Indians than us, that he had a deal with those two Comanche that we encountered up at the San Saba."

"That's the silliest thing I ever heard. Red Overmeyer was a Ranger through and through," Scrap said.

"That's what I thought, but Feders made a solid case for it before we left Austin. Said he thought Overmeyer had a deal with the Comanche so they knew we were coming that way. He thought Overmeyer was a spy for Indians or O'Reilly."

"If Feders was here right now, I'd punch him in the nose for sayin' such a thing. That's not the kind of thing you can say about a man who ain't around to defend his own self."

"He thought Overmeyer was going to split the bounty on my head with the Comanche, but they decided to keep the money for themselves. Which was why they killed him and not you."

"I guess that makes sense, if Red was that type of fella. Didn't even gamble or bet a horse when me and the boys ran 'em up at the camp. Funny thing is, Wolfe, Feders and the boys knew where to find me. Do you think that's just a lucky find, or is there somethin' more to it?"

"I'm starting to think it was more than luck, too. I wondered how Feders knew to find me in Comanche. Rode in just at the right time. And now it sure seems odd that Feders was close by when Juan Carlos was shot, then disappeared south. I didn't even know he was supposed to be involved in this plan of McNelly's. Juan Carlos was tight-lipped about it all. It's almost like he knew everything that was going to happen before it did, and that doesn't make a lot of sense." Josiah said.

Scrap started to say something, then did not allow a word to escape from his lips — which was unusual for him.

Josiah nodded. "Unless Pete Feders was in on all of this for some reason."

"That'd be a surprise."

"It would be a crime worse than any I could imagine, working with that scoundrel, O'Reilly. For what?"

Scrap took a drink of his coffee, looking over the rim of the cup. "You and Feders have always been doin' a hat dance around each other, and the captain's daughter is right in the middle of it all."

Josiah stood straight up, his body tense and tight at the mention of Pearl. "You leave Pearl out of this."

"I'm just sayin' maybe Pete Feders was trying to shift the blame on Red Overmeyer for a reason."

"And what reason would that be?"

"To take the attention off himself," Scrap said. "Maybe he's the spy for O'Reilly — or Cortina. Maybe he wants you to be taken in a bad light. Or dead and out of the way."

Josiah took a deep breath and relaxed. He was surprised that Scrap had said aloud what he had been thinking, what Juan Carlos had warned him of.

He knew that Feders had a reason to get Josiah out of Austin, out of Pearl's life. Even more so now that he and Pearl had spent the night in the barn together. Pearl would never agree to marry Pete Feders. Feders didn't know about Josiah's tryst with Pearl as far as Josiah knew, but maybe he suspected it would happen. Pearl had always been less than secretive about her feelings for Josiah — she showed her desire in plain sight of everyone.

Before Josiah could say anything to Scrap, Dixie Jim hobbled into the cave, sweat glistening from his deep brown brow, his eyes wide open and white with the exception of a fully engaged blue pupil. "Set me a nip of whiskey there, Wolfe. I found a fresh trail."

"You found the company of Rangers?" Josiah asked.

Dixie Jim nodded yes. "They broke off about three miles from here and headed south."

"Broke off from what?" Scrap asked.

"Two horses, heading west."

Josiah sighed deeply, walked over to his saddlebag that he'd taken into the cave, dug out Dixie Jim's bottle of whiskey, and handed it to the scout. "Just one nip, and then we head west."

CHAPTER 41

Dixie Jim proved to be a wise scout, though nearly any man could have found the horse tracks leading due west, since there didn't look to have been any effort made by the riders to hide them. The question remained who the tracks belonged to, but according to Dixie Jim, who was on his knees studying a new set of tracks in the soft, loamy dirt, they were gaining ground on the riders since they didn't seem to be in a hurry of any kind, not riding full out.

"Within an hour, we'll see their tails. Then we will know for sure," Dixie Jim said.

"Know what?" Josiah asked.

"Whether this is your Badger or not."

Scrap was sitting on Missy next to Josiah and Clipper. It was late afternoon, and the sun still burned in a wide, cloudless sky. It was as blue as Pearl's eyes, and Josiah continued to feel like they were all being watched, but he had nothing but gut instinct to prove his feeling. The land all around was desolate and quiet. They had not seen a ranch house, a longhorn, or any animal or human for that matter since Dixie Jim had found the tracks and they'd headed due west. Could have been Apache or Kickapoo scouting them out, or one of O'Reilly's men, keeping an eye on them. Either way, Josiah would have bet his life that *somebody* was staring straight into the back of his neck.

Scrap cleared his throat and scowled at Dixie Jim. "If those tracks do belong to O'Reilly, then why ain't he tryin' to hide himself?"

Dixie Jim stood up. "Seems to me he don't think he has anything to be worried about since Juan Carlos was shot in Brackett. If he knows you fellas, then he knows you ain't no trackers."

"Makes sense," Josiah said.

Scrap continued to scowl. "I can track."

"Sure you can, boy," Dixie Jim said.

Josiah ignored both men. A couple of vultures circled the sky just to the south of them, silently riding the air, not flapping a wing. "You might be right," he said to Dixie Jim, staring at the vultures.

"Am right." Dixie Jim walked to his horse, slid his crutch into the scabbard, then mounted the paint with a hop and a pull, all in one fluid motion. "What you gonna do when you find them two men? You got a plan?" he asked Josiah.

Josiah stared at Dixie Jim, then glanced over to Scrap. "Elliot here is probably one of the best long shots I know. He can hold the high sight, stay back. We can get closer, circle around them, confront them if there's an opportunity, give O'Reilly a chance to come in easy."

"We?" Dixie Jim laughed.

Josiah nodded.

"Not gonna be a we. I find them. That's all I agreed to do," Dixie Jim said. "Just gonna be you and the boy when it comes to that duty. Juan Carlos is a friend, and I owed him a favor, but no sirree, I sure don't owe him my life. If he was here, I'd be gone now. But as it is, once we sight those two and make sure they's the men you be lookin' for, then I'm back off to Fort Clark."

"I have your whiskey," Josiah said.

"I have my own."

Scrap pushed Missy past Josiah. "Told you there wasn't no trustin' a half-breed, Wolfe. Looks like it's just me and you. We can head back if you want, try and get the rest of the boys to help us take these two in."

"We're not going back," Josiah said, urging Clipper on, catching sight of the tracks Dixie Jim was looking at, and taking the lead.

Night was about to fall before Josiah caught the first sight of the two riders. The sun had already dropped below the horizon, but gray daylight still reached up from beyond the curve of the earth. Pinks and reds pulsated on the underside of a few wispy clouds in the sky, drops of fading blood on a growing black curtain. Nary a star dared show itself yet as the day fought its last battle with the overpowering pull of darkness and the coming of night.

It was almost like the colors of the clouds had reached down and touched the head of one of the riders — it glowed red, without a hat. There was no question the man was Liam O'Reilly. But the other rider's identity was not so easy to discern from the distance they were at, and neither Josiah nor Scrap had possession of a sighting scope. For a moment, Josiah thought he recognized the second rider's horse, a tall black stallion, but he was too far away to see any of the markings, so he turned to ask Dixie Jim, who had been riding behind the two men, to see if he had a scope, and discovered that the Negro-Seminole had left their company without saying a word.

"I'll be . . ." Josiah said.

"What?" Scrap asked, looking over his shoulder.

"Dixie Jim's gone."

"Well, it ain't no big surprise to me."

"He could've said something," Josiah said.

"He did. Said as soon as we caught sight of O'Reilly he was out of here. What more you need, Wolfe, a big good-bye?"

Josiah shook his head no. "Just thought he'd be more friendly after spending a few days with us."

"Speakin' for myself, I'm glad to be rid of him. He smelt like he was carryin' a dead fish in his pockets. You notice that?"

Josiah wasn't paying attention to Scrap. The light on the horizon was nearly gone, and the bottoms of the clouds were losing their color so they were almost black. "Damn it," he said. "I've lost sight of them."

They eased their horses next to a large reach of limestone about a hundred feet tall. Might have been taller, but now that night had fallen completely, it was hard to tell exactly how high the rocks and mountains around them really were.

Josiah felt a little out of his element, not knowing the ways of the land this far southwest. He was a long way from the piney woods of Tyler, out among the prickly pear, mesquite, and a host of unknown creatures. Especially at night.

Luckily, the wispy clouds of the evening had pushed on, and the sky was full of pin-prick stars, tiny silver orbs twinkling overhead. Half of the moon was hidden. It would be another week or two before it would show itself completely. Still, even with half of its brightness, there was light to navigate by and plenty of moon shadows to be leery of.

Both men dismounted as quietly as possible. They couldn't see a fire, but Josiah could smell it, and he was sure Scrap could, too. O'Reilly and the other rider were close. Hidden, but close.

There was nothing to hear, no crackle of a fire or voices on the wind. Even far-off coyotes, yipping only minutes before, had gone silent.

"We need to stick together," Josiah whispered to Scrap. He put his index finger to his lips.

Scrap nodded and motioned for Josiah to take the lead. Both men had their six-shooter in one hand and their rifle in the other. As Scrap passed by Missy, he rubbed her rump quickly and gave her an open-handed tap. There were few times Josiah had witnessed Scrap showing the horse affection, but the boy cared deeply about his horse and was always nervous about leaving her behind — especially since his capture by Big Shirt and Little Shirt.

Josiah smiled briefly at this demonstration, then carefully made his way forward, edging along a tall stone face that still held heat from the day.

This was not how he had hoped to come upon O'Reilly, but there was no choice now but to follow the scent of the fire and surprise the two men. Good thing was, Josiah had seen them both from far enough away to know they were riding alone — most likely, considering the direction, heading to Mexico to make contact with Cortina. That, of course, was all supposition on Josiah's part, but he couldn't figure out anything else, or know the whys and hows of what was going on. All he knew was that he intended to put a stop to O'Reilly once and for all. So he would be safe. So Lyle would be safe. So Pearl would be safe.

He had tried to think little of Pearl since he'd left Austin, but every time he closed his eyes, she was fully in his mind's eye, begging him to come back home.

It was a nice feeling to have, a welcome

development over the pull of loneliness and grief that he had held tight for so long after Lily and his three little girls had died. It was far too soon to make too much out of his intimate moment with Pearl . . . but Josiah wanted nothing more than to complete his assignment and personal mission so he could return home to those he cared about.

The rock curved, and Josiah edged along slowly, a tiny glimmer of firelight reflecting off the side of the mountain. He stopped and took a deep breath, then looked over his shoulder and nodded to Scrap, indicating that they were on the right trail.

O'Reilly's camp was just ahead, he was certain of it.

Rounds chambered, guns at the ready, Josiah's heart remained steady. He held no fear, did not sweat . . . until he heard the pull of a hammer and a familiar Irish voice.

"Move one more step, Wolfe, and I'll blow your head clean off."

CHAPTER 42

Everything stopped. There was no wind, no animal sounds, nothing but silence and a beating heart. O'Reilly's voice came from directly in front of Josiah, but he couldn't see a thing, not a shadow, not an outline of a man, nothing but the black of night.

"You, too, there, Elliot. Both of you drop your guns to the ground," O'Reilly yelled out. He was close, a couple of feet away, between a tall boulder and the campfire, hidden so well it was almost like he was invisible.

Josiah knew there were two men, but didn't know who the other man was or where he was. Could be with O'Reilly or behind them. It didn't matter. All Josiah knew was he wasn't about to be captured again, was not going to leave his fate in luck's hand, or the Irishman's either, for that matter.

"I'm not foolin' around with either of

you," O'Reilly said.

"You might as well shoot me now, O'Reilly. If I'm a dead man, I'd just as soon get it over with," Josiah answered. He felt around with his boot and touched a small rock. He kicked it toward O'Reilly's voice, hoping to create a distraction, bouncing it off a boulder, then dropping his body to the ground as quickly and in as swift a motion as he could. He hoped Scrap had the sense to do the same thing, or something else to save himself.

O'Reilly fired into the darkness, the flash exposing his position, missing Josiah by several feet.

The shot had come from a steep buttress of rock. O'Reilly must have been hiding about ten feet up, on a slight ridge, just off the path Josiah and Scrap were sneaking along, toward the campfire. The shot ricocheted off a tight collection of rocks, sending sparks sizzling in every direction.

Josiah rolled on the ground, came to a stop in a prone position against a boulder, and fired back in O'Reilly's direction.

The first shot had been directed at Josiah, giving Scrap time to dive into the darkness. Josiah heard him move, saw his silhouette disappearing, was tempted to ask if he was all right, but didn't have time — and didn't want to give away his position.

"You're a dead man, Wolfe," O'Reilly shouted.

Josiah answered back with a quick blast of three shots. One hit the buttress on the edge, sparking slightly. The other two shots disappeared into the darkness.

"I'm not dead yet," Josiah said.

A flurry of shots erupted from behind Josiah, the percussion loud and deafening.

"Neither am I," Scrap yelled out.

For a moment, no one said anything. A cloud of gun smoke wafted past Josiah, and he sighed silently, relieved and glad that Scrap was all right.

Josiah knew there was another man out there somewhere, knew he was still exposed, but hoped like hell Scrap had his back covered. There didn't seem to be a way to ease closer to O'Reilly without putting himself more out in the open.

"You should have stayed in Austin, Wolfe," O'Reilly said, the lilt in his voice measured with anger.

Josiah fired a round. Hit the rock. "I'd rather be where I am right now."

"If you were a better shot, I would have never made it out of Comanche alive."

"I got what mattered. I'm sure that bank's got a bounty out on your head and a rope waiting for you for killing the sheriff."

"Wasn't much of a sheriff, was he?"

"Should have sent you packing with that kin of Hardin's."

"More to be made runnin' a town than robbin' a bank, Wolfe. That's always the last bit of business before movin' on. You ought to know that."

"You're stopped now. And you haven't reached Cortina yet. One of us isn't getting out of here alive. That's all I care about."

O'Reilly shot back, the repercussion echoing off into the night, the bullet about a foot off from the imaginary target on the center of Josiah's forehead. "You don't know what I've reached, Wolfe."

Scrap jumped up, pumped a full load of six shots in O'Reilly's direction. "You've reached the end of the road. That's what you've reached!"

O'Reilly fired back, and the shadow that was Scrap jumped back into the darkness just in time.

A second later, a pebble pinged Josiah in the leg. He looked over his shoulder. He could barely see Scrap, who was motioning his head in the opposite direction, then pointing his finger up. He was obviously willing to take a chance and wanted to circle around to the other side of the rock, find a

425

way at O'Reilly that the outlaw wasn't expecting. Josiah nodded his head yes.

"That boy's gonna be your death, Wolfe. You need to find a better riding partner."

"I'm tired of your threats, O'Reilly. The bounty on my head is up, for what good it did you."

"I gave you too much credit, Wolfe."

"Did you have a deal with Red Overmeyer? Was he a traitor?"

"Overmeyer? That Indian-lovin' scout?" O'Reilly laughed, then took another shot at Josiah. "I don't know anything about a deal. You'll have to ask those Comanche about that."

"One of them is dead, and the other is on display in the Austin Opera House, last I heard."

Josiah didn't know whether to believe O'Reilly or not about Overmeyer. He just wanted to keep the man talking, distract him, to give Scrap a chance to find his way to a better shot.

"If you've already made a deal with Cortina, what are you doing out here, heading west?" Josiah asked.

"You ask a lot of fool questions, Wolfe. Charlie Langdon should have killed you when he had the chance."

"Is that what this is about? Langdon? He

426

met the rope. You can expect the same thing."

"Ain't never gonna happen. But I owe a mite of respect to ole Charlie."

"Respect or revenge?"

"Call it what you want."

They exchanged another volley of gunshots, both missing, at least as far as Josiah knew. He pulled back against the rock and reloaded the Colt Frontier, then looked to the sky overhead and took a deep breath. There was no way to know where Scrap was or if there was even a way to get close enough to O'Reilly for a decent shot, but Scrap would find it if there was.

Back up, ready to take another shot, Josiah took a breath, tried to sight in anything out of the ordinary, tried to see a shot that would put an end to O'Reilly and free Josiah of any worry about that threat to his life in Austin.

There was nothing to see, no hope of getting the shot, until he heard another voice — the second man riding with O'Reilly, he presumed — yell out and say, "Give it up, O'Reilly, they've got you cornered."

Josiah knew the voice. It was Pete Feders's.

Scrap walked into the firelight, pushing Liam O'Reilly in the back of the head with

427

his rifle.

Pete Feders stood on the opposite side of the dwindling fire, unwrapping a heavy rope with his right hand. "Good thing you boys came along when you did, or I would have been a dead man."

O'Reilly spit. "You are a dead man, Feders. He's your traitor, Wolfe. Not that damned scout."

Josiah was standing next to Feders, uncertain about trusting the man.

Pete looked like he'd been held captive and had maybe just broken free as O'Reilly spied Josiah and Scrap coming along. Feders wasn't wearing his gun belt, and his hands and feet had obviously been bound. There was a gun belt hanging over the saddle of the black stallion that Mrs. Fikes had given Pete, the gun still in its holster.

Feders unwrapped the last of the rope from his ankles, tossed it off into the darkness, and walked over to his horse.

"He's lying," Feders said, grabbing the gun belt off the saddle.

"Why in the hell would I lie?" O'Reilly yelled. "You and I —"

The Irishman didn't have time to finish the sentence. Pete Feders pulled out a gun, a very familiar Peacemaker, from the holster hanging over the saddle, and fired one shot, hitting O'Reilly square in the solar plexus. Another rapid shot caught the man in the shoulder, sending him reeling backward, knocking Scrap off balance.

Feders fired one last shot to finish off O'Reilly, shooting him in the throat, right above his Adam's apple, before the Irishman collapsed to the ground with a solid and unmoving thud.

Scrap continued to stumble backwards. "What in tarnation?"

Pete Feders turned to face Josiah, pointing the gun directly at his heart. But Feders had not counted on Josiah being fast enough to pull his own gun, Charlie Webb's Colt Frontier.

"You better explain what's going on, Pete, or you're going to die right along with your friend here. You shoot me, Elliot's got a bead on your head, and you know he won't miss."

Feders's hand trembled. The scar above his eye twitched, and sweat ran down his face, cutting through the trail dust like a mud puddle lining out its way after a quick spring storm. "How'd you know?"

"O'Reilly gave up way too easy. I've been in a cat-and-mouse game with him more than once, and he's no quitter. Coming in, on your suggestion, didn't seem like enough unless you got some power over him. If that's the case, then I had to wonder who was really in charge. O'Reilly was always a follower, but I never figured you'd be the one he would let tell him what to do. You've been giving O'Reilly the orders all along. Sound about right?"

"Something like that," Feders said, still holding the gun on Josiah.

"You step in after Charlie met the rope, Pete? I figured O'Reilly filled that role, but I was wrong. I just don't know why a man would throw away everything good he's done with his life to saddle up next to a lowlife scoundrel like O'Reilly."

"You've got no right to know," Feders said.

"He moves an inch, Scrap, you shoot him without asking, you understand?"

Scrap nodded his head, biting his lip all the while, an astonished look on his face, as he was starting to figure out what was going on.

"You set Overmeyer up, didn't you? He must have figured out somehow that you were giving orders to O'Reilly. So you sent him out to make a deal with those Comanche, and they killed him to keep his mouth shut, on your orders. That's why they left Scrap. He was innocent of your plan. Knew nothing about it. That was honorable of you."

"If you say so."

"That's my gun, Pete. Why are you carrying it?"

"I took it off the Comanche you killed. I thought you might want it back."

"You had a chance to give it to me in Austin. More like a trophy, isn't it? Proof when you go back that I'm really dead?"

"Maybe."

"Why, Pete? After all of these years, why?"

"You know why."

Josiah exhaled deeply. "Pearl."

Feders nodded yes.

"You need my gun to prove to her mother that I'm really dead and out of the way."

"Major Jones will need proof," Feders said. "Pearl's mother has nothing to do with this."

"I don't believe you."

"Doesn't matter. You have no proof of anything. I am doing what I'm doing for love, nothing more."

Josiah tensed up, glanced over at Scrap out of the corner of his eye to make sure he still had Feders in his sights. He did. The boy hadn't moved a muscle.

"For the love of money," Josiah said.

"It's all the same." Another bead of sweat

cut a rivulet through the dirt on Feders's face. He flinched.

Josiah pressed the trigger of the Colt just a little harder, just to the edge of pulling it.

"No," Josiah said, "it's not."

Pete Feders blinked, swallowed hard, and his left hand twitched. Josiah pulled the trigger before he did.

The bullet caught Pete Feders solidly in the chest. Blood exploded outward onto Josiah as the Peacemaker flew out of Feders's hand. He fell to the ground in a heap.

Josiah stumbled, then regained his footing, shocked at what he had done, certain that Pete Feders had been going to pull the trigger and shoot him.

But even now, seconds afterward, Josiah was already questioning himself, whether he had just killed a man he'd known for a long time over simple jealousy. He had no answer . . . but knew the question was not going away anytime soon.

Feders groaned and rolled on his side, curling up in a fetal position, grabbing the wound. The gun was well out of his reach.

"Damn, Wolfe," Scrap said.

Josiah shot Scrap a look that was not hard to mistake: it meant keep quiet.

"I was never going to have her as long as you were alive, Wolfe," Feders whispered.

"Why O'Reilly?"

"I needed him to help me grow the herd once I had the Fikes ranch. I needed to prove to Pearl's mother I was worthy, that I had the kind of money Pearl was accustomed to — without money I would never have her as my own, as my wife. The old woman needs money, Wolfe; the financial collapse and Captain Fikes's death have left her nearly penniless. Her way of life is at stake, and the only true asset she has left is Pearl; she has mortgaged the estate to the hilt, with little means to pay her debt. I was willing to do anything to have Pearl, to have that land, and the life I have always dreamed of. I was never good at being a captain, you know that.

"I needed the bank money from Comanche to give to Cortina as a down payment for a large herd, and that was the fastest way to get it. I gave O'Reilly a generous cut, and he knew as long as he was riding with me that he would always be protected by Rangers. He was free to do whatever he wanted, and I didn't have to do the dirty work. I am no Charlie Langdon. Surely, you understand that I wanted nothing more than Pearl's love in the end?"

Josiah shook his head no. He didn't understand that kind of love and greed. All he knew was the difference between right and wrong, and the whole thing concerning Pete was . . . wrong. It didn't make any sense to him. "Did Pearl's mother put the bounty on my head to get me out of the way?"

"She's desperate, Wolfe, but she's not a murderer, though I often thought it would be easier to kill her than you. You have a talent for staying alive."

"You would have killed me for Pearl? Left my boy an orphan?" Anger was coursing through Josiah's veins upon hearing the cold truth.

Feders tried to answer, but he didn't have the energy. Blood was leaving his body quicker than it could clot. He struggled to breathe, then gasped, clutching his heart. His hand fell to the ground, his eyes fixed on the sky, and in the blink of an eye, Josiah knew that Captain Pete Feders was dead.

CHAPTER 43

The cold November rain pelted Josiah's face as he rode up to the grand Fikes house. It was late evening, darkness coming earlier and earlier in the day as winter bore down on Austin. Gloomy days lay ahead, and Josiah could already feel the change of weather deep in his bones.

He hitched Clipper to the post in front of the house and walked up to the door, his shoulders slouched, each step taken, heavy and unwilling, though there was no question that he had to do what he was about to.

The door opened before Josiah came to a stop and prepared to knock. Pedro was standing there, an expression on his face equal to those usually seen at a funeral or a wake: sad and reflective. "It is good to see you, Señor Wolfe."

"I'm not sure I believe you."

"The hour is late, and you were not

435

expected, so your presence is news to us, your survival a relief. The last we saw of you was at the dinner, then you were off on another assignment in South Texas. There is always worry when our Rangers take to the road. Captain Fikes came home dead in the back of a wagon. Why would we not expect the same to happen to you?"

"All of you are relieved?" Josiah asked, peering over Pedro's shoulder, wondering what the Mexican butler actually knew about the trip south.

The grand hall of the house was dimly lit, a few hurricane lamps burning low, casting soft shadows on the walls and ceiling. Down the hall, the dining room, where Pete Feders had asked Pearl to marry him publicly, stood in complete darkness. More out of function than in mourning, since, as far as Josiah knew, word of Pete Feders's demise had not yet reached Austin.

"I have just returned to the city," Josiah said.

"How is your son?"

"Fine, thank you, and not happy to see me leave again so soon after arriving home, but I need to speak with Pearl."

"Like I said, Señor Wolfe, it is late, can this not wait until tomorrow?"

Josiah shook his head no. "I have news for

436

her that I wish to tell her myself. Tomorrow will be too late."

Before Pedro could respond, Josiah heard a shuffle of footsteps coming down the grand staircase. Again, he looked past Pedro. Disappointment coursed through his veins as he quickly figured out that the person raised by the voices at the door was Pearl's mother, the Widow Fikes, and not Pearl herself. Josiah had been hoping to avoid a meeting with the widow.

"Who is it, Pedro, disturbing us at such a late hour?"

"It is Ranger Wolfe, ma'am."

"Wolfe?" The widow pushed by Pedro, who retreated quickly into the nearest alcove. "You, sir, are not welcome in this house. There, I have made it official. Now, please leave."

"I would like to speak with Pearl," Josiah said.

"Did you not just hear me ask you to leave?"

"I did. With all due respect, ma'am, I would like to speak with Pearl before I do so."

The widow was more than a head shorter than Josiah, so he had to angle his neck downward just to look her in the eye. She had obviously been preparing for bed, wrapped in a black robe, still mourning, still wearing her widow's weeds, of a fashion, to the very moment she crawled into bed. Her brittle gray hair was unfurled from a tight bun and fell over her shoulders, hanging down almost to the small of her back. Her skin was nearly pale white. She looked like a ghost herself, albeit a well-fed one.

"Your persistence is not appreciated here, Ranger Wolfe. I don't know what my husband ever saw in you, but I rue the day you stepped foot on this property, the day my daughter first laid eyes on you. You are a blight on my life. Do you understand that, sir? A blight."

Josiah restrained his tongue, pushed it to the roof of his mouth. He wanted to respond, to participate in the fight she was laying the ground for, but he did not take the bait. He had the advantage of seeing the shadows behind the woman, saw what was coming before she heard it.

"Mother! What an awful thing to say. Josiah does not deserve such vile treatment," Pearl said, descending from the final step, then hurrying to the door. She rushed past her mother, a smile on her face, the glow nearly lighting up the darkness of the night that lay beyond Josiah.

Pearl was wrapped up in nightclothes, too.

There was a fragrance about her that quickly infiltrated Josiah's nose. Cream of some kind, a freshness that smelled of spring and womanhood. He almost turned and ran away, but he didn't, he held firm. Seeing her took his breath away.

"Why are you here, Josiah, is something the matter?"

"I would like to speak to you, in private," Josiah said, his voice monotone, any emotions held as deep in his stomach as he could manage.

"There will be nothing done in private between you and my daughter, Ranger Wolfe. Do I make myself clear? If you have something to say, say it in front of me, as I will not leave you to a chaperone of any type," the Widow Fikes said.

Josiah drew in a deep breath, and Pearl glared at her mother harshly. Her sweet cornflower blue eyes were harder than he had ever seen them.

"I would like a moment alone with Josiah, Mother."

The Widow Fikes's feet were set as solidly as the rest of her body. Her face was frozen in a state that offered no hint of negotiation.

"I did not come here to cause an argument," Josiah said. "It is bad news that I bear, and your mother will hear it soon enough, too, Pearl. Maybe this way is best."

"Something has happened to Juan Carlos?" Pearl said. "Hasn't it?"

"That is part of it, yes."

The widow Fikes stood firm, her glare never breaking away from Josiah. Pedro stood close by in the shadows, close enough to hear everything.

"Juan Carlos was shot in Brackett," Josiah continued. "We were ambushed just outside of the sheriff's office there."

"He's dead?" Pearl gasped, tears welling in her eyes.

Josiah shook his head no. "He is still hanging on, recovering in the doctor's care in Brackett. He's too weak to be moved. It was a gut shot that he took. A lesser man would have died straightaway. Not lasted a day. But Juan Carlos has a strong will to live. I didn't want to leave there, alone, but I had to return to Austin immediately."

"That man is despicable," the widow sneered.

"Mother, that *man* is your husband's brother."

"So he says. I say he's a half-breed always on the lookout for a handout so he can go off with one of his whores and live like a lazy king."

"Mother, please," Pearl said through gritted teeth, then dabbed the corners of her eyes with a pure white handkerchief that she'd produced almost out of nowhere. "Good, I am glad he is still alive. Thank you for the news, Josiah."

"That is not why I have come here tonight, Pearl," Josiah said. "I don't know how to tell you this, but Pete Feders is dead."

"Dead?" Pearl whispered. "I wasn't expecting that."

"Peter is dead? Dead?" the Widow Fikes yelled. "I don't believe it. He can't be dead. How did he die?"

"I shot him, ma'am. I killed Pete Feders in self-defense."

Pearl's mother barreled past her, knocking Pearl out of the way, and stopped within inches of Josiah, pointing her finger at his face, waving it like a mad sword. "I meant what I said. You are not welcome here, ever, not now, not tomorrow, not ten years from now, do you understand me, Ranger Wolfe? I will make your life miserable. Your days as a Ranger are numbered. I know people. I know *important* people. You will be lucky to get a job as a stable boy in this town after I've had my say. Now leave. Get off my land."

Josiah did not move. He stood watching

the tears stream from Pearl's eyes. His own mouth was dry, and his feet were firmly planted, unwilling to move, even though he wanted them to. There was a chill in the air, and Josiah felt downright cold. He wanted to reach out and touch Pearl, offer her some comfort, but he dared not touch her.

"The papers will have the story tomorrow, Pearl. But I wanted you to hear it from me first." Josiah lowered his head. "I still must answer for what has happened. Major Jones, Captain McNelly, and the adjunct general, William Steele, are set to decide my fate. It is my word against a dead man's. Ranger Elliot is a witness, but whether they will take his account of what happened is still questionable."

"I said leave," the Widow Fikes demanded.

"Mother, for the last time, keep quiet. Let Josiah speak," Pearl snapped, her face hard and twisted with grief and danger now.

"Well!" The widow turned to walk away, the look on her face akin to having been slapped by Pearl. She stopped at the stairway, still within earshot, glaring and whimpering like a sullen pup at the same time.

"Tell me, Josiah, tell me what happened."

Josiah drew in a deep breath. He caught a glimpse of Pedro, who had not moved, and who was not showing any emotion other than surprise. "Pete was desperate to win your love, you know that?"

"I do," Pearl said, softly.

"He was also desperate for money. I do not know the hows, whens, or whys, but when the outlaw Charlie Langdon was hanged, Pete stepped in to fill the void. He took control and began accumulating money. He wanted enough to buy a large herd of cattle and have a pot of money to win your mother's favor and to pay her debts. From what Pete said, she, too, is desperate for money. He and Liam O'Reilly were forging a relationship with Juan Cortina, a cattle rustling scheme that would have made them very wealthy, very quickly. I was sent to stop that union. At the time, I only knew of O'Reilly's involvement. But I didn't know Pete was involved. Not then."

The Widow Fikes suddenly appeared at Pearl's side, almost like she had flown there. "You, sir, are a liar. Now, I will not ask you again. Pedro, have this man removed from the property. That's an order!"

"I'm sorry, Pearl," Josiah said, ignoring the widow. He was bound and determined for Pearl to hear the rest of his story. "Pete pulled his gun. I have never killed a man that I didn't have to. It was me or him."

Pedro stepped out of the alcove, his

443

shoulders squared and a rifle in his hand. "Señor Wolfe, please respect the madam's wishes and leave."

Josiah nodded, and he stared directly into Pearl's eyes and said, "I'm sorry," one more time, then turned and walked toward his waiting horse.

Just as he was about to climb up onto the saddle, Pearl rushed to Josiah and threw her arms around him, burying her tearstained face in his neck. "Don't you see, Josiah, we are free. This is not bad news," she said, in a soft voice so only he could hear her.

"No," he whispered. "We're not free, Pearl. I have only made things worse for you. Not only has a division been drawn between your mother and you, you now know the truth. Your entire way of life is at stake, and there's nothing I can do to help you." He pulled away, quickly kissed her on the forehead without lingering, then climbed up on Clipper as quick as he could.

Pearl trembled, the tears flowing heavily, as she crumpled to the ground in a pile of sobs. Pedro and her mother rushed to her as Josiah moved Clipper slowly away and headed down the path, urging the horse to go as fast as it could once he was certain that he wasn't going to flip dirt or mud on the trio, fighting the whole time not to look back, not to turn back, not to sweep Pearl up and ride off with her forever.

Ofelia sat on the porch, waiting, as Josiah hitched up Clipper. The moon had risen high in the sky, and there was not a cloud to be seen. A soft glow emanated from inside the small house, and the familiar smell of *menudo* wafted on the cool night air. There was a solemn look on the Mexican woman's face as Josiah made his way to her.

"It's good to be home," he said.

"For a short time, again, señor?" Ofelia asked. There was hardly ever a change in her appearance. She was the one constant in his life. Her clothes — a simple skirt, apron, and white blouse — were always the same, and no matter how many days passed, her face did not acquire wrinkles, and her hair did not seem to add any new gray strands. She was as ageless as a rock . . . at least to Josiah.

"I don't know what the future holds, Ofelia. Do you need more time away, now that your family is here?" Josiah stiffened, feeling a little unsure if Ofelia were going to leave — or wanted to. He wouldn't blame her. She had sacrificed so much for him, for so little in return. The guilt he felt about that was immeasurable.

Ofelia smiled. "*Usted está mi familia.* You are my family. You and Lyle. I do not know what the future holds, either. But I wish only happiness for you, señor."

"Happiness seems as far away as the moon," Josiah said, releasing a breath, relaxing.

"I see you happy when Miss Pearl is near."

Josiah shook his head and sat down next to Ofelia. "I am happy when I am here, with Lyle. And you, of course."

They both looked out onto the empty street. A train blew its whistle in the distance, and Josiah knew that before long, the house would rumble as the train pulled into town. He was not used to the sound and the shake of the house, but he got the impression that Ofelia and Lyle paid little mind to the comings and goings of the trains. They had adjusted to city life, while he had not, was not sure he ever would — or that he ever wanted to.

"Someday, Lyle needs a *mamacita,* and you need a soft place to fall into after you have exhausted yourself. This life you live will make you a hard man, señor, and that is not the true Josiah Wolfe that I know." Ofelia looked up at Josiah, a knowing look on her face. "Miss Lily would want you to love again. It is time, señor, to leave the past behind."

"I don't know what to think about that," Josiah said. "There's a storm coming."

"The sky is clear."

"Oh, trust me, it's coming."

The train blew its whistle again. This time, Josiah felt the first vibration under his feet, felt the shake of the earth grow stronger, closer, and he knew all he could do was sit there and wait.

EPILOGUE

The town of Comanche sat on the horizon. Josiah eased Clipper to a trot. Lady Mead followed closely behind, tied loosely with a rope.

It was a comfortable day, a bit cool as December came on, but nothing that would kill you if you slept out in it, like all of the stories he'd heard about up north. He hoped to go there someday, see deep snow and real winter for himself, but he had other things to do at the moment.

He carried Charlie Webb's clothes and Colt Frontier in the saddlebag, and he was wearing his own gun, the Colt Peacemaker, and carrying his own Winchester in the scabbard. Somehow, he'd managed to put himself back together.

The Webb house was just up the road a bit, and Josiah was glad to see a thin line of smoke snaking up out of the chimney.

It was dry, unlike the last time he'd been

at the house, nearly a month back, when the ground was soaked and muddy. A lot had happened since he'd sought refuge in Billie Webb's barn, endured a storm, and helped deliver her baby. He hoped it had been a happy month for Billie, though he knew it would be hard for her raising a baby on her own.

There was no hurry to Clipper's gait, and Josiah didn't push the horse. He took his time riding up to the house, more relaxed, especially after seeing the smoke, than he'd felt in a long time. He aimed to deliver the things Billie had given him to survive, say his thanks, see to it that she was in fine shape, then head back home to Austin.

The bright sun beamed down on the house, and it was nearing midday. Chickens clucked around the front of the house, and a cow grazed in the pasture, chewing a thick cud of grass. The place hadn't been worked much since Josiah was there last, but there were signs that some kind of order had returned.

Josiah rode up to the house, eased off Clipper, and tied the horse to a wobbly hitching post.

When he turned to head up to the door, Billie was standing on the stoop staring at him with a slight smile on her face.

She'd obviously lost her belly, and Josiah almost didn't recognize her. Her curly brown hair was brushed across her shoulders, matching her deep blue eyes, and she was slimmed down in a yellow cotton dress that hugged her body tightly. In her own right, Billie Webb was a pretty young woman.

"I never thought I'd see you again, Josiah Wolfe," Billie said.

"Had to bring Lady Mead home."

"You coulda kept her."

"Didn't seem right. Brought you Charlie's gun and clothes, too."

Billie didn't say anything at first, just stared at Josiah and frowned at the sight of the package poking out of Josiah's saddlebag. "Heard that Mick, O'Reilly, is dead. You kill him?"

"No, I didn't have the chance. Would have liked to have brought him back here to hang."

"They like hangin' folks here." Billie stepped off the stoop and walked to Josiah and slid her arms around him. He stood stiffly as she hugged him and pulled his body tight against hers. "I thought about you every day."

A baby's whimper came from inside the house, and Billie stopped and cocked her head, making sure everything was all right. Satisfied, she returned her attention to Josiah and angled her face up, like she expected him to kiss her.

Josiah stood back, pulling away from her embrace. "There's a woman that I care for back home."

Billie's face grew hard. "You got married?"

"No."

"Engaged?"

"No, we're just . . . well it's complicated. I'm not sure what we are. I got myself in a bit of trouble that still hasn't been settled, and it's not right to drag her into something that isn't finished." Josiah scratched the back of his neck. He suddenly felt like a schoolboy.

"Complicated, you say?" Billie asked, scrunching her forehead.

"Yes."

"You love her?"

Josiah drew in a deep breath and shrugged. He didn't know what to say, hadn't said he loved Pearl to her or himself out loud. He hadn't thought he could ever say those words again, after losing Lily.

"All righty then," Billie said. "Guess you need to decide that. I'm not one to tell a man what he should do or feel, but I wouldn't wait too long, Josiah Wolfe. Life

451

can change in the blink of an eye. Charlie never got to see that little girl; now look what I'm left with."

Josiah cocked his head toward the barn. "I'll put the horse up, if that's all right?"

The whimper from the baby turned into a cry. "Suit yourself. I'll put a pot of coffee on. You need to rest your horse before headin' back to Austin, and whatever's waitin' for you. Come on in when you're done."

Josiah started to say no, he had to leave right away, but he stopped and watched Billie Webb walk inside the house. The baby quit crying immediately.

He grabbed Lady Mead's reins and walked her into the barn.

It only took him a few minutes to get her settled into a stall, fill her bucket with oats, and take off the saddle. The palomino looked glad to be home.

Back outside the barn, Josiah stared at the house and felt a bit homesick for his old life even though he was a million miles away from it. He could smell coffee, hear a baby giggling, and bare feet pacing on a hard-wood floor, calming the child.

He looked to the sky, searching for an answer about what to do, and realized when he looked over to Clipper that he still needed to give Billie Charlie's clothes and gun.

With more than a little hesitation, he walked back over to Clipper, grabbed the package of clothes and the rifle and headed to the door.

Billie was standing next to the stove, holding the baby, smiling widely, as Josiah walked inside. Josiah didn't look back as he stepped inside the house.

The employees of Thorndike Press hope you have enjoyed this Large Print book. All our Thorndike, Wheeler, and Kennebec Large Print titles are designed for easy reading, and all our books are made to last. Other Thorndike Press Large Print books are available at your library, through selected bookstores, or directly from us.

For information about titles, please call:
  (800) 223-1244

or visit our Web site at:
  http://gale.cengage.com/thorndike

To share your comments, please write:
  Publisher
  Thorndike Press
  10 Water St., Suite 310
  Waterville, ME 04901